P9-DNB-423

IT WILL JUST BE US

ALSO AVAILABLE BY JO KAPLAN

(writing as Joanna Parypinski)

Dark Carnival

IT WILL JUST BE US

A Novel

Jo Kaplan

NEW YORK

This is a work of fiction. All of the names, characters, organizations, places and events portrayed in this novel are either products of the author's imagination or are used fictitiously. Any resemblance to real or actual events, locales, or persons, living or dead, is entirely coincidental.

Published in the United States by Crooked Lane Books, an imprint of The Quick Brown Fox & Company LLC.

Crooked Lane Books and its logo are trademarks of The Quick Brown Fox & Company LLC.

Library of Congress Catalog-in-Publication data available upon request.

ISBN (hardcover): 978-1-64385-449-6
ISBN (ebook): 978-1-64385-450-2

Cover design by Melanie Sun

Printed in the United States.

www.crookedlanebooks.com

Crooked Lane Books
34 West 27th St., 10th Floor
New York, NY 10001

First Edition: August 2020

10 9 8 7 6 5 4 3 2 1

To Jackson and Penny
for being a far cry from evil

PART ONE

THE PARABLE OF THE KNOCKER

1

In Wakefield Manor, a decaying ancestral mansion brooding on the edge of the Great Dismal Swamp in Virginia, there is a locked room. For years it has been inaccessible, closing out from the world all the aborted secrets stilled in its dormant womb. After climbing the main staircase that curves up through the house like a twisted spine, you'll find a hallway with striped and long-faded viridian wallpaper that evokes algae-choked seafoam. On the third floor you'll pass a linen closet, a disused nursery, a bathroom with a cracked clawfoot tub, and a wood-beamed room inhabited by broken furniture draped in white sheets. Then the hall narrows and turns a corner, its high ceiling webbed in shadow, and you are faced with a windowless passage, at the end of which lies the heavy door of distressed mahogany—and whatever lies beyond it.

What I have imagined must live in this locked room, if anything can indeed be said to live there at all, are the agonies of ghostly lives playing out on a dusty stage, the callous whispers of betrayal and the succor of revenge; creatures ineffable and unfamiliar as a lamprey must be to an amoeba, not merely vast but vastly alien, having come from either the distant past or the impenetrable future; or otherwise a black hole that invites the earth to leap inside to its death. These wonders have occupied me with indelible curiosity and, I will admit, a long-standing dread of the end of the third-floor hallway.

Imagine a younger me: a deliberate child, inward-drawn, with those two serpentine braids my mother used to weave into my unruly hair. Imagine that child creeping purposely down the hall while her mother downstairs scolds the older sister for breaking a glass.

Left to her own devices, this young Samantha wonders what lies beyond the door. What delicious secrets does it hide? What immortal trappings might she witness were she to peer through the keyhole, just waiting for a skeleton key to twist it into submission? She dares herself to look. Go on, she thinks to herself. Just a peek.

Where's your sister? a voice from downstairs asks, accusing, then calls for *Samantha!*

Kneeling on the groaning hardwood, she is just leaning forward to press her eye to the keyhole when footsteps thunder up behind her, followed by her mother's voice: "Samantha! Get *away* from there. I've told you how many times? You want to pretend you're deaf, I'll tell you in sign language."

A sharp yank on a delicate arm drags her away from the door.

The look on little Sam's face implies disappointment that her mother has found her so quickly in this dim, remote passage, swollen and close as an asthmatic throat, and perhaps she thinks of all her hiding places and wonders how many of them, truly, her mother has found out.

We may never know, because the hollow gong of a doorbell interrupts us.

Younger me vanishes into the twists and folds of time, and I consider that hallway and the locked door where the ghostly apparition of little Sam knelt. The doorbell rings again, impatiently and heedless of the late hour, unbefitting behavior for visitors. Outside the night yawns breathlessly, cold and still.

The hallway recedes from me as I back away and turn the corner.

"I wonder who that could be?" remarks my mother to no one, rubbing her hands over her chilled arms as she makes her way to the front door.

I descend the staircase that unfurls to the foyer as she unlocks the door, and an uncanny presentiment ensnares me. I call down for her to wait, and she pauses with her hand on the brass knob.

"Whatever for?" she asks in surprise.

I can feel something lurking on the other side of the closed door.

I'd like to explain to her so that she will not think me silly. I'd like to explain to her that closed doors inherently provide us with the potential for threat while offering a simulacrum of cold comfort. Imagine: something is waiting for you on the other side of this door. Perhaps there is a knock, or the ring of a doorbell; you know something is out there, but you don't know what. Or even worse, there is only silence; you think there *might* be something out there, but you cannot know for sure. And while the closed door might offer the guise of security from that indefinite world, it simultaneously creates a deeper dread as it conceals whatever stands just beyond. Something in the wind that scratches its way inside, something that slips between the patter of raindrops, something without form until you open the door and look, until you have to open the door, until you cannot stand anymore not to open the door.

"Perhaps it's Charles Severance," I suggest lightly.

"Friend of yours?"

"No, Mother."

She looks at me blankly.

"Don't you remember *The Parable of the Knocker*? That serial killer in Alexandria who knocked on people's front doors and then killed them? He wrote that biblical manifesto about himself. You *must* remember."

The doorbell shrieks again with an irascible appeal. We are angering whatever begs to be admitted from the night.

"So you reckon there's a serial killer out there ringing our bell?" says my mother in her gently chiding drawl.

"I'm all ears, then. Who do *you* suppose it is?"

"A little swamp creature that's lost its way, ringing to see if we can spare a cup of sugar. Or perhaps arsenic."

When she opens the door, the person beyond remains obscured, and I wonder with a thrill who it could be at this time of night. *At this time of night?* Have I become my mother? It seems so very like a thing she would say. In fact, I'm sure she's said it just now, if I could only remember exactly when. But then, she is the one who's opened the door.

"Oh, this is a surprise," she says, before her tone drops with concern. "What's happened?"

A little swamp creature, indeed—my enormously pregnant sister, not deliberate in the least, barges through the door. Her heavy breathing floods the foyer, which seems too bright against her red-veined eyes. At either side of her extraordinarily round belly she carries two small valises. It has been raining, and the sodden fraying rope of her hair glistens like the night sky.

"Elizabeth?" says my mother. "What on earth is it?"

The raindrops on her cheeks are tears. "*Everything*," she spits out, dropping her bags. "Everything's gone wrong. Can I stay here for a while?"

"Well, sure you can. But what about Donovan?"

Elizabeth's words are brittle. "That's what's gone wrong."

"Oh, honey," my mother says, and wraps her arms around Elizabeth, who crumples into them like a child. From above my sister's shoulder my mother's eyes find me. "Well, don't just stand there. Go put on the kettle."

My banishment to the kitchen offers something of a reprieve from Elizabeth's dramatics. Nothing my sister has ever done could be considered deliberate; she is more likely to react from pure animal instinct than from any sense of calculation, from any sense of decency. When we were children, every splinter and stubbed toe against a fallen log provoked wails of distress. Mountains and molehills are all one and the same, equally devastating to the one who pulls the universe in revolutions around herself.

I sometimes think to myself, proudly, that I am not like her. I will never be like her. I will melt into the walls; I will be careful and deliberate in all that I do.

The kettle squeals sooner than I anticipate, as I have some trouble telling time. It slips away from me here and there, quickly now and slow again, like running water—perhaps from living so long in a haunted house.

When I bring out the tea, Mother and Elizabeth have settled themselves in the drawing room. All these rooms have old names. If it were a modern home, there likely would be only the living, the dining, the kitchen, the bathrooms, and the bedrooms; but here in this monstrosity of a manse, built piecemeal over the course of many years in which the previous owners—well, my ancestors, mad, the lot of them—kept adding on as if to confuse the ghosts that live here, there are simply too many rooms not to have names for each of them, or else how would you ever find each other? That is why this old dark maze has also a parlor, a drawing room, a billiards room, a library, a stone tower room, a reading room, a den, and the Rose Room, named—shall I hazard a guess?—for the putrid floral carpet and the pink velvet draperies, and all the old ornate furniture in there that has been around, good lord, since the Victorian era.

When I return with the tea, my mother is asking my sister the particulars of her departure from her husband, but Elizabeth is uncharacteristically tight-lipped on the matter. True to form, however, with her attentive listeners, she proceeds to divulge a litany of general complaints: "He never wanted to get married—*you* remember, he dragged his feet like a child. He didn't want to be a father. Or he could never decide. He blamed me for getting pregnant." Angry tears glisten and run over. "He said I should have gotten an abortion!"

"That man," says my mother, shaking her head. "Well, it's good you came home. You stay as long as you like. Sam, won't it be nice to have your sister here? And a baby!" Her eyes catch on Elizabeth, whose face is a mask of despair. "You know, Lizzie, this might be a blessing in disguise. Why don't I consult the cards?"

"God, Mom, no," groans Elizabeth. "Can't we behave like normal people for once?"

Mother hides her frown behind the mug of chamomile. "Needs lemon." She bustles off to the kitchen, leaving us alone, two strangers who once spent sixteen years of our lives together, with only each other for companionship in this lonely place.

"How long, you think, before she asks to read my palm?" Elizabeth murmurs.

"Well, it won't hurt if you just let her."

"What else should I have expected?" she says, more to herself than to me. She has a habit of speaking to herself aloud in front of me as if I'm not there, but also with the full intention of me hearing whatever it is she wants to say. If not, she would just think it like the rest of us.

"So," she says, as if realizing we are alone, now, for the first time since I left her house after my brief stay with her and Don and moved back here.

As happens sometimes with sisters, once we were adults and no longer lived in the same house, Elizabeth and I became fond friends, with the kind of connection fostered only between turbulent sisters. We met up regularly for coffee and gossip, or lunch while reading movie reviews, or drinks and card games.

It was a system that suited both of us, these weekly visits, until one evening when two drinks at the bar turned into four. I suggested, half joking, that we were both turning into our mother the older we got; that made her angry. *She* was nothing like Agnes Wakefield, and I had better be grateful for that. I didn't see why I should be. Our sniping took us onto the curb in the valley between streetlights, and I told her she could pretend to be something else, but she had always been a rotten bitch to me, ever since we were children.

"If I'm such a bitch," she said, fishing her keys out of her purse, "then you can find your own ride home."

I watched the taillights of her car shrink away in the darkness. Trees closed in the country road, and she was gone.

As I pulled out my cell phone to call for a ride, it slipped from my unfeeling fingers and skittered across the pavement. Such a brief moment. How many times have I dropped my phone and reached over to retrieve it—something you hardly even think about, it's such a natural act.

But I was drunk, and I did not notice the person coming up behind me.

When I bent down for the phone, there was a sharp crack on the back of my head. I fell forward, landing badly on my wrist—felt a knee in my back, tried to push away the stranger, but he was too heavy. I could not turn to look at him, so he remained a mystery, a dark weight on my back, reminding me of my own shadow as a child, the ghost who used to follow me around, the tall shape of seething darkness, although perhaps darkness is not quite the right word—not necessarily darkness but *nothingness*, a shape of nothingness sometimes glimpsed standing at the top of a staircase or the end of a hallway. The Nothing Man, who even my mother never believed existed. And that, I thought in that wild moment, was who knelt on my back, the Nothing Man, and if I did ever manage to turn my head, I would see the terrible emptiness of him.

As if he sensed my thoughts, his hot breath in my ear said, "Don't try to get up." Of course I tried, but a hand pushed my head down, pressed my cheek into the gritty asphalt, and I felt the chilling circle, a mouth of metal, press into my neck.

Time sagged. Wind stirred litter and dead leaves across the empty street. Dirt migrated from my lips, mashed against the ground, into my mouth. A beetle crawled across the asphalt near my right eye, its wiry legs twitching. The knee in my back was a sharp weight crushing my gut. I smelled my own alcoholic sweat and a man's sour musk blanketing me.

My purse was yanked from my shoulder, and with my hair spilling over my eyes, I heard only the sounds of careless rummaging. He took what he wanted, tossed the empty bag to the ground, where it flopped like a dead fish, an empty and forsaken thing.

"Please don't kill me," I prayed into the asphalt.

It was eternity before the cold weight of the gun vanished from my neck.

"Don't try to get up," he said again, and then the knee was gone as well.

I gasped in dizzy lungfuls of air, hardly aware how much life his knee had choked from my chest, and I waited until his footsteps receded, never looking up, never turning to see his true form. I waited until a lonely car or two blew past on the street. I waited until someone else emerged from the bar and presumed me drunkenly passed out and stepped over me.

He hadn't taken my cell phone, because it had slid away in the dark. He took only my wallet. What small miracles we are granted.

The police dropped me off at my apartment, but I couldn't bear to go inside where I would be alone in the dark. When I finally did, and locked the door, and pulled a chair in front of it, and removed the chair to check again that the door was locked, even then, even with the barricade, sleep eluded me, chased away by every rattle of the loose windowpanes and every scratch of wind.

Elizabeth was full of apologies. In one of them, an invitation to stay with her for a while managed to sneak, perhaps unintentionally, past her lips.

How long has it been since I stayed with them? A year, perhaps? At times it feels like only a few days since I moved back home; sometimes it feels like I have never left at all, that everything beyond these walls has never truly existed.

I look up at Elizabeth. It seems strange to see her here; she hardly ever visits. I wonder how permanent her stay will be.

"Do you think it's over between you two?"

Her face twists. "I don't know." She turns her wedding ring on her finger, around and around. "I don't know."

Mother returns with extra lemon wedges. "I'll go make up the bed. The sheets must be dusty. Sam, would you help your sister bring up her things? She really shouldn't be carrying anything heavy." She sets down the tray of lemons and stands there as if unsure where to settle her hands. "Just think—a baby, here! A blessing in disguise."

I carry Elizabeth's luggage upstairs to her old room, where a four-poster bed holds court with a weatherworn desk and a dresser bearing framed photographs. Soft ragged posters line the walls: Audrey Hepburn, Green Day, *American Beauty*, a Degas facsimile. Artifacts of adolescent angst. The canopy above the bed drapes down in a gauzy cotton-mouthed smile.

"I see she *still* hasn't changed anything in here." She sits down heavily, and the beleaguered bedsprings squeal. "I used to pretend I was a princess locked away in the highest tower of a castle when I pulled down the canopy around me." She sighs. "How's Mom been?"

"Same as ever," I say. "But I can sense a change now that you're here."

She smiles wryly. "Don't worry. It won't last."

She's right. The next morning, which dawns clear and dewy, a sleepy aftermath of yesterday's agony of rain, I find Mother in the backyard sitting in her wooden Adirondack chair and gazing with glazed-eyed nostalgia at the tumble of overgrown greenery and puddled marsh leading windingly to the swamp beyond. A tumorous weed-choked garden has grown wild over a defunct stone fountain, now bone-dry and weathered as a tombstone, ensnared by possessive vines, collecting the odd damp leaf to decay in its bottommost parts. Tomato plants bloom enthusiastically amid bushes that haven't been trimmed in so long they've grown rough and rogue, with an air of neglect that doesn't belong in an inhabited home. But who has the money to hire a caretaker or a gardener in these times, or the energy to keep up such a sprawling, schizophrenic place?

Playing in the jungle-grown yard are two little girls: one small and freckled with two unraveling braids, the other a posh little adult of twelve with dark hair swept coolly over her eyes. The sun cants over them in a goldish halo that doesn't quite touch them at the correct angle because it wasn't morning when this moment first occurred, but afternoon. They chase one another in a game they have invented whose rules are lost to me. A faint smile ghosts my mother's face.

"Look how young we are," I say as I come up beside her.

Young Sam's foot slips into a shallow ditch and she goes sprawling in the weeds, while young Elizabeth cackles with cruel glee.

"Careful, girls," calls my mother, even though the children cannot hear her through the span of time. "My girls," she murmurs with amused pride. "They'll come in covered in dirt and licking their wounds like battle heroes. And here I used to worry that boys would be the bigger handful."

"Lizzie's having a boy," I say, to draw her back to the present.

"Silly. Lizzie's just a girl. Oh," and she turns away from the girls playing in the yard and finally looks up at me as if just remembering how much time has passed since the memory she is watching. She looks into my face and frowns as if surprised to see me all grown up. "That's right. She is." She turns back to the girls wrestling on the ground. Young Elizabeth yanks on young Sam's braid, and young Sam cries out indignantly. "It will be nice to have a boy in the family." A distant smile plays on her face. "We need to finish getting everything ready. There's so much to do."

"Why don't you come inside, Mom." I help her up, though she is hardly so old as to need my aid in getting out of a chair. But something about watching the dance of memories seems to age her considerably. "They're not going anywhere."

* * *

Finding Elizabeth in the labyrinthine house isn't easy, but Mother prefers not to shout our names through the halls lest those shouts ring out at random intervals in the future, echoing from the house's memory so that we wake to hear our names called out by ghostly voices in the middle of the night. This is why the house bears such a tomblike quietude. Occasionally you can hear soft music whispering from empty rooms, music from decades ago playing eerily of its own volition. Once I heard a big-band tune crackling through a phonograph in the billiards room, and it drew me there where I could hear but not see its source. Just an echo of a memory. I danced until the music faded away into nothing and went in search of good omens and other mysterious ephemera of the past.

Sometimes it's auditory—gentle echoes riding in on the waves of time; other times it's visible—holograms of what has happened in the house or on the land in perfect re-creation.

We find Elizabeth in the library, perusing the collection of books that have been accumulating since time immemorial.

"At least I'll have some way to occupy my time," she says, gesturing to the towering bookshelves that lean in close, crowding the room into a claustrophobia of untouched volumes. "How is it you still don't have internet?"

Mother waves her off. "I've no use for that."

Elizabeth looks at me incredulously, and I tell her I go into town when I want to check up on the digital world.

"You're something," she says disapprovingly. "This place is going to eat right through my data plan."

"Come on downstairs, Lizzie, and I'll make us some breakfast."

"Please don't call me that," she cuts in. "I'm not a child."

"All right," Mother says, conciliatory. "Eggs. Poached?"

"I haven't eaten a poached egg since I was twelve."

"I thought they were your favorite."

"They were," she says, exasperated. "When I was twelve."

While we breakfast on fried eggs and toast, Mother gazes off at the doorway to the kitchen or out the windows where memories are stirring with the morning. In the middle of a lengthy rant about swollen ankles, swollen feet, and swollen fingers, Elizabeth pauses with her fork halfway to her mouth, waiting for Mother to respond.

"I'm sorry, what?" She blinks out of her reveries.

Elizabeth lets the fork drop. "Was it the same way for you?"

"Oh," she says distractedly, the sun-yellow orbs of her cooling eggs leaking viscously across the plate. "Why, yes. I suppose it was. I don't remember all that. I just remember looking at your face for the first time and thinking, look what I've made."

"How convenient, to forget all the awful parts." Elizabeth rolls her eyes at me, as if expecting me to agree. She has always expected me to follow along with her in a sort of obligatory mimesis.

"It will be worth it, when you get to hold him in your arms. Just you wait," says my mother. "Sam, would you do the grocery shopping this afternoon? We're low on milk."

Elizabeth offers to accompany me. She looks too large for the kitchen, as if she is caged, desperate to escape.

The drive into town is about twenty minutes on the country road that bears little sign of civilization. Rural areas like this that once flourished now seem to be expiring in the face of urban rush. There is something lonesome about the drive, despite Elizabeth's ceaseless talking, which makes me wish she would shut up so I could enjoy the rumble of movement, because I quite like the lonesomeness, sometimes. The road, flush with light, slices through gold-leafed trees vivid with rain.

The town is called Shadydale, and I don't suppose you've ever heard of it, for it consists of little more than the main street with its dismal shops that sell antique things, and its diner inhabited by suspicious folks hunching over their bitter coffee possessively, and the lone movie theater where hollow-eyed teenagers make their weekly pilgrimage on Friday nights to stave off an existential boredom, the faded marquee calling them forth. I like it, though. Everyone moves at a country pace, like tortoises. We go over a wooden bridge to get there, and it is autumn so the maple trees are shrugging off their painted foliage.

What keeps the place going, I think, is the lifeblood of gossip that pumps through its veins, rumors of intrigue to titillate an otherwise banal and slowly eroding existence. I have always liked to come into town and listen to the people talk, even if they never talk to me, or even if they are talking about me while looking at me from the white corners of their eyes. I will always be recognized as *one of those Wakefields* who live in the haunted house out in the swampland, and I must carry that haunting with me wherever I go.

"Do you always do the groceries?" asks Elizabeth. "What did she do before you moved back home?"

"She had a grocery boy."

"Lord." Her eyes turn heavenward. "If she got hooked up to the internet, she could just order all of her groceries to be delivered and continue marinating in that house like a chicken."

I grab a cart, and we stroll at a more leisurely pace than I usually take on my grocery trips. The store is bright and blooming. Rainbows of fruit occupy large crates before us. Elizabeth grabs items at whim as we pass: kiwi, a bottle of mustard, Swiss cheese, bacon.

"You wouldn't believe the pregnancy cravings," she says while inspecting a box of cereal. "I used to hate mustard. Now I can't get enough. I just want to put it on everything. Popcorn, crackers, bananas. Just everything. It's like having the perpetual munchies."

"So just like college, then?"

Elizabeth gained the notorious freshman fifteen—or maybe twenty—after an affair with a pot dealer her first year away at school, when I was still at home. She dieted and exercised intensely for months before the extra weight started to vanish, and this was only after they broke up for the fifth and final time. I actually liked her more with the extra weight, though. She had less to be self-righteous about, and she was pleasanter, and warm, and when she came home for holidays, she would share her chips with me. When she started eating drab salads, there was no more sharing, only an unhappy shoveling of leaves into her mouth, a glower across the kitchen table.

She picks up another box of cereal and says to the list of ingredients, "No. Now there's a boy inside of me."

"So just like college, then."

The cereal ends up in the cart, and her hands find her hips. "Jealous because you didn't get any?"

"You know I never wanted what you were having."

She stops walking, so I am forced to halt the cart and wait for her to tell me what's the matter. She looks suddenly upset, as if the fragile balance of carelessness and that faint fixed impression of a smile are straining under some ugliness breaking through, the first effervescent bubbles pushing at the surface tension of a pot heated almost to boiling. After a moment, the tension settles, but the laugh that escapes sounds high and false. "You know what's odd? When you're pregnant, everyone wants to touch your belly."

"Do you want me to touch your belly?" We start moving forward again. "Is it for good luck?"

"*Some* people are interested in the miracle of childbirth."

We talk the way sisters talk, I think. Even as we needle each other, there is a kind of enjoyment in it, perhaps in the knowledge that we are playing out a larger conversation that all sisters must have. Little lighthearted barbs intended to prick but not sting, to rile up one another; the common lexicon of women bound by blood. Yes, the way sisters talk to each other—for sisters, above anyone on earth, must become fluent in this passive-aggressive language.

But I won't admit that here in the middle of the fluorescent grocery store, amid shelves of milk and butter, my sister is riling me up the way only she knows how to.

I grip the cart and sigh. "I'm glad you're happy. But can't you just enjoy your happiness without needing me to feel it, too?"

"Happy?" she breathes, and I cannot tell if she is truly wounded or if she is merely behaving so to call out my too-overt aggression; there is a fine balancing act that must be maintained to keep the order of politeness and cruelty intact. "Happy? You think I'm happy? My husband and I separated and I'm almost eight months pregnant. How can I be happy?"

"I'm sorry," I say, even though I'm not sure if I really am, and I wonder, if I'm not sorry, whether that makes me a terrible person.

I have become more conscious now of the people around us doing their own shopping, and I get the feeling they are all looking at me from the corners of their eyes. They are looking at me because I have brought attention to myself in being rude to my sister, and then retreating into that docile and pathetic apology. They have identified us as Wakefields and now are thinking their nasty thoughts. This is why I move swiftly and smoothly through the store when I come alone, like a leopard; as much as I like to listen to the people chirp, I want also to be invisible. Being seen makes me uncomfortable. I look around at all the flat-eyed shoppers as we go, and I think to myself, this town is an angry, dismal blight of a place, and I can't pretend to like it anymore.

The truth is that I know Elizabeth will be fine whether I coddle her with niceness or not. It seems a formality to be nice for niceness' sake. The social convention doesn't draw actual love or care out of us; it only filters out the ugliness, as if to say that because we cannot see it, it must not be there.

And I know Elizabeth will be a good mother without having to sycophantically remind her of that. She knows how to do the right things. She took care of me, after all, when I was too young to realize our mother had failed to. Now she reads baby books and goes to prenatal classes and gushes all the usual pregnancy clichés as if they have become fresh in her mouth. When the baby comes, she will take one look at him and no matter how blood-bathed and wrinkled he is, she will call him perfect, precious, beautiful. She will take a thousand identical pictures of him and post every last one online. She will never abandon him like she abandoned me. She knows she will immediately love this creature that percolated in her womb for nine months because he belongs to her.

Such instant bonding with another creature is something I can't quite imagine. A mother is supposed to feel that way about her child, but what if she doesn't? What if she looks at her child and does not recognize it? What if the screaming infant bursts forth into the world and instead of seeing love, she sees only a bleating incoherent alien?

A parasitic creature that makes her wonder how it lived inside her so long, her gorge rising at the very thought? This is not mine, she thinks. This is not mine.

I hurry the cart forward on its squeaking wheels so as not to think about it. Damn my sister for making me think these kinds of thoughts.

On the drive home she says wistfully, "Things will be so different from how I imagined, without him. I don't know what we're going to do. I just wanted everything to be *right.* Is that so much to ask?" She composes herself in the mirror.

I am thinking now not of her child but of mine, the one that never was. I was young and didn't know how to say no to my date, who was also young and stupid and thought I was on birth control. So much for Elizabeth thinking I never got any. I never told her. Even though I was only eighteen, I knew immediately that I didn't want it, would never want it—him or the baby. Without ever showing him the pregnancy test or returning his calls, I quietly found a clinic and took a taxi there. They tell you that when you leave the clinic you will feel guilty, depressed, empty. Perhaps you will feel like a murderer. Perhaps you will feel unwomaned. The exact horror Elizabeth imagined when her husband told her to get rid of it. I expected to feel ill and ashamed, but all I felt as I walked out into the sun-brightened parking lot still glazed with fresh morning rain was relief. Relief and a lightness, as if I was finally myself for the first time in weeks, as if my treacherous body belonged to me again.

Elizabeth places both hands reverently on her belly. "We're going to name him Julian."

2

I have never slept well. Tonight is no exception.

Rather than lying in bed while sleep recedes from me like a boat pulled away by the tide, I get up and wander on restless feet. I don't even need to turn on the television or grab a book; the house will entertain me.

For all that has ever been, the house remembers.

It is a house haunted by memory; it digests us, all of us, and spits us out again at random. I have seen my younger self from the corner of my eye, just a flash stealing through a doorway and then gone. But I have also seen those who lived in the house before us, the Wakefields of yesteryear.

As I creep past the Rose Room, I glance in to see a familiar ghost: Frances Wakefield, bedridden and gaunt with tuberculosis.

She lived in the nineteenth century, the ailing wife of a mild-mannered patriarch, Everett, and mother to two children: adventurous daughter Constance and evangelical son August. They were Quakers, which I have found out by piecing together snippets of their story told by echoes, voices of the long dead; ephemeral glimpses that have appeared to me out of order. I've tried to jot down the details and rearrange them until the chronology fits, my own little portrait of the house's history.

But seeing Frances on the verge of death makes my skin crawl. Her breathing had grown so labored that one could almost hear a ghost of it all throughout the house, the incessant groaning rattle of liquid in her lungs.

I back away from the doorway and nearly into the ghosts of her family.

Constance, thirteen or thereabouts, is cradling a cup of tarry water, filled to the brim. Blonde hair spills out from her bonnet. Her dress is wrinkled, and she is barefoot. Clearly Constance was not very adept at the household duties she had to take over for her mother; I have seen her prick her finger while mending clothes so many times that I imagine her small digits must be pocked as a pincushion.

Before she makes it to the doorway with the cup, her brother, August, stops her with a heavy grip on her shoulder. She glares at him over the cup as the water sloshes dangerously close to its lip.

"I'll not see thee out there again."

"Out where?" she asks with feigned innocence.

His eyes narrow on the cup of water. "I know where that came from. If you will not obey Father, then hark to me: do not be foolish."

Constance frowns. "You've been to the swamp a dozen or more times. Why shan't I?"

"Sakes alive, Constance, 'tis dangerous, *that* is why!" August lowers his voice. "You know that I go into the swamp to help those people because Father wants to help them. If it were up to me, I would not set one foot in that terrible place."

I know who he is talking about. At the time, there were secret communities that lived in the swamp called maroons—escaped slaves forced to dwell in a place where no one else dared tread. Life in the swamp was a hard, toiling existence, with land too liquid for extensive farming or comfortable dwellings; one feels the heaviness of the air like a hot, wet cloak, infested with ravening mosquitoes and pressing one down into the sucking, sinking morass. These natural defenses kept out intruders but forced the maroons into a prison of their own devising—a deadly sort of freedom.

The Wakefields, with their home at the swamp's edge, had helped fleeing slaves make their way into its depths, guiding the refugees by night.

"Not even to save Mother?"

August looks at the door hanging ajar on its hinges; perhaps he can smell the sickness within.

When he doesn't respond, Constance continues, growing bolder, "The water of the swamp is said to have healing properties. If I only get her to drink—"

August's face grows livid as he slaps the cup from her hands. It clatters to the floor, spilling a puddle of dirty water.

Constance opens her mouth in defiance, but she withers at the look on her brother's face and the coldness in his voice when he says, "Nothing will save her."

I do not stay to watch her clean up the mess.

Constance is not the only one who has ever felt the swamp's strange allure. What is it about things that horrify us that simultaneously attracts us? Like moths drawn to their own demise by candlelight, unable to look away from the burning beauty even as we draw closer, so close our flesh melts and sloughs off. The swamp, shrouded in heavy mists and the odors of decay that conceal lurking predators and invisible quicksand, should warn all to stay away. *This is a bad place*, the swamp communicates to us. *Do not enter.* So what is that voice underneath the warning, entreating us to see it for ourselves? What is this siren song of the swamp? Why is it that we fancy ghost stories that raise the hair on the backs of our necks?

I walk down the old wooden staircase, through a house that looks much as it did in Frances's time. One reason we haven't changed things much over the years—no remodeling, an adherence to old furniture positioned in just the right places—is so that we do not become disoriented when suddenly a room decides to rearrange itself into its past formation, to show us a memory it has dredged up. The house is sufficiently disorienting as it is. Rooms inside rooms like nesting dolls; an intersection of two identical hallways, confounding the unwary traveler who neglected to bring his compass. All thanks to Mad Catherine, of course, my great-great-great-great something or other, who built this mausolean monstrosity.

The house is a nonsensical place, but if you keep to the main areas, you might never understand how strange it is; it is only when you explore further into the recesses that you begin to realize, with a sense of mounting dread, that the house just goes on and on, intending to confuse and disorient, and as you try to find your way out, confused and disoriented yourself, you cannot help but wonder if you are merely going in deeper, toward the heart of the house, wherever that may be, where, one can only assume, the Minotaur lives.

I find myself heading into the kitchen, thinking I might rummage through the cabinets for something to eat, when I spot another ghost. It is a boy of eight or nine, sitting at the kitchen table. I do not recognize him. The moon in the window silhouettes the boy's frame in pale light. His back is to me, and at first all I see is dark unruly hair, his head bent down to examine some treasure.

What is it? I creep around until I can make it out. Upon the table lies a crippled blackbird shifting its broken wings feebly. Detached feathers make a soft bed around it. I wonder what has happened to the poor creature and how the boy ministering to it plans to help. His hands hover over the ailing bird, as if he is unsure of what to do.

I find myself a granola bar and sit at the table across from the boy to watch. Though his head remains bent forward, I can see that he looks sickly, insipid. His eyes are two dark smears of charcoal in the darkness and his nose juts to a sharp aristocratic point; that is all that I can make of his face. I'd like to ask him who he is, but we cannot interact through the span of time. He is a memory; I am not here to him. He would neither see nor hear me. I am an invisible observer.

His fingers find the bird's tiny heaving chest, and he caresses the soft black feathers with fingers that look clumsy but strive to be delicate and adroit. The tender moonlight puts me in a state of calm, and I understand why it is so easy for Mother to get caught up in the past.

He begins tugging gently on the feathers, lifting them to see what lies beneath, to see what secrets they hide. The bird struggles vainly. His tugging grows more insistent. What is he doing? What is he looking for? He yanks hard on a feather, which snaps free, and he brings it close to his night-blurred face, inspecting the fine black filaments curiously, scientifically, before letting it go and watching it drift and twirl back to the table, where it settles among the other feathers.

The granola goes dry in my mouth and I find it hard to swallow. How dare you, I want to tell him. How *dare* you. It is a poor, injured creature, and just because you are bigger than it does not give you the right to be cruel.

The boy continues to divest the bird of its patchy coat of feathers, and more and more skin shows through. He plucks them one by one while the pitiful creature lies prone, its black eyes staring dementedly at the ceiling through the pain of its denuding.

"Stop it," I whisper, horrified, repulsed, even knowing the boy cannot hear me.

He hesitates with his fingers on the next feather, his head cocked as if listening, but the moment passes and he finishes his plucking. He does this methodically, with neither malice nor anger but with a clinical detachment.

When the bird is fully stripped, retaining only a few pitiful tufts here and there, I see what the boy sees, what the boy perhaps wanted to see all along: a scrawny wretched creature that hardly looks like a bird anymore at all but instead like some hideous alien from whose frightful skull bulge round black eyes and a predacious beak. I should feel sorry for the bird, but now I can feel only repulsed by the ugly thing it is. I want it to go away, to die, not to have existed in the first place, for how can such a lovely bird look so hideous in its naked skin? It is not at all like a proud tree shed of its autumnal cloak, stark and spindly; it is sad, vile, unnatural.

The boy takes one mangled wing and breaks it with a sharp little snap. Awful sounds issue from that beak, sounds I have never heard from a bird before. Holding the beak shut as if to quiet the thing, he breaks the other wing.

"Stop it," I say again, and lunge forward, but my own hand passes through air. They are mere echoes, untouchable. Whatever has happened in this moment cannot be changed.

When it seems the boy has grown bored with the bird, he drops it to the floor and stomps. I hear the crunch and creep slowly around the table, expecting to come around the edge and see the pulverized corpse flattened into gory pulp on the floor, but before I can see it, the bird and the boy are gone and I am alone in the kitchen.

I wonder when this boy was here, how long ago. Was he a Wakefield? And if so, are we all doomed to evil and cruelty, like Mad Catherine—are we cursed to be horrible people? Is that just who we are? Some of us had to be good. The Quakers, they were good. I tell myself this as I back out of the kitchen, tell myself that I can be good, too.

The house feels darker. Unsettled. Beyond the window in the overgrown yard, the girls are playing again, framed this time by the moon and their laughter now sounding of the night, of mystery and malediction, playing on an endless repeating loop. Where is their mother now? My mother, the Agnes of the present, is upstairs asleep. But what about the "now" that these echoes inhabit? Why is the Agnes of my childhood never present when current Agnes sits watching memories of the past?

The Agnes of my childhood is in the library, sunk into an armchair and leaned back to where the thin light cannot catch her face. She is drinking brandy from a tumbler with melting ice and contemplating the bookshelves with detached passivity. The half-empty bottle sits near her feet. She is there when the girls come inside, and from there she yells at them to slow down, not to stomp, not to make so much goddamn *noise*, and her nerves unravel with each giggle and shout and childish footfall. Elizabeth wants to keep playing, for she is a queen and Sam is a peasant in this game, but Sam wants to read a story and so she creeps into the dim library, knowing better than to startle her mother.

She stops in the doorway.

"What do you want?" says Agnes.

"A book." She goes to a shelf and picks one out. "Will you read to me?"

"You know how to read. You're not a baby anymore."

Sam hugs the heavy book to her chest. She looks hesitantly at the other armchair.

"Go read somewhere else. I'm busy," says Agnes. Sam doesn't move. Tears glisten on Agnes's cheeks. "I said go somewhere else. Are you deaf?"

"Do I make you sad?" Sam asks hesitantly.

Agnes allows the tears to drain unchecked down her cheeks. Her eyes are glassy and unfocused. She has arrived at an emotional stasis where the tears arrive with no sound, no hitched breath. They exist like two small indifferent rivers gouging valleys down her face.

"No," she says at last. "You don't make me anything."

I pass the now empty, night-blanketed library and its silent sleeping books and feel myself like a ghost wandering the halls of this ancient manor. Are they the ghosts, truly, or am I?

* * *

Come morning, Elizabeth makes a proposal over coffee. Mother brewed only decaf, for her, and I imagine I will be made to feel interminably tired for a month to come, half dozing even in my waking hours. My notebook sits before me, filled with scrawlings of our family history—both what I have uncovered from old records and what I have seen here myself. Who is the boy? I am determined to identify him, add him to my collection of history.

Hands wrapped around the warm mug that steams into her face, Elizabeth says, "I need to get everything figured out for the birth, now that things have changed. Mom, will you come with me for my ultrasound appointment?" She punctuates the last sentence with a sip.

Mother looks at her with surprise. "Oh honey, I'm not sure you need me to go. Why don't I just take care of things around here?"

I don't know why Elizabeth deliberately prods us in our tender spots. It seems callous to continue poking a wound just because you can see it. She must have known what Mother's response would be.

She purses her lips and places her mug on the table with barely contained resentment. "I can't do this alone." Then she sits very still.

"Why don't you take Sam?"

Elizabeth laughs rudely. "You won't even be there for the birth, will you?"

"Well," says Agnes. "Have you considered home birth?"

"No doctors? No nurses? No epidural? No thanks. Besides"—she waves her hand dismissively—"that sounds so archaic."

"You know we're here for you, Lizzie."

"Are you?" she snaps, untethering her anger from wherever it was fastened.

Elizabeth stands up so suddenly that her chair slides across the tile with a screech, and I am amazed that someone so pregnant can move so fast. "You won't die if you set foot outside this house." She shakes her head in disgust. "You've never come to visit me. Not once. You didn't even come to my baby shower. How do I explain that to people? My own mother. I started telling my friends you were dead. Did you know that?"

"Keep your voice down, please," Mother says tersely. "Is this a conversation you want to remember?"

Elizabeth tilts her head back and screams incoherently, just to spite her. Then she fixes Mother with a cold stare. "I don't care."

"That's enough. Go to your room."

"I'm thirty years old!" The shriek is so high-pitched it becomes nearly unintelligible. She clutches at the air as if looking for something to grab on to. Her hair dances frantically on her shaking head and her eyes glint madly. At last she gives a sound like an angry bull and storms from the room, her maternity shirt billowing around her like a curtain troubled by furious wind.

Mother carefully pours a spoonful of sugar into her coffee. "I know how old she is," she says.

We finish our coffee in silence. Outside, birds flit hither and yon in the naked trees and chirp their disinterest in human affairs. I observe my mother carefully. She looks small, plucked clean.

* * *

A girl in an old-fashioned dress dusts the little-used dining room. She hums to herself a heartful tune, but her eyes are sad. Whatever dust there is now on the china cabinet remains. I think I recognize her, but it's too late to place who it is. She is gone before the tune fully dissipates.

My grandmother now stands there, holding a glass and gazing into its depths with profound concentration as if willing it to reveal the secrets of life.

The past is everywhere, here, wrapped up in the present.

It is the past that intrigues me; I am afflicted with an obsession for history. Teaching archaeology allows me to slide easily into the past until I find myself missing it achingly, feeling a kind of nostalgia for a time before I was born. I feel almost as though I can touch an artifact from the past and transport myself there, which is why I collect small tokens from around the house that feel imbued with meaning or history, or both. It isn't, after all, as if time is quite as fixed as everyone else would have you believe. At least, not here it isn't.

I would very much like to go on an official archaeological dig in the swamp, if I could get the funding. I could be the foremost expert on the secret communities that used to live there, reading into a tiny bit of polished stone all manner of tools and meals it helped create. But for now I focus on sharing this peculiar joy with my students: enjoying the slow easy lull of old documents with their baroque prose that implies no one is in any hurry to get anywhere but to the next lovely phrase, the look on students' faces when they begin to understand the subjectivity of the past, of reality itself, of how stories create our reality. But I wonder: is the house an objective source? Are the memories here perfect reconstructions of reality, or are they filtered through the house's perception the way all memories are filtered through our brains, the way I am reconstructing this story for you?

So how can I find out who the boy was, if I can't trust my own eyes?

I fear what it must be like to forget the past, like my grandparents. My mother's parents were both plagued with early-onset dementia. In a house that constantly relives what came before, they must have seen versions of themselves doing things they could no longer recall, strange beings wearing their own flesh. *Darling, did we argue on the night of our twentieth anniversary? Did I make you sleep on the couch? Let's watch and find out. Make some popcorn.* Even the smaller gestures—putting away dishes in a certain order, a moment of indecision in the library with a hand hovering over the spines of potential books, a sharp word on a gloomy evening—must have seemed so poignantly foreign that they questioned whether or not they knew themselves at all. Imagine that life. Familiarity become unfamiliar.

Eventually they decided it best, when they were lucid enough to discuss their options, to stay in an assisted facility. Agnes was still young at the time and had only just met the man she would soon marry. She was an obstetrician, living in a cramped little apartment across town.

When they had Elizabeth, they decided to move into Agnes's family home, where they would have plenty of space to raise children. What did he think when they first crept down the long drive through the broken iron gate? You come up past the ugly cherubic statues shaggy with undergrowth and moss, past the Virginia creeper and wisteria, and you see, emerging from the earth, the sprawling Gothic eyesore where terrible angles meet at sharp and angry glances like an unhappy jigsaw. You see the house, crumbling and perverse, with its brooding walls and secretive windows, grown over with vines as if the earth should reclaim it.

But even beyond that, I wonder what my father's reaction was the first time he saw the ghost of a former resident facing him in the hallway or the light of a candle as someone centuries ago lit their nightly way.

When I was six and Elizabeth eight, he killed himself.

* * *

Elizabeth has shut herself up in her childhood room. A teenager stands in the hallway outside the closed door.

Though he is older now, of a stature that signifies a recent growth spurt that he hasn't yet filled out, he retains the aquiline nose, the spectral moon-washed features overcast by thick dark hair, his face still somehow indistinct, unformed.

Who is this faceless boy? I can make out the dark pockets for eyes and the protruding nose, but that is it, and it makes for a disturbing image, like a photograph that was blurred in the taking, turning your once-familiar friend into a smudged ghoul with a jagged black scar for a mouth and impenetrable holes for eyes. But reality is not a photograph. Is it that the house cannot remember his face? Is this the way we imagine people whose features we can't quite recall? Like my father—if I think very hard, I can vaguely remember his looks, but would my memory reconstructed into life be accurate, or would it contain gaping holes, ghostly blurs where there ought to be defined lines? No, that is impossible; I have seen memories here that are too old for me to remember, older even than my mother and my grandmother, and these are arranged with precise detail.

He faces the closed door as if looking in or waiting for it to open. Inside my sister might be sitting in front of the mirror, unaware of the young man who hovers just outside. I think I ought to warn her, then chide myself for being foolish. Of course it is an echo. Why should I be afraid of an echo? Yet I get an awful feeling from him, this young man so happy to stomp birds to death, and perhaps I am right to have this feeling, for I notice that he is holding a kitchen knife. What would he be doing with that knife up here on the second floor?

I back away down the length of the hall to my own room as he turns around, looking through me with those indistinguishable black pits for eyes, blank like the dead, out of that strangely unfocused face. I walk backward all the way to my room, grateful to find the doorknob in my hand. With a thrill of unfounded fear I close and lock the door behind me, then turn and listen to the slow footsteps creaking across the hall toward my room. Inside all looks just as it did when I was a girl, and it is to the bed with its ruffled blue comforter that I move, where I sit listening to my anxious heart and the heavy approaching footsteps that stop just outside my door. Stop being so afraid, I tell myself. You are being foolish.

Yet I can't help it. I think of that poor bird, and I am afraid of being a small helpless creature, afraid of being fragile and ineffectual. I have always been thin and small like a child, and I always feel, even behind the podium of a classroom, that my students and colleagues must not take me seriously.

Cold autumn sunlight pushes weakly through the heavy curtains behind me. The room is a semidusk of blue though it is not yet midday. On my desk lie a handful of artifacts I excavated from the swamp—a gunflint, a piece of a broken bowl, an animal bone fragment. I palm the gunflint, turn it over in my fingers, hoping it will bring me luck, will keep me safe.

A thud on the door jars my heart. Then something drags down across the wood in a long grumbling scratch, pulls back, and repeats. He is dragging the point of the knife along the door.

I can feel a sick taste in the back of my throat. I am trapped and small and caged like a weak little bird. Why should I be so afraid of this boy except that, even as a teenager, he is already taller than I am? I would like to be large, like a man. I almost envy Elizabeth for her sheer girth. I can only imagine what it must feel like to be that size. To be so huge, to take up so much space.

But here I am, curled up and making myself even smaller, reminding myself that we are not in the same time, that he cannot hurt me. I squeeze the gunflint.

Still, in the hall he looked so solid. The memories are often just as real as the present. It's hard to tell sometimes.

The scratching stops and I think it must be over. Whatever this frightening memory is, whoever this disturbed boy is, it must be over.

Then a low voice calls softly through the door: "Let me in."

My breath catches in my throat. Beneath the door I see the two dark shadows of his feet. His face, his hands, must be pressed against the wood. I sit still and try to make no sound even as I remind myself that he cannot hear me, it's not really me he wants.

"I know you're in there." He speaks in an unhurried, pitchless croak. I hear the tip of the knife tap gently but insistently. "Come out, come out." More scratching now, and it is deliberate; I follow the sound, the motion. He is carving an X on my door.

"I told you I wouldn't hurt you," he says through the door. "Last time was an accident. I'm better now." More scratching, and this time it sounds like his nails. "I'm better now. You can come out." The scratching grows, impossibly, as if a multitude of hands are clawing at the door in livid desperation. "But don't look at me. Come out but don't look at me. You can't see me." A bang, the flat of his palm. "You can't see me." His mouth seems to be pressed right up against the crack between the door and the hinge, and his voice sounds of something awful bubbling up from the recesses of his throat, and he beats his fist against the door.

I close my eyes and press my hands to my ears, pleading silently that the memory will stop. At some point a madman lived in this house, and I shake with sick fear at listening to his deranged railing against my door, his uncontrollable rage trapping me here in this room.

"Let me in! Let me in! Let me in!" he says amid the pounding of hands and the clattering of the knife.

Then all at once it stops.

My heart jackhammers and my breathing comes in gasps, but gradually it all slows, calms.

Then the near-inaudible voice presses to the crack in the door: "Auntie?" *Tap. Tap. Tap.* "I'm sorry. Auntie?"

I can hardly move. My breath is caught in my throat, the gunflint slick with sweat from my palm.

Auntie. I shake my head. It isn't me. No, no, I am not an aunt.

At least, not yet.

3

I cannot expunge the faceless boy from my mind, even in the light of day; he lingers there as we clear away breakfast and ready ourselves for the drive to Elizabeth's doctor. I keep trying to get her attention, knowing that the closer we get to the appointment, the more likely it is I will lose my nerve before I can tell her my suspicions about Julian.

But Mother is still within earshot as we pull on our shoes, and I don't want to have this conversation in front of her—not when she is so keen on bringing this new life into the house. All morning she has been smiling, making pancakes, talking about how to prepare the house for a child. I don't have the heart to dampen her spirits.

Perhaps I should sign to Elizabeth when Mother isn't looking? It would be stilted, fumbling, ungraceful after so many years, but we used to converse in sign all the time. Just as my father and I had secret code words we shared with each other, made-up signs that only we would understand, so too had my silent language with my sister evolved. In the years following his death, however, she increasingly pushed away my attempts at signing. Whereas I thought it was a marvelous secret language, she seemed to think it was foolish, since we could both hear.

But what would I sign? We don't have a sign yet for Julian, so I would have to spell out his name, and then—what? What would I say? That I think her unborn son will be dangerous? That I am afraid of him? I feel deeply lacking, without word or symbol to communicate the unutterable and perhaps incommunicable truth.

I can't even come up with the words when we're in the car, pulling away from the house, my mother's face in the grimy window watching us go. Elizabeth plays with the radio to break the silence between us. She never could stand silence. I have never minded it, though. Perhaps that is why I have always felt more at ease in our silent house, in the silent swamp.

When you enter by canoe, there is a quiet mystery to the Great Dismal Swamp. Gray and hazy sunlight filters through tall thin trees that rise from their own rippled reflections in stagnant water to stand on top of themselves, and the way is veined with creepers and shrouded in the mists of time. Broom straw and river cane stitch the woods. Insects swarm in great black buzzing clouds that electrify the heavy sluggish air with a sense of disquiet.

I try to imagine what it was like for the people who once lived here, the maroons that those then-Wakefields, the ones of the early nineteenth century, helped in their escape.

I learned about one family by listening to the voices of the house—hearing them tell their stories to each other. If you are quiet enough, if you listen hard enough, there is much you can hear from the walls.

Here is what I heard: the father, Jonah, had been at a plantation eight miles from where his wife and daughter lived, and once a week on Saturday nights he would make the trek to see them, promising that soon they would be together—things that his wife, Clementine, did not believe. Once or twice she'd had to chastise him for putting notions in their daughter's head, little Meriday being only ten years old.

But then one day Jonah appeared on a Sunday, wild-eyed and frantic. He gathered them up, told them they were leaving, and they went off under cover of darkness.

They found their way to Wakefield Manor, where Everett Wakefield put them up in the basement until it was safe to leave for the swamp. Constance seemed delighted by the family's arrival, and was particularly taken with Meriday; she must have been unused to having playmates other than her brother.

While Jonah slept deeply that night, Clementine lay awake, gazing at her child's face.

Her former master, John Garrow, was a genteel fellow known for his amiability—not like Jonah's Thaddeus Carrington, who seemed to derive great pleasure from watching the quartermaster dole out beatings and never lifted a finger himself. But what many did not know was Mr. Garrow's predilection for youth. As soon as a girl turned twelve, she would be invited into the house; sometimes she would come out pregnant, or else she would take up in a luxurious bedroom to tend personally to Mr. Garrow's needs.

Clementine knew what would happen in the coming years as her daughter matured into a young lady.

I've seen them in the house—little Meriday and Constance, running together down the hallways, peeking into different rooms and scampering off again, giggling.

I do not believe I have the constitution to *live* in the swamp, but it draws me to it still, like it drew Constance. Elizabeth and I used to venture into the swamp when we were children, and I think how much more interesting a journey that would be than sitting here in the car, on the way to the doctor. The dull and daily journeys of adulthood feel so flat, so lifeless.

We've reached the perfect lull for me to tell her about Julian. Now, now I should tell her, with the sun warming us through the windows, with Elizabeth commenting blandly on the landscape, clearly looking for something to talk about. "Look at those cows, all in a circle around that other cow. You'd think they're forming a cult," she says with her chin in her hand. And then, a few miles later, "What do you suppose a cow cult would worship?"

Julian, I think. *Julian*. Instead, my mouth trips around the words, and I say, "Reminds me of that time we saw all those birds congregating together in the swamp. Just a huge cluster of them. Remember?"

Perhaps Elizabeth doesn't remember those bygone days as fondly as I do, because she makes a face. "Those birds were clustered together because they were all trying to get at the dead deer. Scavengers." She shudders. "Jesus, the thing was half eaten. I had nightmares about it. You don't remember that part?"

I shrug.

The gloomy mystery of the swamp drew me into unchecked, uncharted exploration. Sometimes she came with me; sometimes I went in alone. So often back then I found myself exploring the secretive depths of the swamp. My travels took me gliding along canals, the murky greenish water reflecting me, replicating me, re-creating me. Remembering my face. I trod through perilous unstable muck threaded with cottonmouth snakes and laden with sinkholes waiting to suck me in.

On second thought, I can see why Elizabeth might not think so fondly on it.

"Mom should never have let us roam around in there on our own," she says. "I would never let Julian do what we did."

It does seem different, now, when I see little Sam and Liz creeping into the marsh. What had seemed like such freedom now tastes more of neglect. When you're a child, all you want is freedom. Sometimes you don't realize how much you need your parents.

After my father killed himself, Elizabeth and I took care of ourselves while Mother shut herself away with her grief and her solitude and her self-loathing. She was not there to tell us not to wander too far into the swamp, to warn us of the dangers that lay therein; and when I see her now watching this perverse version of old home movies, watching us as children, watching our memories and echoes flit by, she is always watching what she missed in the first place, when she was too busy with her sorrow to notice or care.

"You can't protect your children from everything," I say, an insufficient defense of Agnes Wakefield. "And, no matter what you do, you never really know how they'll turn out."

"It's just lucky we turned out all right." Elizabeth frowns out the window. "Is that school new?"

I glance to my right as we breeze by, catch the blur of the brick structure with its clean, modern lines. "They tore down the old one last year."

"I guess it's been a while since I've come this way."

"You never visit."

Elizabeth has always made excuses to avoid coming back home. I can't remember the last time she visited. I wonder how long it's been since she last went to the swamp.

I enjoyed the quiet of the swamp in a way that, I think, Elizabeth never did. When she came along on our adventures, it was always noisy—feet sloshing through muck, complaints of mosquitoes devouring her, attempted birdcalls to see if any would call back. Lots of talking. I don't think she could ever really stand the quiet, so she had to fill it with something of herself so as not to feel even the vaguest hint of being alone. I was more like my father; I never minded the quiet, and sometimes I wanted to push her face into the muck just to shut her up.

My father was not born deaf, but he was deaf for as long as I knew him. I remember learning sign language very young, right alongside English, bred to be bilingual so I could communicate with him. I was precocious, as some children are. I appreciated the silence of our conversations, talks that could be quiet but at the same time filled with a world of words and ideas. The deft movements of his liquid hands, as if fingers could dance, communicated the tone of his voice as much as spoken word. I could pass a day without speaking if I was on bad terms with my mother and Elizabeth. You see more, you hear more, and you appreciate the quiet.

I do not know whether my father appreciated the quiet like I did, but then I hardly know if he even experienced it by then, he had been deaf so long. And what is silence to the deaf?

When you live with sound, going without must feel incredibly painful—a sense of absence, of missing some vital aspect of life, of withdrawal. But when you live without it, somehow it must seem natural—the silence comfortable rather than terrifying, so comfortable it ceases to exist. When silence exists, there is something awful in it, something awful in the emptiness and void of it, but when it is everywhere and it no longer exists, it can no longer do any harm.

We fall into another lull in the car. Up ahead, just there, is the doctor's office, another clean modern building emerging from the wild landscape and its proselytizing cows. The road rumbles gently beneath us. The turn signal clicks as I slow to enter the parking lot. An advertisement murmurs from the radio. Even in the quiet, it isn't really quiet after all.

And the swamp is never quiet either, not really. It is filled with a constant song of many voices, the voices of the birds and the trees and the insects and the wind culminating in a sighing, humming, buzzing, trilling soundscape, a music of the earth. Perhaps I can appreciate a certain kind of quiet, but when the swamp goes silent, that's when I feel the most uneasy, as if someone is turning down the volume of the world.

Somehow the quiet is calming. Somehow the quiet is frightening.

I do not know why I am going on about this. Sight and sound.

Yes. I do know.

* * *

"There he is."

A distinct gray shape appears from the pixelated darkness. There in the pulsing womb we see Julian's emergent form appear as if sound made visible, like a spectral voice coming through radio static. His nascent self, almost complete.

I know we are not really seeing him. We are seeing the echoes of him, hearing with our eyes, and I wonder what my father would have thought of that, what he thought when he saw the ultrasounds of his own daughters before they were born. How it felt to him to hear with his eyes. Julian is still hidden, though. We cannot see him secreted away in Elizabeth's womb, but we can hear his edges, his form, his shape.

Elizabeth cannot contain the smile that she shares with the monitor and then turns to me, to which I must respond in kind although I cannot shake the sick feeling that has come over me at the sight of him, making him real. I see him in that ashen gradient of the machine, not quite human, and I think of the boy dragging the knife down my door, calling me *Auntie*, marking me.

"Look at him," says Elizabeth. "Just look at him."

The ultrasound technician points out his body parts like it's a scavenger hunt: a hand, a foot, a knee.

"He's perfect," says Elizabeth. "Isn't he perfect?"

The lights are too bright and I feel a headache building behind my eyes.

"I'll meet you out there," I say, and move blindly from the room while Elizabeth calls after me to see what's the matter. She will be angry that she cannot continue to share this moment with me, for sharing moments, to her, is much more agreeable than experiencing them on her own. If she has a moment all to herself, she must wonder, what is the point?

I emerge into a long corridor and make my way toward the lobby. That sick feeling hasn't left me, carries my feet down the tiled floor, past multitudes of closed doors behind which anything might be happening. Behind those doors lie rooms where a woman is finding out her baby's sex, where another might be doubled over with terrible cramps, where someone is getting the worst sort of news. Rooms imbued with the mystery of birth and death. Whatever lives in those rooms remains a secret to me, hidden behind their many doors.

Yet there is something different about the door to my left. All of these other doors are a light, pleasant oak, friendly and neutral, but this one is darker, heavier. The wood is battered and ancient, grained and scuffed. I know this door.

Somehow it has followed me to the hospital. Whether it is just the door or the contents behind it too, I cannot possibly know. Yet how can a locked room suddenly appear in a different place entirely? Do you think I am going crazy? I stop before it, gazing on its impossible provenance, place my palms flat upon the rough surface. It feels the same. Thinking I might hear something, some clue, I lean my ear against it, but there is only silence. My hand finds the dull brass doorknob, but it doesn't turn. Below it, there is an old-fashioned sort of keyhole; if I only press my eye against it—

"Excuse me, dear. Are you lost?"

I turn to find a middle-aged nurse clutching a clipboard, staring at me beneath raised eyebrows and thick red hair, the dye fading at grayish roots. There is a speck of blood on her blue scrubs, and I find myself fixating upon it, wondering where it came from, wondering if she realizes it is there.

I look back at the door, but now it just looks like any other door here. Did I imagine it?

"No," I tell her, and continue down the hallway until it opens up into the lobby.

The hospital feels unnaturally *now*, all white under surreal light, metal fixtures, murmuring televisions hanging from ceilings, torturous-looking wheelchairs, two satisfied women with pregnant bellies reading magazines as they wait their turn.

I have been back home only a year and already the real world feels less real to me, strange and foreign and locked in time. It feels false, shallow. All that matters here is what is happening right now. The births and deaths of the past are irrelevant, as someday the births and deaths of the present will become irrelevant, each receding into the great chasm that lies at the bottom of time. I wonder if they realize this. If *then* doesn't matter, then *now* can't either, because soon it will become *then* and all will be the same.

I sit down across from the pregnant women hiding behind their magazines, feeling self-conscious and wishing Elizabeth would hurry up so we can leave this awful place. I don't know what to do with my hands. There is no magazine rack, so the women must have brought their own, and the television sleeps on, black screened, in the corner. I cross and then uncross my legs. *Oh, hurry up, Elizabeth.*

Since I do not know the names of the women, I will refer to them by their most defining characteristics: one is blonde and the other is wearing red lipstick. The blonde leans over and whispers to her companion while the other titters, and then they both smile private little smiles, stealing glances at me from the white corners of their eyes. They lean back, rustling the pages of their reading.

I want to ask them what they are giggling about. What could be so funny here? But I have a terrible feeling they are whispering and snickering at *me*, and there isn't a thing I can do to find out what it is they've found so amusing. I'd like to ask them. Just open my mouth and ask them what exactly they find so funny about my presence. After all, I am the only other person in this lobby.

I wonder if they planned their pregnancies together. How puerile! They have probably done everything together their whole lives. Most likely they spent high school lounging in one another's bedrooms with their hair hanging down over the side of the bed; daydreaming about the same boys; sharing their deepest secrets, which they never realized are entirely shallow; holding each other's hair back when one of them got so drunk she had to crouch gargoyle-like over the toilet to vomit; painting each other's toenails with silly colors; one of them intimately wiping away the other's tears with her bare fingers after her dog was eaten by a coyote. They will probably grow into old ladies together, their husbands only vaguely aware that they have always come second.

A little girl who cannot be more than four rushes over to the woman with red lips and tugs impatiently on her skirt.

"What is it, darling?"

"I'm bored," says the little girl in her little-girl voice.

Why bring her here, I wonder. This sterile prison of needles is no place for a child. And all the doors! There are so many doors behind which she might get lost forever. Too many doors for a child, surely.

"You'll just have to entertain yourself, sweet pea. We're obliged to wait until the doctor is finished with the other patients." Her eyeballs roll up in their sockets to glance briefly at me as if to say, *Who are you? Are you the one who is holding us up?* I quickly look away.

"Here, play with this," and she hands her an electronic device that looks like a small plastic tablet, which the girl carries away to play on. The women resume paging through their magazines, glancing up every so often, murmuring to one another from the sides of their mouths, looking at me, I know, without *really* looking, until I can't stand their little whispered conversation any longer.

I uncross my legs and slap my hands down on my thighs. "Do I know you?"

Their beady eyes latch on to me as their voices die, offended by my abrupt rudeness.

"I'm sure you don't," says the blonde.

Somehow the brunt of their direct attention strikes me as worse than the unconfirmed suspicion that they are gossiping about me. If only I could puff myself up and proudly take up an imposing amount of space, but instead I find myself shrinking away into my own body, in danger of shrinking away into nothing.

"I don't recall seeing you much in town," adds the woman with red lips. "I suppose that makes you one of those Wakefields?"

She says it without surprise. They must have realized already; they must have been speculating about *those* Wakefields, the witches, the swamp people, this whole time, knowing who I am by virtue of not recognizing me, for it is true, I do not spend much time in town, I am like a ghost here.

"And what does that make you?" I snap back. "How would you like it if I sat here snickering and whispering about you? As if I had nothing better to do."

Both women now fix me with looks of such vapid affront that I almost laugh in their faces, but we are interrupted by Elizabeth, enormous and full of easy courage. "Making friends?"

The woman pinches her red lips as if sucking on a lemon. "Another Wakefield, I suppose."

Scornfully, Elizabeth replies, "I'm not a Wakefield anymore." Then, as soon as the words have tumbled from her mouth, her face goes ice-cold and still; I can see the realization blooming in real time. If a divorce is imminent, then will she be a Wakefield again? Will she revert to her maiden name? Who will she be, she wonders? Elizabeth Hill or Elizabeth Wakefield?

We are Wakefields, all of us, even in this patriarchal world. Even when my mother was married to my father, she kept her name, and they debated long and hard over which name their daughters would take, eventually settling on my mother's family name, allowing us to inherit a lineage that would otherwise be lost to time and X chromosomes. Perhaps it does not matter, anyway. Perhaps the Wakefield name will die with us after all. It is so hard to keep a thing like that alive.

Maybe the house will keep it alive for us.

* * *

When I first came to stay with my mother, my intentions were for a short-term lease. A few weeks, perhaps, to regain my equilibrium. A month at best.

I should have known: once this house has you, it doesn't let you go.

I slept on Liz and Don's couch for about a month after I was mugged. Each night sleep tugged gently at me like television static, and just as I let my eyes slip closed, a windblown shutter would beat against the window, or a neighbor's dog would bark to be let out, and I would snap awake and lie wide-eyed in the dark with my ears attuned to every minute noise that crept or cracked or whispered: the hiss of a passing car, the rustling of a bothered tree outside, or perhaps the patter of footsteps, some stranger stealing onto the porch, rattling a lock pick until the handle of the front door jiggled metallically, and the creak of the door swinging open, and that pungent odor of musk and sweat and my cheek pressed into the cement and the gun pressed into my neck—

Unable to take it, I would rise from the couch, check all the locks, make sure the windows were closed, and then, wired with nervous energy, I would spend the next several hours straightening up the house: pairing shoes and lining them side by side against the wall, alphabetically organizing DVDs, putting empty glasses in the dishwasher—and once I was so bored and fidgety that I moved all the furniture in the living room four inches to the left, just to see if they would notice in the morning.

Surprisingly, they didn't care for my midnight labors.

One morning, when Don was getting himself set up at his rig to work, he started digging through the drawers of his desk with increasingly sharp movements, until he yelled out, "Where the hell are my headphones?"

I had to retrieve them from wherever it was I had placed them the night before during one of my shambling, zombie-eyed organizing sprees, and he snatched them from my hands. "You shouldn't put things where they don't belong," he snapped, before closing the headphones over his ears.

Often I would catch a few hours of sleep close to dawn, when I had exhausted myself silly with all the nighttime working. But until then, I got to know that house intimately, saw into all its secret shadowed places that Don and Liz never saw, as they tended to sleep through the night. Until that last night, of course.

It was sometime after midnight and I was lying awake, running through possible tasks in my mind to see if I could fall asleep just by imagining I was doing something, when inevitably there was a petulant creak, which at first I chalked up to the house settling. But when I tried to go back to my mental exercise, there was the creak again, this time unmistakably the sound of a footstep, weight shifting on the floorboards.

Someone was in the house.

My breath caught in my throat as I listened to the slow, heavy footsteps creeping down the hallway, footsteps that didn't belong there. I tried to remember if I had checked all the windows and doors that night, but I couldn't recall doing so, and let's face it, Don and Liz were fairly careless with that sort of thing, so who knows, there could have been a wide-open invitation somewhere for an intruder looking to steal inside. My gut twisted, sick with dread.

I reached out and felt around the coffee table to the left of the couch until my hand met the cold glass encasing of a candle. It smelled cloyingly of apples and spice, some heady autumn scent, and I pulled the heavy candle close to me as I sat up. On fleet, silent feet, I prowled over to the hallway and lay in wait for the figure's passing. When the shape of him stepped out of the hall and into the living room, I shouted and swung the candle.

The man cried out and doubled over, one hand on his left eye, and with a sinking feeling somewhere beneath my furious heart, I recognized the sound of his voice.

"What the *hell*?"

The hall light blinked on as Elizabeth came stumbling out in her pajamas, hair mussed with sleep. "What is going on?"

Don straightened, still holding a palm over his injured eye. The candle lay somewhere on the floor.

"What were you doing?" I demanded, my voice rising defensively.

"I was going for a smoke," he confessed, and sure enough, he had a pack of cigarettes in his hand.

"Damn it, Don," said Elizabeth. "Are you smoking again?"

When he finally pulled his hand away from his eye, we saw the purple blooming over the swelling lid. It was lucky he didn't lose the eye. His brow ridge absorbed the worst of the blow, leaving him with a ghastly black bruise and a burst blood vessel that turned the white of his eye red.

I was lucky, too. They didn't press charges, didn't even want me to cover the medical bills. They just wanted me to leave.

Perhaps it was time to go home, but when I thought of home, I didn't think of that lonely apartment I had been living in for the last several years; I thought of the mansion on the edge of the swamp with its proliferation of rooms and towering bookshelves. And even though I intended to go back to my apartment, truly I did, when I started my car and crawled away from their suburban bungalow, I imagined myself settling into bed that evening alone, surrounded by the darkness within and the darkness without, figures creeping around outside my windows, shadows with nothing visible but the whites of their eyes, breaking through the front door, stealing into my apartment, pushing me to the floor, pressing death to the back of my neck. Before I knew it, I was driving in the other direction.

I drove up the winding roads, through hilly forests and leafy vales, and when I arrived at the house, it welcomed me as if I had never left.

My mother, answering the door, looked at me like a stranger. She opened it only a crack, giving me a slivered view of her wary eyeball.

"Yes?" she said.

The porch light wasn't on. All was dark, and I a shadow.

"Mom," I said.

She flipped the switch, and the low yellow light buzzed to life.

When I stepped in, she padded away in her slippers to fix some tea. I brought in my things, and from the foyer I heard the distant murmur of her talking to someone in the kitchen. By this time, my mother had been living alone for nearly ten years, ever since her youngest child flew the coop for college and other worlds—her only company the house itself and whatever it deigned to offer her.

When the teakettle started screaming, I found the kitchen abandoned and the kettle rattling with a volcanic expulsion of steam, which only calmed when I shut off the burner and went searching through the labyrinth to find where she had gone.

As I turned through the lonely halls, a terrible sensation came over me—the strange uncertainty of this house, the inescapable feeling that I had never actually left, but that I had been wandering these halls and finding in them doorways to other places, unreal places, dorm rooms and cafeterias and movie theaters and coffee shops, as if my life outside these walls had never actually existed but only been a twisted sort of pretend, the house making up the whole of my reality.

When I found my mother, she seemed to have forgotten I was there, inciting my fear of dementia—that she would lose her memories, too, like her parents before her, the house sucking them away to keep for itself as if feeding on her mind. But she was only confused. The memories confused her, she confessed after the fact, so that she had thought me a memory as well, wasn't sure if I was real or not, as the memories had become more real to her than anything else in this world.

It was easy to fall into the comfortable habits of home, and easier still to tell myself I had to stay for my mother—a sharp, clever woman, but anyone will grow dull and muddled if they are left on their own for too long with their own mind. So I broke my lease, moved the rest of my things in, took over the grocery shopping and other necessary trips into town, and found there the very same people of Shadydale I had left behind, their flat profiles, the infinite corners of their eyes.

These people would never invade Wakefield Manor, however, and so I felt safe from them. They never ventured that far out toward the swamp. They left us well enough alone.

And then I remembered who I was in Shadydale: not just a small, meek, anonymous creature, the way I was out in the world, but *one of those Wakefields.* Most of the time I kept to myself, tried to make myself invisible, but sometimes I stood outside the post office after mailing the gas bill and stared at the woman walking her dog until she shuddered from my gaze and hurried away, yanking the leash after her. Or I stopped at the diner for a milkshake and sat in the shadowy corner booth, slurping until long after the drink was gone, until that empty bone-rattling gurgle of the straw made the young couple at the next table call out for the bill, throw down some cash, and scurry away whispering.

Sometimes it is a pleasure to be *one of those Wakefields*. If everyone leaves me alone, then I have nothing to fear.

* * *

When we returned from the doctor's office, Elizabeth had that cracked smile on her face, and she wandered about the house like that, restless, trying to rein in some terrible identity crisis burbling just under the surface, which those smirking women had managed to stir loose. She handed the ultrasound photo to our mother, whose delight seemed not enough for her, as she kept urging my mother on with questions about every little visible part of the child's body—*Don't you see his foot there? And his head? And what about . . . ?*—until even my mother gave her a look of alarmed confusion, said he looked like a healthy baby, and handed back the picture to put a period on the conversation. She then went about cleansing the air of whatever negative energy Elizabeth had brought back with her by lighting up a variety of incense. She hummed all the while.

I suspect the person Elizabeth really wanted to show the photo to was the child's father. At dinner, I found myself wanting to see the faceless boy again, and I kept checking the doorway in hopes that he might walk through and reveal himself. I needed to know who he was. If only I had the right talisman, the right ritual to summon him. But I waited in vain.

* * *

I wonder if the house dreams.

Its regurgitations of memory seem accurate, as far as I can tell; and if they are accurate memories, then they are unlikely to be dreams.

But what if the house dreamed? Would the memories distort the same way our dreams sometimes twist reality? Would it begin showing surreal images of things that never were and never would be? And what monsters might be lurking in the shadows of these dreams?

Is the faceless boy a dream?

I wonder, because my dreams are always so strange.

In this one, I am as pregnant as my sister; my belly protrudes unnaturally from my angular frame, and from within that aching globe of flesh press tiny hands, pushing up, pushing free. I am lying down and watching mesmerized as two little hands appear, distending the flesh. At first I am intrigued by the sight, but then two more hands appear, and two more, until myriad tiny hands are pressing up from the inside of my belly and fear grips me as I wonder what is inside of me, and I begin to shout *please get it out, please get it out*, but there is only a dark figure lurking in the corner of the room—and I call out to this figure but he does not move, merely watches as the tiny hands burst through flesh and reach their bloodied fists into the open air and one by one climb out and away, trailing umbilical cords, and the figure steps closer holding a knife and the figure is Julian—

No, of course it isn't. I wake, feeling foolish, pressing both hands against my stomach.

After the nightmare, I cannot get back to sleep. My brain feels wired, keyed up with electricity. Lying in bed makes my stomach churn, so I get up and tread quietly into the dark hallway, the floor sighing disconsolately beneath my footfalls. I make it only a few steps into the hall when I feel suddenly that I am not alone.

A creature creeps low against the floor toward me.

It crawls with long narrow limbs like a spider, its elbows protruding into the air. Instead of crawling strictly on its knees, it keeps picking them up to use its feet, pushing itself forward by extending its legs out behind and repeating. All I can see are pale limbs and black hair hiding a face that is turned down to the floor, a face I know I would not be able to see even if it were lifted in my direction, and I beg inwardly, *Please don't look up, please don't lift your head, please don't fix me with your black eyes trapped in an indistinguishable face.* I wanted him to appear again, but not here, not in the middle of the night. What seems fine in the daylight becomes infinitely more grotesque when encountered at midnight upon opening one's bedroom door.

I step back into the open doorway as he crawls past, so close he might reach out and brush my bare feet; I curl my toes in revulsion.

The floorboards groan beneath him. I turn on the bedroom light so that it floods the hall, but he is already past me, and the light only illuminates his path from behind.

Though he looks young, he is clearly too old to be crawling. This child should be able to stand but instead continues his hypnotic spider-scuttle.

"Elizabeth," I whisper, knowing she will not hear me, wherever she is, likely asleep in her own room—but I am too afraid to shout, fearing, again, irrationally, that he will hear me across the span of time.

Frantically I decide I must run down the hall and shake her awake, drag her back here to see, with her own eyes. Who is he? Would she recognize him? But he is moving too quickly now, and I fear if I lose sight of him he will vanish altogether.

I follow a few paces so as not to lose him as he slithers up the stairs. Up here, in the quiet of the third floor, the only light is from a window calling forth the moon. He creeps and creeps down the narrowing length of the hall. Maybe when he reaches the end he will turn around and come back. The mere thought sends a wave of nausea into my throat. *Please do not come back.*

Instead he slithers one hand up to the brass knob of that heavy locked door.

He will not be able to open it. No one ever has.

But impossibly, the knob turns, and the door swings inward to reveal a gaping black pit.

I have to blink. It is like seeing double, although it is so dark I can hardly see at all. He is going through a door from a different time; the door of *now* is still closed, is still locked, and I can see the door closed at the same time I see it open, like a photograph overlaid with the ghostly imprint of something else. The darkness of his open door reaches out as he climbs inside, into a darkness the feeble moonlight behind me cannot reach out and touch.

Then he is gone, but the doorway remains.

At first I am repelled by that terrible emptiness, as if that complete absence is sucking all light from the world, but I have to know—I have to see.

I hurry down the hall, the seething maw of darkness opening before me like an abyss, but as soon as I reach it, the open doorway vanishes. My hands and eyes meet solid wood, and nothing more.

If only I could arrest my heart. On trembling legs, I descend the staircase all the way down, thinking of cold water, a nip of whiskey, something to calm my nerves.

Instead I discover, again, that I am not alone.

The television is on in the sitting room, and Elizabeth sits bathed in its blue glow in the otherwise dark room, holding a glass of wine.

For a moment I am invisible in the dark. I could go back upstairs, but I do not. "Elizabeth?"

She startles, looks momentarily betrayed, perhaps wondering how long I have been standing here watching her.

"Have you seen him?" I step into the room, but I can't sit; the vision of the crawling boy is fresh in my nerve endings. I wonder if that's why she's down here at two o'clock in the morning, distracting herself with infomercials. "Please tell me you've seen him."

"Seen who?"

In the artificial light, she's aged by the moonlike glow, as old as she has ever been and older still by the minute. But she is calm, unafraid. I tell myself to be calm, to be unafraid. She lifts her wineglass to take a sip, then hesitates with it inches from her mouth. "The doctor said I can have one," she murmurs defensively.

"One glass or one bottle?"

"*That's* funny."

The dark figure crawls through the back of my mind. "Look, there's something I have to tell you."

She waits for me to continue, then lowers her glass. "Well, spit it out. Or are you going to keep dancing around it?"

Maybe I should just keep dancing. Just dance away, down the halls, and never speak of this again. I don't know who he is, after all. The boy could be anyone.

And yet, I feel it in my gut. I *know* who he is.

"I've seen Julian."

She rolls her eyes. "Yes, I know. You were at the ultrasound."

"No, I've *seen* Julian. Here, in the house."

A short round laugh escapes her, and her face invents an expression of bottled annoyance, amusement, contempt—clenched teeth behind closed lips.

"Julian? Here in the house?" she says with determined levity. "How could you possibly have seen someone who hasn't been born yet?"

"Lizzie." She scowls at my infantilizing her name. "You *know* this house. What if . . . ?"

"I don't believe you." She takes an angry little sip. "Mother, I can understand. She's always had a few marbles loose. But please don't tell me you've bought into her New Age mumbo jumbo."

"It isn't mumbo jumbo."

"Please. In any case, how is it you've come to recognize my unborn son, when you've only just seen a fuzzy little gray picture of him?"

"He called me Auntie."

"Oh, of course, that explains it."

We're at a stalemate. If we continue on in this way, sooner or later one of us is going to crack. I hope it isn't me.

"I'm afraid there's something *wrong* with him." I look around, wishing for him to appear again. I need him to show himself, to show Elizabeth what I cannot possibly explain with mere words. Maybe she would be able to see his face. "You'll see." I look around, half expecting him to come crawling toward us out of the shadows. "I just saw him upstairs, not ten minutes ago."

"This is just like your ghosts. When you were a kid," she says, with more wonder and disbelief than spite. "Remember those? You were so scared that we looked through our family's whole genealogical record, but the people you saw never lived in this house. It was all made up."

"I'm not making this up."

"Sure you aren't. And there really was a man who lived here once who didn't look like anything, and an old woman with Xs for eyes." She laughs, but it is a mean sound. "Come on, Sam. You scared yourself because you let your imagination wander away from you, and, well, nobody could blame you, could they? Not in this place. But you *have* to get a handle on what's real and what isn't. When you mix those up, you *hurt* people." The words etch a scowl on her face.

"If you open your eyes, you'll see him too," I tell her, ignoring her comments on my childhood ghosts. "Just wait."

I want so desperately for her to believe me that I wait as interminable seconds tick by, waiting foolishly, hopelessly, for the boy to show himself, and every second that he doesn't I feel my credibility shatter a bit more. But I wait, anxious and eager, because I cannot stand any more of Elizabeth's condescension. She must, she *must* believe me. The air crackles expectantly. A minute drags into eternity. The television drones in the background, bothersome and insistent, until Elizabeth snaps up the remote and douses us in an abrupt dark and quiet.

"Are you finished?" she says coldly.

"Why don't you ever listen to me?"

"Why would I listen to bullshit?" Her voice is harsh and low; I hear the slosh of wine in her glass. "You don't know what you're talking about."

I fumble my way to the light, trailing broken sentences behind me as I go. "I do. Jesus, Liz. I'm trying to help you. So you can . . . I don't know . . . *do* something."

"Like what?" she snarls. "Get an abortion?"

I pause beside the lamp. "Well, it's a bit late for that."

"You're still angry with me," she says. "For kicking you out of my house. That's what this is about."

"I'm not angry about that," I tell her, which is the truth.

I turn the switch and a harsh light pierces the air, glaring on every surface and illuminating Elizabeth's furious face in a cold white. Her pupils hastily retract into glossy irises. Red wine drips over the lip of her glass and onto her hand.

"You attacked my husband. What else was I supposed to do?"

"I told you, I'm not angry about that," I insist.

"Then what?"

"I'm not angry about anything."

"Oh, don't lie."

I shred a piece of lint in my pocket until it disintegrates in my fingers. "How could I be angry with you? You only left me there." The words stumble free, cottony in my mouth. "You only left me out there alone, to get mugged—to be pushed to the sidewalk with a gun to my head, thinking I was going to die."

"How on earth was I supposed to know that was going to happen?" she replies, her voice rising indignantly. "You can't blame me for not predicting the future."

She finishes her wine in one long pull, slams the glass down on the table so hard I'm surprised when it doesn't shatter, and pushes herself to her feet in what is supposed to be a sharp rise but turns into a laborious toddle. "Anyway, you're an adult now. It isn't my job to take care of you. Frankly, it never was. But I did it anyway, because Mom wouldn't. You can't expect me to look out for you forever." Her eyes are iron. "Making up stories for attention won't make me feel sorry for you. Poor, neglected Sam. Always has to have some invented problem. Well, some of us have *real* problems."

She stalks away before I can think of anything to say.

4

Elizabeth has locked me out of her life now, refusing to talk to me. I have made myself an enemy, and now she will defy me in her spite, retracing her childhood footsteps of rebellion, which always came so easily to her and so hard to me. Rebelling against Mother, against the house, against the quiet.

She used to do this to me when we were kids, sometimes even quite literally locking me out of the house.

Once, when I was fifteen, I stayed out late with my study group, and when I returned the house was dark, dormant, the front door locked. They were supposed to leave it open for me, but Elizabeth and I had been fighting that day, and I knew she must have crept downstairs and locked the door at some point to get back at me. I circumnavigated the house, tried the back door, tapped on forbidding windows. I looked up to the second floor, begging for a light to shine through the draperies—Mother awake reading, Elizabeth sulking in her princess bed. Their rooms were dark.

Moonlight made a mystical landscape of the swamp, which seemed to whisper its mysteries to me, saying, *Don't worry if you can't get in there, the swamp is always open, we'll let you in.* Why I thought the swamp might want me to wander, lost, through its narrow creeks and sorrowful trees must have been the fanciful workings of an overactive teenage mind, one fraught with the anxiety of being trapped out in the darkness, barred from home, from the grace of light.

I went around picking up small pebbles—small enough, I hoped, that they wouldn't damage the old windows, which even then had seen better days. Feeling like a cliché—I am a boy who is in love with a girl but we are only sixteen so I will throw pebbles at her window—I tossed my little prizes here, and here, but my aim was terrible. One of the pebbles flew off course and hit the window overlooking the back corner of the house. The only one that is truly inaccessible from the inside: the window of the locked room.

A heavy curtain hangs there, never touched, never opened, leaving the window perpetually black even in broadest daylight. But then, one can hardly tell the difference from any other room. All the house feels encased, enclosed, with its heavy draperies pulled over each orifice as if to keep the outside world *out*.

What a fool was I, wasting a pebble on entirely the wrong window.

But then, of all things—the curtain moved.

At first I thought it must be a trick of the moonlight, the swamplight, that strange eerie glow that inhabits the darklands of the country, a glow that's likely just the eye trying frantically to see in such nonlight where there is nothing to refract against the pupil, where everything looks grainy and strange no matter how desperately you squint, as things fuzz and fray and disappear, pursued relentlessly by the failing eye. But it was no mistake. The curtain's dark sensual curves fluttered and began to draw back to one side.

The heart-stopping sight flooded me with terrible anticipation—*there was someone in the locked room.*

It could not be my mother or Elizabeth, I reasoned, since neither of them had the key, the lost key, the long-gone key.

There was someone *else* in the locked room.

Thrilled with this new fear, I suddenly lost the old one; being locked out was not so awful after all, even out here in the darkness, for at least I was *out here*, at least there lay a solid windowpane between me and whoever, whatever, was drawing back that black curtain with its bony fingers, whereas my sleeping mother and sister were inside, locked in there with *it*.

I wish I could describe to you the face that loomed out of the empty dark within, but I could not make it out from below, and the moonlight was too afraid to touch whatever lingered in that lonely room, leaving me with only the vague impression of a face with pits for eyes, like a demon.

In a moment, the curtain swished back into place and went still.

And then I was at the front door. I was pounding desperately, madly, to be let in. I was hesitating with my fist an inch from the wood, abruptly terrified to be let in, wanting in that sick moment to remain out in the familiar confusing dark, perhaps to go live in the swamp now, away from the house, when the door opened, and my mother ushered me inside with a mixture of irritability and fondness, assumed my panic was at being locked out. She made me an indifferent cup of tea and went back to bed.

I don't know how long I sat in that kitchen, clutching the mug of cold dregs, trying to convince myself to move, to ascend the stairs, to get to my room where I could cower beneath the covers like a child.

Eventually I did.

I never liked to see the memories at night—something in their ghostly appearance has always unsettled me during the moonlit hours—but then I saw, inexplicably, my father, just standing there cleaning his glasses. Seeing him gave me a warm rush of relief, enough so that when he vanished, I had the courage to run upstairs.

By the next morning, in the light of day, it all felt like a dream, and eventually I came to the conclusion that I had imagined the figure. But perhaps it did not matter whether I had imagined it, for the room was locked and no matter how many times I pressed my ear against the door, I never heard a thing.

* * *

In the morning I frantically, belatedly iron out my lessons for the week, trying to catch Elizabeth's eye as she lumbers past. I've planted myself in the drawing room, a book spread out on the table before me, the drapes pulled open to let in a bit of light. She ignores me.

My mother is upstairs, picking through dusty boxes of old toys and blankets from when Elizabeth and I were children. I had to come downstairs after trying to work in my room, because every so often she would appear in the doorway holding up two stuffed animals worn wretched with age and ask me what I thought. “For Julian,” she said when I only stared, dumbfounded, and it was all I could do not to tell her we shouldn’t give him any animals, even fake ones, not if he’s going to destroy them, like the bird. I bit my tongue, shrugged, thinking my silence would protect her. Eventually I could no longer take her constant interruptions.

Julian, I think, *why will you turn out so cruel? What is it that could produce such a disturbing child?*

I shiver, feeling trapped by the question, and wonder how long it will take him to pick up a knife for the first time, crawl his way to my room in the middle of the night, and beg for his auntie to let him in to play.

Elizabeth comes into the room again without looking at me and picks up a set of headphones, plugging them first into her phone and then into her ears, the better to ignore me with.

I always had the sense that Elizabeth was afraid of the cold depths of silence, and afraid of being alone—the silence of loneliness. She has always tried to fill the world with bright sounds, sought out distractions, noise, delightful chaos. Her most memorable rebellion against the eternal tomblike quiet of Wakefield Manor came when she was thirteen, loud, talkative, restless; she brought home a yard-sale mint-green Fender Strat, a junky guitar with warped strings she did not know to replace and pick scratches from unrestrained clumsy strumming. As soon as she plugged it into the cheap amplifier she’d picked up, she started playing feral nonsense—dissonant nonchords of the purest teenage rage. After a day or two they morphed into actual chords as she started to learn by reading tabs, and soon she was playing punk rock that echoed throughout the house as yet another seeming anachronism that lived there.

No surprise, then, that the screaming guitar and its unholy choir of demonic chords sent my mother into a towering drunken temper.

I remember hearing her footsteps overhead and the pounding on Elizabeth’s door and her shouts. “Do you want to hear this noise the rest of your life?” Then more shouting, on either end, until there was a door slam and the cold, ringing, uncertain silence that hovers in the wake of a fight.

The next day when we got home from school, me with a dandelion tucked into my hair for good luck and she sulking her way from the bus stop with her backpack slung over one slouched shoulder, a posture that later put her at risk of scoliosis, we came into the house to find a little girl peering anxiously out the windows, which I knew from photo albums was a younger version of our mother. The real one, the current one, was nowhere to be found.

"Who cares?" said Elizabeth scathingly, still annoyed with her yet simultaneously displaying something other than mere annoyance, something I did not recognize then—whatever veiled emotions recoil within a teenager whose mother frequently yells admonishments at her over a glass of something opaque.

(I recognized this reaction much later, when this memory returned to wander through the house and I had the opportunity to study it from the outside—to study the childish carelessness and the complex succession of rancor, hurt, and regret that passed fleetingly across my sister's face with all the whispery impermanence of a hummingbird's wings—and to understand the truth behind our behavior.)

Eventually we found our mother in Elizabeth's bedroom. Well, I should say Elizabeth found her; she had run upstairs to her room while I deliberately counted my steps, as I was fixated on counting at the time, and there were certain magical numbers I had to reach in my counting if I wanted good fortune—in particular, seven, eleven, and twenty-one. I had just reached nine, counting my steps on the way up the stairs and having pocketed seven for later magic, when I heard the thump of Elizabeth's backpack hitting the floor and a wordless shriek that sent me racing up the rest of the way in a flurry of curiosity. I found Mother sitting on Elizabeth's princess bed, the sorry guitar flat on her lap. Each of the strings had been removed, tied into terrifying metal knots, and cast onto the floor.

As children, we were shocked and appalled at the defacing of the guitar, but really, it wasn't as though she'd smashed it into pieces or damaged it irrevocably. If only we had known how easy it was to change strings—or known, in fact, that guitarists change their strings all the time. Strings get old, after all. They lose their vibrancy. They fray. Old strings sound like the muted voices of damned souls whose cries you can only hear coming up through the floor vents. And those strings were *old*—imagine one of them snapping in Elizabeth's face the next time she put the full force of her teenage fury into her strumming. It might take out an eye.

"How *could* you?" Elizabeth shouted.

Agnes picked up her drink and smiled. The ice that remained, nearly melted, clinked against the sides of the glass. "So pick a new hobby."

"Like drinking?" Elizabeth shot back.

(She did pick a new hobby shortly thereafter, in fact, and one that seemed at odds with her brief foray into the rebel-punk life: ballet. A rebellion against her own rebellion. Playing classical music from her stereo, she practiced her graceful movements. Sometimes, though, when Agnes had vanished into the house or into her own head, Elizabeth played her punk CDs and danced a dizzying mélange of ballet and the frenetic energy of crunching guitars—a paradoxical art. It was only much later, when she was older and more sensible, that she realized the very best rebellion against our peculiar family was to become, in fact, a terribly sensible, down-to-earth, and altogether normal human being.)

My mother held out her glass, taunting. "Go on, then. Give it a taste so we can see if this is the hobby for you."

Elizabeth knew better than to take the glass, but she didn't know better than to knock it out of Mother's hand, where it thudded and spilled its contents over the floor, the room erupting in the acrid smell of alcohol.

It reminds me now of August Wakefield knocking the cup of tarry water out of his sister's hands, letting the floorboards drink the dark elixir. Elizabeth had the same cold look on her face when she knocked the glass to the floor.

The sound of a slap left a bright handprint on Elizabeth's cheek. She and my mother both looked momentarily stunned, and then Elizabeth shouted, "I *hate* you!" She swiveled but my mother reached out, grabbed her arms as she thrashed away, and held her fast, making crude attempts at apologies. Elizabeth struggled, shouting, "I hate you! I hate you!" through her tears.

They were retreating from me now—but it was only because I was backing away from the room, away from the shouting, my hands over my ears. I told myself I could not hear them. I closed my eyes so I could not see them either, but I nearly tripped over one of the knotted strings cast onto the floor, tied like a soft pretzel. I stumbled over it, and it sprang free of the careless knot until it was once again a curved line, dented periodically from years of pressing into frets. I picked it up and carried it with me to my hiding place.

I was there for hours, hiding among the white-sheeted shapes of old furniture, playing with the steel string. Beyond the arched window the sun set, plunged me into nightfall. No one came to find me. No one called me down for dinner. My stomach grumbled, and I crawled out from under a sheet covering an old piano, accidentally taking it with me in a plume of dust. The ancient piano with its yellowing keys grinned back as the falling sheet plinked out a few sour notes.

Worried that Mother had heard—that she would come yell at me for my music, too—I threw the sheet back over the piano and crept out of the room, peering around for any sign of her. The hall was dark with dusk.

No one was in the kitchen. I was hungry, but I didn't know how to cook anything, not really, so I went looking in my mother's favorite drinking spots. In the lightless parlor, I saw someone sitting on a chair against the far wall. "Mother?" I called out. "I'm hungry. Can we eat now?"

She didn't respond.

"Please?" I stumbled around, feeling the wall. "Can you turn on the light?"

She was laughing low, in the back of her throat, a terrible old chuckle, and suddenly I thought, *this is not my mother.*

Instead of searching for the light switch, I fell back against a curtain and dragged it open, filling the room with uneasy twilight.

She sat in a wheelchair—an old woman, older than my mother, with black Xs where her eyes should be. Her hands were plagued by fingers bent and crooked as if broken and allowed to heal at contorted angles, and though her lips were sealed shut, she was laughing still, that dark chuckle behind closed lips. Gray wisps of hair wilted against her gaunt face. Her feet were bare, wrinkled, callused; she was missing several toes.

A scream rose in my throat, trapped behind my tonsils.

I ran from the room, bumping into walls; a stiff old portrait fell down when I slammed against it, landing sideways in its gilt frame, staring up at me from the floor. Scrambling away, I darted around the corner of the hall, my breath hitching fast—

And I ran right into a warm, solid shape, which wrapped its arms around me.

"Samantha! What has gotten into you?"

It was my mother, and I clutched her house robe, pressed my face into it, inhaled her sharp oaky scent. "There was an old woman," I moaned into her clothes.

She ripped me away, bent down, saw the guitar string I was still clutching in my fist. "This isn't a toy," she snapped, pulling the string from my hand.

From the parlor came a creak like rusty wheels, and the string slipped out of my mother's grasp.

She sighed. "Throw that away and go to your room," she told me.

I peel myself away from the past. That was then. I am not a child anymore.

I remember standing there, though, my heart racing, thinking there were things in this house I didn't understand, things that maybe I didn't *want* to understand. I would have to take the long way around to the staircase, too afraid to pass the parlor, too afraid at the moment even to look up from the floor. My eyes were locked on the fallen guitar string, a line that seemed to divide the past from the future, that existed somewhere in between.

* * *

Elizabeth never believed me about the old woman. I guess it isn't a surprise that she doesn't believe me about Julian, either.

But that old fear comes back to me now, when I think of him. The fear of what might be lurking in the shadows of this house. It is a fear hard to shake with autumn dragging daylight away sooner and sooner, night encroaching on us in the afternoon, and earlier still within the curtained, closed-up house.

Even out of the house, though, the uneasy feeling follows me. It doesn't help that it has been raining.

A storm has blundered through town, carelessly throwing branches to and fro and driving insistently against the roof of my car. It crashed into existence just as I was making my way home from teaching, stretching the forty-odd minute drive to more than an hour as I crept through the deluge. The rain puts me in mind of myths and legends; of ghosts and witches.

All I want is to go home, but first I have to stop in Shadydale to pick up eggs and coffee. I duck into the grocery store, shaking the downpour out of my eyes as it drags my hair into a wet tangle, and grab my purchases as quickly as I can.

The cashier knows me, just as she would know anyone else who frequents this market, but she acts as if she doesn't, politely handing me the receipt without looking directly at me. As soon as I step away, I hear her whispering with the next person in line.

I'm nearly back to the door, back out into the rain, when I stumble around two small children playing at the front of the store, waiting for their parents to finish shopping. The boy looks up at me and calls out, "Hey, Wakefield!"

I make the mistake of acknowledging him by stopping and looking down. I can feel eyes on my back from the woman who was behind me in line.

"I heard your mother's a witch," the boy says.

His sister nudges him and asks, "Who?"

"Agnes Wakefield."

The girl's eyes go wide. "Oh. I thought she was dead. But she still haunts the house."

"No, she's a witch. She put a curse on the house. And she eats children."

The girl turns her eyes to me. "Is it true?"

I consider telling them to stop saying such things about my mother, who is frightening to them only because she never comes out of the house, but instead I pull my lips into a grin, though it is really more a baring of teeth. "Yes, that's right. And if you get too close, she'll eat you up."

Their eyes bulge and they turn, dart away from me, behind their parents' legs at the register. The parents glance up at me and then away again.

I pull the back of my sweater over my head and rush out into the rain, throw myself into my car, wet and dripping.

A witch. I shake my head, start the car. They are confusing the tales about Wakefield Manor with the legend of the swamp. My mother is not the Swamp Witch—that's an old legend, passed down through the ages: a way of warning young ones to stop them from straying. Isn't it funny how we humans have evolved? Animals seem to know instinctively, but we must tell each other stories to warn of danger. And for that reason, folktales live in the swamp, just like the water moccasins that slither through the wetlands and the bobcats that skulk in the log fern.

As the legend goes, since time immemorial, the witch has haunted the swamp, leading wanderers astray in the form of a hovering light that guides them to quicksand, where they sink into the underworld. She is always seen as a dancing flame, for the witch's true form appears only in reflections, so terrible is it that it cannot be tolerated by the unshielded eye.

I imagine the maroons telling each other these tales by the fireside in the olden days. The house has whispered things to me—about Jonah and Clementine and Meriday's experiences in the swamp. And a Cherokee man they met, whom they called Wind Walker. He must have told them about the Swamp Witch.

Though there were real and present dangers in the swamp, I imagine it was the witch that haunted their dreams; that made the shadows twist crookedly in the firelight of a warm summer dusk.

Perhaps Wind Walker also told them of a mysterious tribe of Cherokee that lived in an even more remote part of the swamp—a place that has never been found by anyone, a place so isolated he wasn't even sure it was real. It was said that the cult there had broken off from the rest of the tribe long ago, had gone to the center of the swamp not in fear of the witch, but to try to conjure her. They believed she had come to return their land to them, to kill and drive out the white man; to rupture the movement of time and begin a new world for them, one that exists outside time itself.

I wonder if those children sit around with flashlights telling stories about the Witch of Wakefield Manor. What would my mother think of that? Of having herself immortalized in legend?

Though I can barely see past the wipers swishing rain from the windshield, out of the misty distance the looming outline of the house appears. It is no wonder children tell ghost stories about this place.

I may be living in one.

* * *

Once I arrive home, I am stuck inside while the rain pounds the roof. And though my mother and sister are also trapped here by the storm, we have hardly seen one another. It is such a very large house for three people that we might spend all our time in separate rooms, blocked off from one another by a labyrinth of walls, and never even know the others are there. All the doors are closed, as my mother likes to keep them; all the many doorways, in a house with too many doors, fastened tight against the dismal halls.

I fear that one day I will open a door and what I am expecting to see beyond it will be something else entirely, somewhere else, a place that isn't in this house at all—that I will open a door and fall into the abyss of outer space. And while these are fears, they are also fantasies, for wouldn't it be perfectly adventurous to step through a doorway and go somewhere else, somewhere wild and strange and beautiful, and never return?

In any case, it is easy for us to avoid each other, in the way family members who live together find ways to do. And when you live in a house of twenty-seven rooms and numerous winding corridors, of hidden staircases and secret circuitous halls, it is almost easier not to see each other.

But inexorably there is the collision; I find my mother in the kitchen, one of our few areas of congregation, grown irritable with wine. "Storms do nothing for my nerves," she says by way of explanation, as if we are always needing to explain to one another why we all drink.

"Could you pour me some?"

She does, slides it across the table slowly, shrewdly. "Something on your mind?"

"Am I that transparent?"

"As a ghost."

I could tell her about Julian, I reason. She would listen to me. But it would break the spell of joyful anticipation that has come over her. She would slide into the place that constantly tries to tug her back down, back to drinking heavily in dark rooms.

And if she doesn't believe me—if she tells me I cannot be seeing someone who hasn't been born yet—what will that mean?

How will she look at me then?

I take a large ungraceful gulp and put down the fragile glass rather too indelicately. "All right, mind reader: mind read."

She closes her eyes and presses fingers to her temples in exaggerated concentration; then she takes my hands, turns them palm upward, frowns at the lines, lets them go. She is only playing. A moment later she looks into my face and says, "Frustrated with your sister?"

"Good guess." I choose my words carefully. "She won't listen to me."

"Listening was never her strong suit."

The glasses swirl with red. The corkscrew, an abysmally old thing with a nasty spiraled spike, sits open on the countertop, pointing at us. Evidence of carelessness, or frequent use. I am looking for a black feather sweeping across the floor, or a muddy footprint the size of a child's bringing the swampsmell, that odor of rotting vegetation, into the house. For totems of proof that what I have seen is real.

You cannot know how maddening it is to be so sure of what you have seen but to have no evidence of its existence, and no way of verifying that it ever happened, because it hasn't happened—not yet, at least. But that it hasn't yet happened does not mean it didn't happen. Does that make sense? Am I crazy anyway? The images leak away in sips of wine and grow fuzzy, unreal. Did I see the boy after all, or have I really imagined him, like the Nothing Man, like the old woman with Xs for eyes?

You do believe me, don't you?

Instead of a feather, I see a bottle of prenatal vitamins left on the counter, promising healthfulness.

I am always looking for good omens, meaningful artifacts. That must sound silly and childish, this desire for small magical enchantments in ordinary things. Perhaps I am foolish to believe that the house is cursed or the swamp is under a dreamy spell of dark vegetal magic, but if I did not believe these things, then nothing would make sense to me. Everything would be so hard and cruel. Please do not think me whimsical, though.

I do not think it is whimsy that makes me ask my mother to give me a reading. It is something else.

She looks pleasantly taken off guard by the request, and I remember how wonderful it is to please her. It has been ages since she's given me a reading. When I was a teenager, she would pull me aside every so often, tell me in no uncertain terms that I was in need of a reading, sit me down, and give me one against my will, with frequent interruptions of, "Samantha, are you paying attention?" Sometimes I thought she might be making up the meanings of the cards to fit whatever narrative she'd invented about my life—reasons I was struggling in chemistry, for instance. Yet looking back, I realize all those unwanted readings veered, at least in the end, toward the optimistic; and against my will I left them with a sense of hope for the future, a feeling that things might turn around, that the friends who had abandoned me would return, or that I would eventually find a boyfriend—which was true, although it turned out later I didn't want one after all.

Maybe it is because teenagers always think they can find their own answers to life's questions, even though our parents have been around longer than us and likely know more than we do about life. We still think, when we are young, that they are old and out of touch, that we do not need their antiquated guidance even if we do need their approval, that what we really need is to figure things out on our own. And then, when we are older, we return to that childish desire for parental wisdom, but we must request it in oblique ways that play into that grand game of pretend in which all adults participate, pretending that we have any clue what we're about. It is not so much the reading I want but my mother's reassurance.

On the second floor, adjacent to the dreadful Rose Room, tucked into the haphazard floor plan, is my mother's reading room—not for reading books, mind you, but for reading tarot cards. It is a small, oppressive room, bundled tight in its thick tapestries like a cocoon. In the middle sits a circular table with S-shaped legs, covered in a purple cloth. An old curio cabinet looms against the wall, filled with uncanny items: an owl skull, vials of lavender oil, incense, stray books on the occult, and mismatched religious ephemera including a small brass Buddha, a wooden crucifix, and a steel pentagram. A rusted horseshoe is nailed upright to one wall; on another hangs a copy of the painting *The Garden of Earthly Delights* by Hieronymus Bosch.

Before we begin, Mother lights a white candle and some sage, the scents of which mingle intoxicatingly. She waves the flame off the match as smoke curls inquisitively from the candle, then takes out the cards and begins to shuffle the deck. "I suppose I'll do the five-card horseshoe spread. Good for working out problems."

A certain calm comes over the room, a nearly stifling calm, or the room is too warm, thick and humid like the swamp. The rain outside becomes white noise.

"I want you to think about what's been bothering you," she says as wind berates the shuttered window. "The first card represents your present position." She flips it over.

The moon gazes somnolently down at a dog, a wolf, and a lobster between two towers.

"The Moon," she says, "is a card of intuition, alienation, and the unconscious. There are two sides to this card: on one side insight and clarity, and on the other confusion and anxiety. I suspect you're somewhere in the middle, searching for answers."

"Aren't we all?"

"Hush. The next card represents your present desires." The card that appears displays six golden cups of white flowers and two children before a medieval castle, all bathed in a happy yellow glow.

Agnes smiles. "The Six of Cups. Nostalgia, memories. You have a desire to return to happy times from the past."

Unfortunately, I lack my mother's rose-colored glasses. What the house shows me often destroys even my tempered memories with the harsh light of truth, of how things really occurred. I'm not sure I can believe this card's assumption of the endless supply of happiness that the past delivers. The past is no different from the present, as dark or as light.

Is it my desire that the past be granted that happy glow? Or that my experience of the past be like everyone else's—that softly filtered recollection afforded by memory, and memory's ability to alter perception, to smooth out the rough spots? Do I wish, perhaps, that I did not have to live with actual recreations of the past wandering through the house, ruining the perfect nostalgia that comes with no longer having to experience it firsthand?

In any case, I wish it were a seven instead of a six. Seven is a much better number, round and whole. Six is too symmetrical.

"The next card represents the unexpected." She flips the card and frowns. Landing upside down, it depicts a man on a gray throne in the middle of a crashing sea. "Typically the King of Cups represents balance and control." She taps the card with her finger. "But when it's reversed like this, you see, it embodies emotional manipulation and volatility. While many of the cards relate to your inner life, the Court cards usually indicate someone else's involvement—in this case, a man in a position of power, most likely."

"Not my division chair, I hope. He is a royal prick, although you can't argue that he isn't as predictable as a cup of coffee."

She shakes her head. "No, I feel it must be either the appearance of someone you haven't met yet, or someone you haven't thought about in a long while. Watch out for someone who seems calm on the outside. He is not what he appears to be."

Her expression has become one of unhappy contemplation, and the candle flickers and fills me with its heady, cloying scent.

"Don't worry. I'm not in the habit of entertaining wild men."

She gives her head a little shake and smiles. "You know I wouldn't mind it if you *did* entertain a man, for a change. He doesn't have to be wild."

"Wouldn't that take all the fun out of it?"

"I'm only saying, if your goal is to become an old maid, then you're on the right track."

"Mother."

"What?"

Seemingly, she will not flip the next card until I have provided her some satisfactory reply. "It isn't as if the relationships in this family have worked out very well, is it?"

"Well," she hedges, "we don't know for certain whether things with Donovan are really over. Though to be perfectly honest with you, I was never terribly fond of him." She leans in close, conspiratorially. "Don't tell your sister I said that."

As much as it pleases me to share secrets with my mother, I think to myself that Elizabeth would, in fact, be thrilled to hear it. She would feast on the knowledge of our mother's disapproval, which would likely drive her right back into Don's arms. It would be just like her to do that.

To be honest, I could never tell whether I like Don or not. I can recall times when he has been something akin to a friend, the kind you might casually share a beer with—but I can think, too, of times when his easy mood soured all of a sudden and he turned his vicious sights on the nearest available target. He is the kind of man you might tiptoe around, enjoying his presence when he is in a good mood but always wondering, in the back of your mind, if the wrong word will ruin it. The world is full of these men, having told them long ago that they are entitled to the sea and the stars and all manner of life beneath.

Still, in some ways I know I am indebted to him, as uncomfortable as that makes me. I did almost take out his eye.

My mother flips the next card. "This one represents the immediate future."

The words are hardly out of her mouth when she nearly sucks them back in: riding across the tarot card on a white red-eyed horse is a skeleton clad in a suit of armor, who goes by the name of Death.

"Now, before you get upset," she says in a rush, "the Death card is the most misunderstood of all the cards. It doesn't necessarily signify physical death, but other kinds of profound change, the kind of change that destroys what came before."

The words do nothing to mitigate the unease in her voice.

Behind the skeleton holding his flag of death, the sun sets between two towers, above which a gray purgatorial sky presides over the corpses that lie in the horse's path. "These are the towers from the Moon card," she says. "That means there's a connection between your current confusion and the change that's coming."

A stark thread of lightning illuminates the window like the crackling bony hand of Death reaching toward us through the curtains, followed almost instantaneously by thunder that I can feel reverberate in my chest. I am afraid now to look again at the skeletal rider, fearing that this time he won't have a face.

"We left the wine in the kitchen," says my mother, apropos of nothing. She goes to sweep up the cards in her hands, but I grab her wrist.

"We aren't finished."

She shakes her head. "I'm getting a very negative feeling. I think the electricity in the air is throwing off the energy. This was a bad time. We ought to try again another time."

"Just finish it. I have to know."

"What is it you're hoping to see?"

My hands are itching for a good-luck charm; I nervously bite my thumbnail, tear off a pearly crescent, and put it in my pocket. Mother is watching me, expectant. Can I tell her without spoiling it all?

"What if I told you I've seen the future?"

She picks up the deck, contemplating. "I would say you've finally opened yourself up spiritually. That you're finally understanding this place."

Her words send a bolt through my heart. I force myself not to chew on my other nails. "I'm not talking about telling someone's fortune. I'm talking about . . . literally *seeing* the future. It's not possible, though. It must be something else. Some*one* else." I laugh without humor. "That, or I'm losing my mind."

My mother only nods. "You aren't losing your mind, Sam. The future, in this house . . . I admit, it's rare. It only solidifies as time progresses. But once a certain choice is made or a certain event takes place, then the future decides itself. And just as memories of the past drift through these halls, so too does the future, in glimpses and shadows." She fixes me with her gaze. "But it *is* there. The future is all around us, just as much as the past. If you've seen something that hasn't yet come to pass . . ." She shrugs.

My stomach has twisted itself into a knot like one of Elizabeth's old guitar strings. If my mother is right, then that means my faceless boy is who I think he is after all.

I could hide from this, pretend I'd never seen him, but that would be cowardly. I cannot turn my back on the truth. Better to stare the future in the face, then, even if the future has no face. Better to face it myself and spare my mother the heartache.

"Flip the last card."

My mother seems reluctant to continue, now that we've gone down this rabbit hole. "I'm telling you, Sam, we really oughtn't take this reading to heart. The air . . . the storm . . ." She trails off with a sigh when she sees I'm not going to budge. "The last card is the outcome."

A woman sits up in bed, hands over her face, nine swords perched horizontally on the wall behind her head.

Lightning, again, and this time the thunder so close it occurs simultaneously, right on top of us, a great clash of angry gods, and we are plunged into gripping darkness, blind, with the wind and the rain pounding to be let in.

Fuzzy candlelight imbues Agnes with the ethereal look of a ghost. Somehow everything feels closer in the darkness; even with the rain, the room is quieter.

"You ought to check the fuse box," she says in a hush.

I don't want to get up and wander into that abyss. Unseen things creep in shadow behind me. "What does the card mean?"

"The Nine of Swords," she says. "Have you ever had the sensation of waking from a bad dream . . . only to discover you're living a nightmare?"

There is nothing in the darkness behind me. I know there isn't. But it *feels* like there is, like there is someone, or something, back there with eyes burning into my prickling neck—or perhaps Xs where eyes should be—and with it comes the surety that if I turn around, I will see whatever it is. *Oh don't turn around, don't turn around and see it, if you don't turn around maybe it will turn out there is nothing there after all.*

What you have seen is real, is what the card tells me. Julian is real, it is all real—not a dream, not a nightmare, but reality, if there is any difference indeed between them. You have seen what Julian will become. I see the cards now like a kind of code, revealing their secrets, looking into the layers of reality to show me the truth.

The rest of her explanation haunts me, though:

"The Nine of Swords symbolizes all of your fears, your regrets, your inner anguish. Your knowledge that whatever has gone wrong in your life—it is, in some respects, your own fault."

Candlelight shivers over her face looming in the darkness. I feel spooked by the look on her face, by the cards on the table making an arc of dread, by the dark that encloses us.

"There are more candles around here somewhere. Some in the dining room. And the basement, I believe." She begins packing up the cards. Beads of melted wax drip down the candle between us.

Must I? I suppose I must. I will not send my mother blundering about in the dark, much less Elizabeth. It will have to be me.

My skin is alive with dread as I make my way downstairs, feeling my way through the shadowed house, over the groaning floor, to the dining room where I search in vain. No candles here. I turn, dreading the blind trip into the basement, but my path is blocked by a figure.

"Elizabeth?" I whisper, even though I know it isn't her.

I can hear the figure breathing in the dark. He is wet, muddy; stinks of swamp rot, buzzes with flies. My breath catches.

"Julian?"

The figure doesn't move. For a moment, he doesn't breathe. Then he says, "Sometimes I feel so cold and so still, like I'm really dead. I think if I just go still enough, I'll be dead."

Lightning flashes in through the window, lighting up the faceless boy—fourteen or fifteen, now—and I see red caked into the swamp water soaking him. Gore crusted under his nails. Strands of hair in his fingers. My gorge rises. Darkness returns, and he speaks out of it.

"I thought we could be dead together, but I don't like the way she stares. I put her in the basement," he says. "With the others."

Gagging, I reel away as another crash of thunder shakes the house and blares its lightning into the room, making every corner livid, showing me the muddy footprints on the floor and a streak of red, something dragged. I don't know where he went, but I cannot see him anymore.

We are not evil, I tell myself. The Wakefields are not cursed with madness and murder. Some of us are good. Some of us have to be good.

I find myself in front of the ancient cellar whose door swings inward on aching hinges and opens up to an abyss. What will I find here? Candles, or the *others* that Julian put in the basement? I gaze like one gone blind and feel myself unable to step into the nothingness that lies beyond the doorway, where an ancient staircase will lead me down into the depths.

A damp, rotten smell emerges from that darkness, as if the swamp is eating away at the house from underneath; I force myself to take one step down, and another, but still I can see nothing, am enveloped in the all-consuming perfume of decay.

Isn't it strange how familiar spaces become unfamiliar when one loses a sense? I have been in that basement a thousand times, collecting gardening tools, jars, and other sundries; and, knowing where the candles must be, I assume I will be able to find my way to the far shelf in the dark; but now I feel lost—as though the basement has disappeared around me, as though I may reach out for the shelf and feel something else altogether, as though once I step out into the flat expanse I will never be able to find my way back to the stairs again.

Which may be a reasonable fear, after all, as there are several doors in the cellar. Any one of which, if left open, might lead me down one of the strange secret passageways that tunnel below the house, most of them flooded for all time thanks to the swamp, left to rot half-steeped in muck. The tunnels were originally used as part of an elaborate system of hiding escaped slaves, but I can hardly imagine a person wanting to creep down one of those low, narrow, black passageways, wondering where it may lead, if there even is an exit, or if it will only lead them endlessly into the entrails of the damp forbidding earth.

Here at the bottom of the stairs, the smell is stronger, and when I take that last step to the floor, I understand why. Unexpectedly, cold water sloshes over my ankles, shocking me, and I am back up the stairs panting before I recognize the simple fact that the basement has flooded in the storm, as it so often does.

In the hall closet I find rain boots, and in the kitchen, rummaging blindly through the drawers, I come upon a flashlight. All is eerily quiet in the house, as if the darkness has turned off all sound but for the creaking of floorboards under my feet, and I switch on the flashlight to guide me back down and assess the damage.

I feel the cards following after me as I go, like bad omens. I see the Moon in the ethereal circle of the flashlight's beam against the stairs as I descend again into the black ocean the basement has become. And in the middle of that ocean, perhaps, there is an ancient faceless man sitting on a throne, the swampy waves crashing around him—the King of Cups, brooding over his cruel domain.

I shine the flashlight over the opaque water. As I slosh through it, I decide it must be at least three inches deep, but I feel with every step I take that I might slip into quicksand, or a bottomless pit, and never emerge. Gratefully I find that the doors leading to the underground tunnels are all closed.

The far shelf is made of old wood that I fear may collapse in the damp, moldy air. For now it holds, and I find the candles collecting cobwebs. I ignore whatever appears to be floating in the water below; it is merely old junk that the water has swallowed up off the floor and carried along with it. It is not a body from the future. It is not a head with hair floating around it.

When I turn back for the stairs, my flashlight catches a figure standing in the middle of the room.

It is not the faceless boy but a girl, perhaps eleven years old, dark skinned and wearing a beige dress.

"It's her," she says, her whispery voice ripe with the silken strains of fear. "She's coming."

Framing her with gold light, the flashlight begins to flicker; I whack the side of it with my hand, regretting that I did not check the batteries. She wavers in and out of existence, the light shining on the terror in her eyes until it dies completely, leaving us in darkness.

I recognize this girl, and before I know it I am sloshing my way out of the basement to follow her, wondering if I will finally see the Swamp Witch—if I will find an answer to the evil that plagues this house. The same evil, perhaps, that plagues Julian.

Let me explain.

There is more to the story of Jonah, Clementine, and Meriday that I haven't told you; pieces of the story I've heard secondhand from the echoes of the house, the timeline scrambled; things too strange and frightening to be real. But now that I know what I've seen here is real—now that I know *Julian* is real—anything seems possible.

I am afraid what I'm about to see when I follow the girl up through the main hall and out to the backyard won't make a lick of sense to you unless you know the whole story leading up to that moment, so I am going to tell it as best I can, hoping you will understand this is just my own re-creation of what I have heard.

PART TWO

THE SWAMP WITCH

5

They were smuggled into the swamp under cover of night.

August led them stoically through the dark, where they crisscrossed through the brush in narrow switchbacks, up to their knees in spongy soil. The chittering of nocturnal creatures rhapsodized on the soft wind that troubled the trees above, shrugging their signature of leaves against the silvery moon. Apart from that riddle of moonlight, the only illumination afforded to them against the night was August's yellow lantern.

Until another light shined through the trees.

Meriday saw it in the distance, bobbing as if it were on the move: an orange flame.

"Mama," she said. "Look."

"Hush, child," said Clementine, urging her forward. "You just keep following Mr. August and we'll be there soon."

"But there's a light," she insisted.

Jonah and Clementine froze and looked at August with the sudden wary coldness of distrust. "Is it the camp?"

August shook his head. "We are not yet close enough."

"Have we been *followed*?"

Again, August rejected the idea. They could not have been followed, and what's more, the light was ahead of them, not behind—it was deeper in the swamp than they.

"It's there," said Meriday, pointing. They all looked.

Jonah saw the concern on August's face before he schooled himself. "Fox fire," he explained.

Unsettled, the family was eager to get to the camp as soon as possible, but after another hour passed, they seemed to be going in circles—around the flame that now refused to move or disappear but hovered in the air, burning a hole in the world.

Several times, August tried his compass; each time he put it back in his pocket with a shake of his head. Compasses don't work in the swamp, you see. They get confused. There is something strange in the magnetic field.

"Come," said August. "The Lord will guide our way tonight."

* * *

At last, after hours of slogging through near-impassable marsh, they made it. August left them to retrace his lonely steps while shadowed figures crept out warily to greet the newcomers.

That first night, Meriday could not sleep.

They were given beds of broom straw, surrounded by the log cabins of the settlement, some with raised floors and porches for when the floods soaked the higher ground. They would soon learn that nothing stays dry in the swamp; one must get used to being always damp. Meriday's feet were still wet and sore from the trek, the straw rough on her back, and she felt lonesome and afraid of this new place with its foul stench and its unfamiliar denizens. She gazed up through the thicket of trees into the fractured moonlight and the stars beyond, listened to the sounds of critters roaming in the dark, and wondered if she would ever feel safe.

By and by, however, Meriday came to love the swamp.

What had, in those first grueling insufferable days, seemed a hellish isolated place filled with myriad dangers scarcely imagined by the girl, came to feel more and more like home. Each night the bleating of frogs and buzzing of nightly insects became more familiar, and she learned to navigate the flooded areas around their dry island, although her parents warned her never to stray far, and certainly not beyond the barrier of vegetation that grew densely around them, or into the surrounding marsh where footing was treacherous amid the slick snarl of roots and quicksand.

There were other children to play with here, and in the evenings everyone sat around the fire and passed a white clay pipe, smoking and laughing and sharing fantastic stories.

Jonah went to work building their new home with the aid of several young men. Clementine traded recipes with the other women as they cooked up the hogs and fowl that were either raised or hunted, or shucked the corn they were able to grow in the acidic soil, or gutted fish they caught in the rivers. Everyone pitched in, and they were glad to do so. The work, though hard, was happy, independent—all manner of things Meriday had never known. That work could be joyous, could be done for one's own self.

Living alongside the colony was a Cherokee tribe that had been in the swamp for many years. It was from them that Meriday learned that the stones they used as tools had been refashioned out of Indian arrowheads, that some of their pots were repurposed from Indian pottery, that all they used here was either from the swamp or recycled from those old societies that had long survived in this mystical land.

While the house was being built, Meriday slept on the carpet of dead leaves that covered the island, enjoying this strange freedom, the naturalness of it, while her parents bunked on their makeshift bed of straw.

Several times she had caught her mother standing or kneeling on the edge of the island, staring out into the water and the creeping vegetation, her eyes glazed with unrealized tears, and she wondered if her mother was crying.

Yes, Clementine was crying. Of course she was. Not from something as simple as sadness, though; until now, her body had been owned, had been possessed, by someone else. This power structure had defined her life, had defined the very way she perceived her own body. But now she was taking ownership of herself. She was reclaiming herself. In a world that would seek to control her body, this body was *hers*; in a world that would seek to silence her, this voice was *hers*;

and she vowed, in that very moment, kneeling on the bed of the creek with tears breaking loose from her eyes, that she would never be possessed by anyone ever again. She would rather die.

When Meriday dared to break her out of this reverie and ask what was the matter, she took the girl into her arms and said, "Nothing at all is the matter, Merry child." Clementine brushed a hand over her eyes and said, "Go on now. Go on and play. I hear Mr. Charles is making a flute. Would you like to hear him play it when he's finished?" Meriday nodded. "Go on, then. Perhaps you can offer your help. Make yourself useful."

Meriday nodded again and took off, glancing back only once to see her mother kneeling on the ground, a hand over her mouth, staring into the hanging vines with divine wonder.

It was one of the last times she saw her mother alive.

* * *

They were in the camp only a few weeks when Clementine disappeared.

Certainly, she shouldn't have gone off by herself. Particularly in the dark of night. But she couldn't sleep, said Jonah, who had noticed her tossing and turning as he drifted in and out of consciousness. One moment she was there beside him and when next he opened his eyes, she was gone.

He hadn't been immediately concerned; sometimes she grew restless at night and went out to look at the stars and think whatever nighttime thoughts came to her mind in the secret hours before dawn.

But when he woke again in the dark and she still wasn't there, an ill foreboding filled him. He rose to find her. She wasn't anywhere in the camp.

Jonah took a lantern and tried to imagine what would compel his wife to venture into the swamp at this time of night.

"Clementine?" he called out. He searched for the better part of an hour, nearly stumbling to his death tripping over angry roots, and when he found her, the first thing he saw wasn't even his wife but the fox fire that had lured her out there.

It appeared as a pair of small glowing flames that hovered before Clementine's beguiled face. She seemed hypnotized by the dancing light, for she did not acknowledge Jonah as he drew nearer, set down his lantern, and reached out to her.

But before he could take hold of his wife, he made the mistake of glancing into the water below, over which the fox fire floated.

Illuminated vaguely by the moonglow and the tiny flames and the lantern that sat perched on a small grassy knoll, he saw a figure reflected in the water that did not exist above it—and its eyes were two flames, the flames into which his wife was gazing with mad ecstasy, two flames perched within the sockets of a terrible ancient face, a face that was not a face, of a creature that appeared, in the reflection, to be hovering above the water and reaching one twisted arm like a gnarled tree branch toward Clementine, whose name Jonah cried out in horror, who turned to look at him with surprise, like a sleepwalker abruptly jolted awake.

But the look lasted only a moment.

In the next, Clementine was yanked by unseen hands into the water, which swallowed her whole.

Later, the others would gently suggest to Jonah that she had lost her footing. The mud here was treacherously slick. People slipped all the time.

Jonah did not hesitate to dive into the sludgy water. In a moment, he was enveloped by the cold black as he blindly fought his way down through the weeds. What he found when he got to the bottom, however, was not his wife; he found an underwater hole that opened up into some dark recess below.

Would he have happily descended into that bottomless pit if he'd believed he would be able to drag his wife back to the surface? Of course. But he thought of sweet Meriday awakening the following morning, frightened and alone. He swam back to the surface, pulled himself coughing and wet onto the bank, and watched the water desperately in hopes that Clementine, too, would find her way back. But it was not to be, and the longer he sat waiting, the more hope dwindled.

Mad with grief, Jonah raced back to camp, hardly caring about the branches that scratched his face. By the time he woke two of the men, they gazed into his raving eyes with a small measure of fear. But they were quick to rise and follow him back out, and, being good men, both jumped into the water to see if they could fish out Clementine's body. They both drew the line at the underwater hole, though. Neither was willing to dive that deep.

They sat together, swamp water mingling with Jonah's tears, the chirp of wakening birds mingling with his friends' words of consolation. By and by, the sun came up, and they all knew there was not a chance in the world Clementine was still alive. She had been underwater for hours.

Just as the men were preparing to make their way back to camp, a burst of bubbles broke the surface above the underwater hole, which froze Jonah in his tracks. He stopped and stared, mesmerized, at the cloud of bubbles, signaling movement, a release of air.

Then a hand reached up out of the water and dug its claws into the muddy bank.

The men were so startled that they did not even reach down to help. The hands pulled laboriously and a muddy head emerged, followed by a torso, and then a full body made almost unrecognizable by the mire.

But Jonah recognized her. Of course he did.

He would recognize his wife anywhere.

Later, Jonah would think back on this moment with a sick look on his face and stumble over the telling of it in the Wakefield house. The woman who crawled out of the swamp, smelling like death, was his wife . . . but at the same time, not his wife. She was changed.

Beneath the mud her eyes were strange—glassy, reflective, like two pools of dark water. Clementine walked heavily, dribbling continually out of every orifice.

When she spoke, her voice warbled as if underwater. "Jonah?"

The two men crossed themselves and called her the devil, but Jonah took her in his arms—feeling her cold, slimy flesh against his and the tangled ropes of her dripping hair—and was filled with a relief so profound it overshadowed even the truth that she had been underwater for hours, that she could not possibly be alive.

"It is a miracle," he said.

They returned to camp, the other men hurrying ahead. Jonah helped Clementine, who moved rigidly as if her limbs were planks of wood. Much as he tried to warm her, she remained cold to the touch. Her skin was loose and waterlogged.

Back at the camp, the rumors spread quickly. By the time they arrived, the men and women out breakfasting already knew about Clementine's fall, and their eyes showed fear. While Jonah found Clementine some dry clothes, the two men told the others in hushed tones what had occurred.

In their little house, Meriday saw her mother and was glad. She had heard the rumor that her mother had had an accident, and she had been sitting there hugging her knees to her chest. But her mother brought in with her that awful, rotten smell, and Meriday did not want to go near her. She listened, however, when her father asked her mother how it was possible—how she was alive.

"The witch sent me back," said Clementine through muddy lips, and Meriday had the sensation that she could hear her mother's voice before she even spoke, in a kind of watery echo. "I saw the place where she comes from," she continued. "A place at the beginning and the end of the world. Come with me and I will show you."

By now Jonah was experiencing such a mixture of emotions he could not hope to untangle them—joy, relief, fear. She reached out for him, dry, wearing dry clothes, and when he grabbed on to her outstretched wrist, the skin began to flake off like bits of paper. Calm as ever, she got up, went out to the edge of the island, and dunked herself in the water until she was sufficiently wet again.

All the rest of that day, Clementine was the terrible marvel of the camp. By that evening, Jonah had agreed to let the Cherokee hold a purification ritual to cleanse her spirit. They burned herbs and chanted in their native tongue while Clementine sat before the fire, which lit her slick skin ghoulishly.

Smoke billowed up from the fire and the damp burning herbs like a spell of demons, the smoke conjured by wet things. Clementine grinned with a mouth blackened by mud, which oozed out between her teeth. At first it seemed her glassy eyes reflected the fire, but in truth her eyes themselves now burned like flames.

Wind Walker saw within those hellish depths something that froze him with dread.

"Would you like to know the truth?" said Clementine. "She comes through a crack in the world. A hole. Comes from a place you could never imagine. She's been in the swamp a long, long time." The fire in her eyes danced and shivered, and Jonah felt a cold rush of fear. "She does not mean to hurt us, though. She wants us to experience the world like she does, in all its splendid glory. Here we are, stuck in our little minute, in our narrow little window of the world, when we could see everything—everywhen, the magnificence of it all."

The tribe's chief chanted louder.

The undead woman looked at her husband. "She says there will come a time when our people are free. And there will come a time when the Indians take back what is theirs. But that is all far from now, and we shall never see it in this lifetime. Don't you want to be free?"

"We *are* free," Jonah said, through his budding tears. "We are *free*."

"The only way to be free, truly free, is to die, to cast it all off," she said. "Life binds us to our here and now."

Jonah shook his head.

"I will help. You and Meriday—we shall all go together."

He stood up. "*No!*"

Before he could grasp her by the arms, shake her, call forth his wife from wherever she might yet live buried in that unholy flesh, a plume of smoke obscured her from him, and in the confusion he lost sight of her.

Then she was standing before the chief, grasping his throat as gouts of dirty swamp water issued from his parted lips, an impossible geyser, his eyes popping as he shuddered. When she let go, he fell still, water trickling gently from his mouth to seep into the soil.

The others scattered, the wind carrying off their screams in their desperation to escape.

Another burst of smoke from the crackling flames, and Clementine skittered off again.

Jonah stood beside Wind Walker, both frozen with shock.

The moment of silence was broken when Jonah remembered what Clementine had said about him—and Meriday.

* * *

They had told Meriday to stay in the cabin and not to come out, no matter what she heard. Naturally, she had pressed her ear against the cracks in the wooden wall to listen to what was going on outside. She heard drumming and chanting but could not make any sense of it, so she retreated to her bed, where she sat playing with a doll her mother had made of straw. She was content in her play until she heard the door creak open, but it was dark inside and she could not make out anything but a figure in the doorway, outlined by the fire still burning outside.

"Come, Merry child," said the figure, holding out a hand. "I promise it will not hurt."

There was nowhere else to go—only one door. When her mother walked over to her, where could she have run?

But the hand she took was cold, with the muculent feel of a tree root that's been submerged for many years, and though this sodden woman was her mother, yes, she was afraid.

* * *

By the time Jonah arrived at their cabin, he knew something was wrong.

The door hung askew like a yawning mouth, inviting him into the darkness within. His flickering torch revealed a floor covered with muddy footprints and no sign of Meriday except her doll, which lay abandoned on the floor.

Jonah let out a sound like a wounded animal. Wind Walker, adept at tracking, knelt down in the dead, wet leaves and told Jonah to follow him.

They tracked Clementine and Meriday into the swamp, far enough that Jonah lost all sense of where they were. When he found Clementine and Meriday standing hand in hand at the bank of a root-choked river, he shouted for his daughter.

"Daddy!"

But Clementine did not let go of her hand, and now Jonah could see the two small flames hovering in the air.

"Let her go," said Wind Walker. He took the torch from Jonah, who found himself too afraid to move, to startle his wife, or whatever she had become.

"My daughter will be free," said Clementine. Meriday did not struggle but stared at her father, eyes wide as dreadful moons.

"You cannot listen to the witch," said Wind Walker. "She is an evil spirit. Now let go of the child."

She only tightened her grip.

Wind Walker thrust the torch into Clementine's back.

Meriday was able to break free. She fell in the mud and scrambled for purchase as Jonah grabbed her around the waist and hauled her up to him.

Pieces of Clementine's clothing caught fire, but otherwise she was too wet and only smoldered in the flame, releasing a heavy black smoke while her eyes burned in their sockets.

"It is a blessed thing she ended up in the swamp," said Clementine through her mouth of mud, her flaming eyes laughing at the dropped torch, which the water quickly consumed and made impotent. "If she lived on dry land, she would burn a hole right through the world wherever she walks."

She seized Wind Walker's throat with her clawed fingers. For a moment he was enveloped in the putrid stench of mold and rotting vegetation, and his mouth filled with hot swampy liquid, but he managed to break free from her grasp, shove her away, where she fell into the water. Spitting out a mouthful of sludge, he turned to meet Jonah and Meriday, and all three of them took off into the forest without a look back.

Soon it became clear that in their mad blind dash through the midnight swamp, they had lost their way. Spectral pine and sweetgum oak towered above them, shrouding the sky and the land beyond, barred with an endless vista of trunks emerging from marshy soil. They turned and turned, knowing with dread deep in their hearts that the swamp was vast and eternal, and they were lost.

They walked all night and into the next morning, when the mystery of the dark gave way to the thick heat of day, and finally the trees began to thin; and Jonah recognized this place and knew which way to turn; and they found themselves heading out of the swamp and toward the looming shape of Wakefield Manor.

6

All of this was told to the rapt Wakefields in the course of one sitting, but as for my telling of it, I have had to reconstruct the story from the bits and pieces I have heard whenever the memory shows itself to me. This house does not care for the nuances of storytelling; it spits things up here and there and tells you *go on, tie up the threads yourself.*

They tell it by candlelight, having taken refuge in the basement, where the flickering light etches lines of horror on their faces, fear gleaming afresh in their eyes. Most of the story is told by Jonah, but occasionally Meriday chimes in to add some detail, and when those two are overcome, Wind Walker steps in to fill in the gaps. All told, it is a wild puzzle of a tale fit together by several competing voices and perspectives, and I was never sure whether I believed it at all.

But now I think I do.

What happened next, I can't really say. For a long while, this part of the story remained unfinished, like unraveled yarn, but I think that now I will have the rest.

If you have been paying attention, you will know who the girl is that I see in the basement.

"It's her," she says, her voice floating on the dark. "She's coming."

I follow Meriday out of the basement, trailing water from my rain boots, still holding the dead flashlight in one hand and the candles in the other, trying to keep up with the girl.

We emerge from the house into the backyard, where the storm rages violently, shuddering the black trees in the distance as lightning sears the sky in arresting patterns. Rain blankets the distance.

Then I see her.

Not the Swamp Witch—*Clementine.*

Here she comes, lurching stiffly toward us, lit with an unholy glow—but it is only, I realize, the sun, for it was daytime in that other when. She appears brighter than the world around her, coming to us in the guise of a terrible angel, exuding her own inner deadlight.

Words seem inadequate. This is the first time I have seen, with my own two eyes, the woman herself, and have known that the story is true. It is true, just like Julian, just like the future.

Clementine beckons to Meriday, who refuses to move closer. She says, in that warbled, watery voice, "I will protect you from what will happen to you. If you come with me, we can stop it. I will make you safe."

Meriday shakes her head, terror in her eyes.

Then August emerges from the house, raises a gun, and shoots Clementine three times in the chest.

The shots do not kill her; she is already dead. Dirty water pours from the holes in her chest like a perverse fountain.

The others retreat. Meriday will not go with her mother. Clementine, seeming to understand this, lets them go.

She turns her dead eyes onto me, now, with a steady gaze, and I am surprised to find she is not looking past me, or through me, or slightly to the left of me—no, she is looking *right at me.*

And she says, in a muddy voice that I can yet hear over the rain, "Who are you?"

Before I can respond, she is gone, and I am left once again alone, standing in the pouring rain, soaked and chilled to my bones. Holding a wet flashlight and wet candles like failed totems.

This is a moment I will have to mull over for hours.

She should not be able to see me. The house shows us visions of what was (or will be—yes, I know that now), but it does not transport us there. It bends time but doesn't break it in half.

So why is she able to see me with those haunting fiery eyes? How could she possibly?

Behind me, I hear my mother call my name. I should go back inside and shut the door that is banging on its hinges in the wind and letting in the rain.

I know what I should do, but I cannot move.

Far in the distance, where the swamp rises menacingly out of the earth and its unhappy trees swoon in the wind, a small light pierces the dark and hovers in the air orange-gold, the color of flame.

It is fox fire, I tell myself, which I know is merely a bioluminescent fungus that lives in decaying wood. But the light that I see is not bioluminescence but flame, floating on the air despite the deluge that would extinguish any normal fire.

Before I can stop myself, I am running toward the swamp, away from home, pounded incessantly by rain, my boots sticking and sucking in the marshy soil, hoping the light will not vanish or retreat deeper into the labyrinth. When I get to the first of the trees, the light is still far away, tucked deeper in the forest than I imagined it could have been, for me to have seen it all the way from the house. But I press on, sheltered from the hardest of the rain now beneath the canopy, blinded momentarily by lightning that feels too close, that makes the twisted cypress trees look like the roots of something else—some ghoulish tentacled creature that lives under the swamp and puts out its strange feelers toward the sky. My feet slosh through heavy brown water as I fight my way toward the light that grows infinitesimally closer with every laborious step.

I am far enough into the swamp now that I may have trouble finding my way out again, but I am not thinking of that. I am thinking only of reaching that light before it goes out—or lights, I should say, for now, as I approach it, the light resolves into two twin flames.

Even knowing what happened to Clementine, I want to see what she saw. I want to know how she can move through time. Maybe if I can figure it out, I can reach out to Julian somehow, talk to him—ask him why he killed those girls, if that is what he did . . .

The lights are close enough for me to reach out and touch, but I feel no heat emanating from them. The rain pours down around me, roiling the surface of the water in which I stand ankle-deep, making it snap savagely at my boots. Making a reflection in its surface impossible. Something grabs me around the ankle, like a claw made of tree roots, and I slip forward into the deeper water, shocked by the sudden cold as it slides up to my waist.

In my mad rush to the swamp, I've felt only flickers of excitement or foreboding, intangible as a shadow cast from a flash of lightning. But now as I am dragged into the water, just like Clementine, I have the opportunity to feel true panic. Where will I go? And will I come out like her? And—no, no, I don't want to die, but the bank is muddy and slippery and my hands can't find purchase to pull myself back up.

But someone else's hands do; they grab me from behind and pull me from the water until I lie gasping on my back in the sludge, my vision blurring with stray raindrops until a face looms over me. It is too dark to make out who it is. The fox fire, I realize, is gone.

"What in God's name were you thinking?" My mother's pinched, angry voice greets me from above.

When I drag myself fully from the water, I notice a snarl of thin roots tangled around my boot. My mother helps me pull it free and leads me back home.

* * *

The three of us sit around the blazing fire. Mother has piled an immoderate amount of blankets upon me until my teeth stop chattering, but deep in my soul I still feel the watery chill of the grave. We sip hot tea, tea the color of the swamp water, and listen to the crackle of the fire and the tinny drumming of rain on the roof.

"Well?" says Agnes, as if she has been waiting for me to speak. "Are you going to explain your spontaneous dip in the swamp?"

"It's kind of a long story."

"We've got all night, haven't we?"

"Leave her alone, Mom," Elizabeth cuts in. "Sammy's crazy; you can't fault her for that."

"I'm not crazy," I mumble under my breath.

A faint buzzing fills the quiet in the wake of this pronouncement. Elizabeth's phone rattles on the table, shifting several millimeters to the left each time the buzzing commences. She turns it over, looks at the screen, and puts it back down.

"Aren't you going to answer that?"

She purses her lips, perhaps tasting Donovan on them, tasting his words. "No."

"Oh for heaven's sake." Agnes sets down her tea and casts her eyes to the ceiling.

We sit within our own thoughts for some time before Elizabeth says, half-seriously, "Well. Board game or charades?"

Any games that might yet lie in storage here are likely in the basement, so I tell them it is flooded. I don't mention that I lost the candles and the flashlight somewhere in the swamp, probably devoured by the hungry waters that wanted to suck me in, but I make a mental note to replace them. We cannot, *cannot* be without these sacred totems of light and warmth.

"We'll deal with it in the morning," says Agnes. "I'll get paper for the charades."

We end up playing several riotous rounds, coming up with more and more outlandish things to act out. We are some of the best charade players you'll ever meet. Some of it feels rusty, though, like pulling out old clothes that have lain in the attic for years, that now fit stiffly and smell of mothballs and are no longer familiar, comfortable.

Throughout it all, my mother casts me furtive looks that she must think I don't notice, looks weighted with indefinable emotions too complex to be explained in such simplistic terms as grief or anxiety—the looks of a woman whose husband killed himself and whose daughter nearly killed herself, whether intentionally or unintentionally, this very night. What has she seen of the future in this house? I wonder.

And the thing that must be trapped in the back of her mind is haunting her too, the tarot card I can almost see hovering behind her eyes, the one with the skeletal rider and his red-eyed horse trampling over the dead.

7

We spend the next day emptying buckets of dirty water from the basement. The power comes back on around noon, by which time Elizabeth is already throwing out rancid food from the warm refrigerator and looking constantly on the verge of vomiting. It is evening before the basement is dry, or as dry as it will ever get, I suppose. The floors still smell of mildew and the faint ripe odors of the swamp, which no amount of lemon-scented cleaning solution can fully eradicate. Old wet magazines and holiday decorations and other debris that ended up floating in the water are added to the growing pile of garbage on the side of the house.

When I haul out another bag to the trash bins in the long shadows of twilight, the ground still wet and spongy from last night's rain, I find a little boy sitting on the grass, surrounded by a half circle of dead frogs as if performing an esoteric ritual.

"Ribbit. Ribbit," he says. "You're dead. You can't see. Can't talk. Only I can see and talk. Ribbit. Ribbit."

He pokes them with a stick. They flop wetly, baring white bellies and limp, sticky limbs. Then he stands, a boy of seven or eight with a blank, shadowed face, and steps on the frogs, leaning his weight into it. They crunch under his shoes.

His childish notion of death disturbs me in its superficiality, as if death were merely a lack of vision and vocalization, with mental processes remaining intact so that one becomes imprisoned in one's cage of flesh. How terrible, I think; how much more terrible than actual death must be, when those mental processes cease. Perhaps he simply cannot fathom that cessation, not while the world is his.

"Julian?" I say, then feel foolish. He cannot hear me. But I cannot help myself. "You wouldn't hurt your auntie, would you?"

The boy faces the swamp, and I am grateful his back is turned so that I cannot see the indistinct blur where a face should be, that unsettled vision of inhumanity, a face that is not a face.

Without turning, he says, "You're supposed to be dead."

He could be speaking to the frogs, I think as I drop the trash bag and hurry back into the house. He could be speaking to the ghosts in his head or the voices of the swamp or whatever else exists in his mad world.

Or, a voice suggests in the back of my head, he could be speaking to me. Like Clementine.

* * *

For a time, I am distracted by the classes I teach as an adjunct at the local college and the armload of essays I have to grade, but it is all I can do to stop myself from venturing back into the swamp. I have gone over the story again and again in my little notebook, searching for answers, and I have had to grapple, too, with the inadequacy of my reiteration, knowing all the while that I haven't gotten their voices quite right, that there may be some blanks I've filled in myself, some things I may have gotten wrong. Well, we do our best with what we have. I suppose a certain number of imperfections are to be expected in any story.

I have been keeping an eye out for Clementine, though, holding my breath as I open closet doors, half expecting to see her dragging herself out of the basement, crossing the barrier of time in her undeath. When I hear footsteps one night while grading essays in the cozy parlor, I flinch and drop my pen; Mother, lighting incense nearby, pauses to stare at me.

"Everything all right?"

"I could ask you the same thing."

Ever since the power outage, my mother has been obsessing over her witchy rituals. The house has become sleepily perfumed by incense. Once she went around the whole first floor counterclockwise with a smoldering bundle of sage, which exhaled smoke into every room. Then she did the same with cedar, then sweet grass. Elizabeth, sorting through boxes of baby clothes she had picked up at Goodwill and dutifully ignoring her buzzing phone, warned her not to burn the house down.

"It's just a good thing we live in such a damp place," said Elizabeth, sticky with humidity, "or this house would have been a pile of ash a long time ago."

After being dissuaded from burning anything else, my mother turned to cleaning, which is out of the ordinary for her; she tends to allow plumes of dust to billow up from couch cushions and grime to creep across windowsills and mold to spore in the bathtub before she finally relents and goes in search of a dust rag. Now, though, she has been scrubbing the old hardwood floors back to a color they haven't been in years and making the windows clear again, humming to herself while she works, elbow-deep in a bucket of soapy water.

She was humming a familiar tune yesterday while hunched over the toilet cleaning the crevices behind, one I couldn't quite put my finger on as I walked past until she started adding the lyrics, singing in her sweet, lilting voice: "*Oh my darling . . . oh my darling . . .*"

"Why are you singing that?" I cut in.

"Why shouldn't I be?"

Perhaps the detriment of an analytic mind is the inability to take a coincidence at face value. I know now, thinking back on that moment, that my mother was ignorant of Clementine's story. Had I heard her singing that song several weeks ago, it wouldn't have registered in my mind—but once a name or a word is at the forefront of your brain, it suddenly becomes impossible *not* to notice it everywhere, like learning a new word and immediately hearing it on the radio, and then on a TV show, as if the word didn't exist until you learned it but now that you know it, the world has permission to use it around you. Strange phenomena like that occur all the time, and while it seems more meaningful to ascribe the mystery to some greater purpose, some deeper narrative you know you must be participating in, it is usually, and unsatisfyingly, only coincidence.

At the time, though, none of this crossed my mind, as my mind was too wrapped up with Clementine. But that conversation comes back to me when my mother startles me while I am grading.

She is evading my question, refusing to tell me what is the matter, though I can sense a desperation in her tight movements. Even though I kept my secret about Julian, I haven't managed to keep her from one of her moods. "Mom," I prod her again. "What is it?"

"Whatever do you mean?"

I gesture to the stick of incense leaving a languid curve of smoke in the air. "All these bizarre rituals."

"Well," she says, straightening a pile of pregnancy magazines. "I didn't expect Elizabeth to notice, but you . . ."

"Me what?"

"You haven't felt it?" she asks. "The energy here has changed. I'm doing all I can. If we could just go back to the way things were—"

"Stop trying to do that," I snap.

"If you girls . . . if you hadn't . . ." She shakes her head, tight-lipped.

"What is it? If we hadn't what?"

"You brought it with you." The words tumble from her lips. "Both of you. You went out, lived in the world, and absorbed all the negativity that lives out there. And then you brought it with you. You brought all of that outside energy in *here*. I'm trying to clean it out."

Her face twitches with repressed emotion. I want to slap it. Here I am, trying to keep her happy despite the terrible secret in my gut, and she can't even do that. Leave it to my mother to realize something is wrong even when she doesn't know what it is.

"Please," I scoff. "There's been bad energy here forever. You just pretend not to notice."

She stands abruptly and stalks from the room. Distantly I hear the pop of a cork and the liquid trickle of a glass filling. I realize that while she has been on her intensive cleansing spree over the last four days, she hasn't had a single drink. And I realize too, with a kind of vicious satisfaction that morphs into guilt, that I am the reason she's just gone for a drink now.

* * *

And now my mother's rituals have invaded me. I have arranged artifacts around my room to ward off bad energy—piles of my favorite books like philological talismans, a smooth rock I found in the swamp when I was a child, a mug of blue pens, a candle holder shaped like an owl, a dream catcher I made in high school. I have taken out the clock that once lived here. It seemed like a bad sign.

As I pass Elizabeth's room, I cannot help but hear the conversation she is having on her cell phone—the kind of livid whispers that would be shouts if we weren't so good at keeping our voices down in this house.

At first they are wordless, harsh slithering sounds, but when I stand closer to the door, I can make out some of it.

"Where do you think?" she hisses. "As if I had anywhere else to go!"

The pause allows me to imagine what the person on the other end might be saying.

"No. I don't want to see you." She goes off on a whispered tirade at this point that is impossible for me to understand, but it ends with two words weighted with the heaviness of the earth as it depresses and curves space-time around it: "A divorce?"

There is a long pause after that.

"No, of course not," she says at last. "I don't know. I don't know." And then, "Of course I do."

I can almost feel her words crackling in the air.

Elizabeth and Donovan have always had a tumultuous relationship. Perhaps all of her relationships are like that. When they first started dating, they passed smoldering looks to each other; they couldn't get enough, ravenous for the other, but they bickered, too. When I stayed with them, they could go from a terse conversation out the sides of their mouths while watching TV on separate couches to a full-blown screaming match to a half-weeping, half-laughing reconciliation in an hour or less, whereupon they might snuggle back together on the couch to finish watching whatever was on TV. It was strange for me to behold that riot of emotions; I could not imagine behaving in such a way with another person. The more riled up I get, the quieter I become, and the more insistently someone asks me what is the matter, the more cagey my response. But Elizabeth is a tidal wave, a whirlwind that pulls up pieces of the house around her until whatever has had the misfortune of her focused wrath has no choice but to explode in equal measure.

Curiously, when they were not together, Donovan seemed remarkably more at ease. There were days when Elizabeth would don her fashionable pencil skirt and heels to go into the office while Don, a coder, elected to work from home in his sweat pants, and if it was an off day for me, then I would stealthily observe how quiet and calm the house became, how it settled into its foundation with ease, like a sigh as one slips into a warm bath, how readily Donovan might toss me a casual joke. I thought that if love was such an unpredictable thing, then perhaps I didn't want any of it after all.

But I did love Elizabeth, even if the love of sisters, too, could be wild and tumultuous.

When we were children, I made Elizabeth a necklace of arrowheads I had dug out of the mire, which I presented to her on her fourteenth birthday as if it were gold and diamonds and not a jagged mouth of sharp rock strung together on twine. She could have tossed it back at me like the junk it was, or thrown it away, or even simply draped it over the snarl of necklaces that adorned the top of her dresser and left it there to tangle, but instead she put it around her neck and wore it almost every day that year. It was one of those kind things she had a habit of doing that made me love her again.

My childhood with Elizabeth was predictable in its unpredictability. One day we might be warriors together, traversing a long-lost domain to slay invisible dragons in the name of our mother, the queen. She would encourage me on those travails and request my advice on how to proceed, as an equal. Then on other days I became, inexplicably, her enemy. We might venture into the swamp, and she would throw a rock at me when I followed too closely, narrowly missing my face with the muddy missile, and yell at me to leave her alone. After the rock, I might shed some tears, and she would tell me to go cry to Mother, who had sequestered herself away again with her drink and her silence and her loneliness.

Now that I think of it, that smooth rock in my bedroom is one that was thrown at me, and I kept it so long because it carried with it a curse that I thought, one day, I might hurl back at my sister.

Elizabeth was always a force of nature: benevolent when it pleased her, conspiratorial with me when she liked, and abruptly fearsome or vengeful when the mood struck.

As we grew older, her vindictiveness smoothed out to a kind of niceness, on the surface, even when she was being scornful. Those are the ones you have to watch out for. People who are outwardly aggressive are easier to predict; you always know what they are feeling. Elizabeth was the type that forced me to go back over our conversations to determine what, if any, cruelty might underlie the polite words, what criticisms, what barbs, what condescension.

I find it much easier, in general, to despise Elizabeth. Her incuriosity. Her self-centeredness. Her cattiness. But I mustn't let myself hate her. To hate is so easy, so comforting. To love is much more difficult.

But I loved her when she wore that necklace of arrowheads. I wonder whatever happened to it.

The house feels stuffy. The air is thick with secrets.

I follow the dark, narrow hallways and creaking staircases down and out to the backyard, the cool wind berating me as I join the shrubs and trees that shiver against it. Overgrown grass blows flat and stands up again, hiding whatever lies in the soil beneath. I think about the treasures Elizabeth and I found when we were young, rooting around for additions to her necklace.

I don't see echoes of us, though. There are others here.

Clearly we are not the only ones who dig in the dirt as children, who dredge up enchanted artifacts from the mystical swamp like sacred tokens of childhood. Such possessions of seemingly magical provenance, of a history so ancient as to seem folkloric.

But who are these other children? Who is the boy mining the mud, playing with a girl dressed in an old-fashioned frock and bonnet holding in wisps of escaping blonde hair? Who are they, these two mysteries so close to the swamp, happily digging together?

From a distance, it is possible to think nothing of the scene. It is an echo of history, a pleasant reminder that childhood play is timeless. Would that I could turn from the happy vision without curiosity, with acceptance of whatever it is, or was, or will be. But how can I? Who else am I but the one who creeps closer to make out their faces?

Only the closer I creep, the less I see, for the boy has no face.

He kneels, scrambling with his narrow hands as if looking for bones, the bones of the creatures he has buried. I can almost see the dirt caked eternally under his fingernails.

And the girl—she is not from the present. She is not from the future, either, but the past. When she turns her head to me, I cannot help but recognize the features of Constance Wakefield, not much older now than when I last saw her.

What else could it be but that Constance is playing alone in her own time, and the faceless boy in his, and they just happen to be playing at the same game, in the same place, as I see them in this fractured moment?

I feel like my mother, watching the ghosts of children unaware of the future.

The faceless boy pulls out a sharp black arrowhead from the dirt and presents it to the girl in his outstretched palm, showing off his treasure. Constance turns, her face lights up, and she leans over to look at the artifact, nodding in approval. And time has been ripped apart and resewn together, fused imperfectly such that a girl from the nineteenth century and a boy who has not yet been born might interact, might even touch, since she is reaching out now for the arrowhead still clumped with soil and bits of grass, to see it with her fingers, to feel it into existence.

I reach out as if to tell her to turn away, not to touch it, not to touch him.

It turns out, I don't have to worry about *her* touching *him*.

The faceless boy—no, let us call him by his name—Julian rises to his feet, grass stains turning his knees a sickly green, and as he stands he thrusts the arrowhead at Constance with violent momentum, which carries the sharp rock into the girl's neck.

Constance reels back with the arrowhead protruding from her flesh like a hard black tumor. She gapes at Julian—the boy who is capable of slipping through time to invade and alter the past.

Poor Constance does not know enough to leave the stone in place—I am not in the right time to tell her; I am out of time, or perhaps I am the only one within time—and from her convulsing throat, she yanks the stone free. A gout of blood blooms from her neck, her slippery neck, grasped by slippery hands, but there is no keeping it in; it streams from her mouth and from the pulsing gash, red, redder than a sunset. She falls, her throat gurgling. She coughs blood, like her mother. She pulls herself across the grass, away from Julian, who picks up a rock—Constance on her back, now, gasping at the sky—and he brings it down on her face. The rock craters her left eye, pooling red, cracking her skull like an egg.

Finally, she is still, but I've taken her trembling into myself.

Julian drops the stone and looks at the girl; his face is blank, a nothingness.

Then, from out of the swamp, a woman dripping with brown water, vines and soaked foliage tangled in her hair, slogs over to him, trailing her sodden dress on the ground. She walks stiffly, her limbs moving in a way that suggests they are rusty with disuse or with rigor mortis, her skin moving wetly as if disconnected from the bones beneath.

Clementine approaches Julian and takes his hand in her own. She gazes down at the body of the girl. She breathes a long, slow death rattle of air into drowned lungs and exhales.

"Bury her deep," she says. "They took my daughter. We'll make it so they don't find theirs." She looks to a spot in the shadow of a red maple, nods.

After a moment, Clementine and Constance vanish, but Julian remains briefly afterward with his arm still outstretched as if he continues to hold her invisible hand, staring out in my direction but giving no indication whether he can see me, whether he knows I can see him.

PART THREE

MIRRORS AND DOORWAYS

8

Over the centuries, many people have lived in the swamp, and several determined archaeologists have managed to find fragments of their existence—reworked arrowheads, clay pipes, and the like—but do you know what no one has ever found in the swamp?

Human remains.

What happened to those who died in the swamp? Surely, there are many who have perished there. Hundreds or thousands once occupied its remote interior. And, just as surely, those who died were not removed for a dry burial; many never had any contact with the outside world. Is it possible that the acidity of the swamp literally disintegrated the skeletons, ate away any remnants of human existence? Or is there another explanation? It makes you wonder, doesn't it?

When Mother asked me what I was doing, I told her it was part of my archaeological work. I was digging for artifacts.

"Well, just don't tear up the whole yard. And be sure to close up those holes when you're done."

"Of course."

By now I am thigh-deep in my third hole, hillocks of moist earth piled up around me. The first, empty. The second, empty. Perhaps what I saw was only a dream. Perhaps it didn't happen at all, and Constance Wakefield lived to a ripe old age. And I am digging holes, endless holes, like a lunatic.

But I have to know.

I am on my fourth hole, the sun bearing down through the cold air, through the exposed branches, their red leaves scattered and curling in their death throes, when my shovel strikes something hard and unyielding. Kneeling to dig with my hands, I find it is only a tree root.

Despite the cold, I've removed my jacket. My skin has a sheen of sweat. I lean my back against the maple, my arms aching, torn between frustration and relief. One more hole, I decide. Five is a nice round number; I will dig one more hole, and that will cement it for me.

Deep within the fifth hole, I strike again. There's something here: a hardness in the soil. My hands scrabble at the grime, pushing it away, until I am staring at two sockets in a dirt-caked, tawny skull.

Dusk has settled by the time I've uncovered the entire skeleton, careful not to disrupt its position. Forgoing the shovel, I dig with a small trowel the rest of the way, then use a brush to expose the bones.

Calling forth what I can remember from the forensic anthropology course I took in grad school, I examine the pelvis; the wider subpubic angle and concavity, together with a sharp ridge down the ischiopubic ramus and a ventral arc, identify the skeleton as female. Based on the size and growth of the bones, it is clearly a young girl, prepubescent, perhaps twelve or thirteen.

It is more difficult to be clinical as I examine the skull by the diffuse moonlight and failing sun that dwindles beneath the horizon. The left socket has been cracked open, a gaping hole, and around it the skull is fractured with radial cracks splintering off from the site of impact. I close my eyes and see her eye bursting like a cherry tomato beneath the bludgeoning stone. I open them and stare into the skull's dark sockets, and think of the vague black pits of his eyes.

I fill in the holes, close Constance back into her bed of dirt; it doesn't seem right to disturb her remains any further. I will not document this find. She isn't an artifact to me—not when I've seen her running down the hallways, vibrant, full of life.

* * *

Whippoorwills cackle with derangement at midnight, when I am tired and aching from my dig, but I can't sleep for listening to them. They call their names again and again, unable to stop the incessant echo affirming their identity. Doesn't it seem as if the night, of all times, with its lonesome mystery, is when we desperately repeat our names into the abyss, hoping to come out the same person by morning?

The knowledge that Julian killed, kills, will kill Constance—and others—eats away at me. That he can kill through the span of time. That he can hurt me, even now, even though he isn't yet born.

My mother already knows something is wrong, even if she doesn't know what. Maybe I should tell her. She'll believe me. She won't tell me I'm crazy.

But what exactly will she do? It will only disturb her.

I need to understand. Maybe if I can talk to Julian, I can find out why he is the way he is, and I can stop him from ever turning out this way. But I'm not my mother; I cannot call up echoes at whim. I need help.

My mother taught me a ritual designed to, in her words, "commune with the spirit world." It must be done in the dark of a basement, with a mirror and a candle. It's not exactly the spirit world I'm looking for, but it will have to do; if anything can summon Julian, bring him into the present here with me, perhaps it is this.

Because I lost the candles from the basement, I have had to borrow my mother's white candle from her reading room. The mirror is another matter. The one in my bedroom is immovable from its place on the wall, and my sister's vanity includes a mirror as part of the furniture. The seven bathrooms—only three of which are in any state of use—all have mirrors affixed to the walls. In my search, I find myself stepping into the Rose Room with a shudder at the floral carpet that imbues the room with a kind of unpleasant saccharinity, at the air that is warm and stuffy, like a fever.

What would life be like without mirrors? Imagine the course of history in which identities must develop without ever glimpsing themselves reflected in a pane of glass. Who am I but that I know what I look like?

I wonder if Julian will be made to live without mirrors. Perhaps I will smash all the mirrors in the house, and then he will never know his own face. And then the house will never know his own face.

In digging through the drawers, I come across a hand mirror with an ornate silver handle carved into floral designs. The dusty surface reflects my prying eyes. I try to wipe it clean with the sleeve of my shirt, but the mirror nearly slips from my grasp at the sound of a cough very close to me.

Carefully I hold it up and use it to peer behind my shoulder. I think to myself, *There is no one else in this room. There is no one else in this room.* Yet the sensation persists—the feeling that someone is standing right behind me. If I turn around, they will vanish as if they were never there. What is this sense that we all have, this sense of knowing when we are being watched?

When I look into the mirror, I am certain I see a shadow standing just there—Julian, murderous Julian, come to slit my throat—but when I turn my head, it is gone.

The cough comes again, wet and wretched.

This was the sickroom of Frances Wakefield, many years ago. Her illness clogs the air with remembered disease, that peculiar feeling that must linger in disused hospitals and abandoned sanitariums. It is her history that lives here.

Each room in this house has its own peculiar history—the yellow nursery, which I avoid for the ghosts of babies whose cries resonate along the patterned walls; the stone tower, accessible only from a spiral staircase tucked away in a black hallway and seemingly instilled with the spirit of Gothic castles; the library with its memory space of books; and on and on.

Is it my imagination, or do I hear the death rattle of Frances Wakefield just to my left?

If I should run into my mother or Elizabeth right now, I think I would go mad from the shock. But it is late, and dark, and they must be in bed.

With my acquired tools, I descend. I have come to the basement to call my name into the darkness and see what answers.

The old wooden chair that I place in the center of the room stinks faintly of fungus. The darkness is unbreakable beyond my little candle, and I hold up the mirror to my side so I can see it only obliquely.

Do not look directly into the mirror. Terrible things will happen if you do.

Sitting in the dark with strange stirrings in a mirror that can be glimpsed only at a maddening angle, from the corner of your eye, is nearly unbearable. I wonder if I ought to ask the house to show me something, but the house does not listen to me as it listens to my mother, who calls up her happy memories whenever she pleases.

Abruptly I notice a change in the basement's odor. The smell of decay has intensified. Rotten swamp water, a vaguely fishy, vegetal smell. Where there wasn't before, there is now a presence beyond the tepid glow of the candle that flickers double in the mirror.

"Are you here?" I whisper. "Julian?"

From the corner of my eye, I detect movement in the glass, too subtle and too dark to make out. My eyelids peel themselves back and I stare determinedly ahead, trying not to look directly into the glass, not to break whatever connection I might be forging with the house or whatever else lives in it, for we are not alone here, not with all of time unspooling around us, and all the other creatures who have lived here or will live here creeping through the dark.

The other creatures, indeed, who are whispering now all around me.

My voice feels too loud, even though I speak with the merest breath. "Julian? Is it you?" I steady my voice. "I want to talk to you, Julian. Come out, now. Let's just talk. Can you tell me . . . what did you do to the girls you put down here? Why did you hurt them?"

Still no clear answer but for the indistinct vocalizations that I hear from the walls, or perhaps from the mirror, susurrations of history, haunting us here.

I am waiting to see him creep out of the shadows, into the shivering candlelight. I hope he doesn't have a knife.

Instead I see vague movement in the mirror, and I feel, like a whisper of the swamp, warm muddy breath on the back of my neck. A low throaty sound begins chattering beside me, and I see now that there is a face in the mirror, although I cannot make out any of the features at this angle, only the shape of it, the impression of eyes and a mouth. It takes all my willpower not to turn my head.

"Hello?" A pit of dread opens in my gut. As awful as it is to think of speaking with Julian, I am unnerved by the possibility that I've opened a doorway to something else entirely. "Who am I speaking to?"

The voice intones only guttural nonsense syllables. It is like listening to a garbled television submerged in a fish tank. I must not look into the mirror.

"Julian." Without shouting, I raise my voice—what I think of as my teacher's voice. It echoes through the basement like a slap.

The only way to change the future is to understand it, but I'm starting to wonder, the longer I wait in the dark, how much more there really is to understand. I keep hoping to see a sliver of humanity in him, something to reach out to, but what if it isn't there?

I think of the way he brought the rock down on Constance: deliberate, unemotional.

A door in front of me—one of the doors to those flooded tunnels that snake through the damp earth—creaks slowly open, exhaling with it the black stench of death. Now I cannot take my eyes off the doorway, even though I am blind to whatever lies within. I must watch. I must not look into the mirror, but in its surface the face opens its mouth as if to laugh, and a low slithering voice emerges. *How long will you wait before you stop him?*

Now I can sense something in the tunnel, creeping down the throat of earth toward the basement on its hands and knees, or on many legs; I can hear the slosh of water, sucking feet in mud; yes, something is coming.

Will you wait for him to begin mutilating animals?

The candle fights to maintain its potency, but its flame flickers in the damp air moving in from the tunnel.

Will you wait for him to begin murdering children?

I can almost see a figure now, in the darkness, pressing against the doorway, but it is only my imagination conjuring him up. The distant sounds of the tunnel might be nothing at all—might be rodents or frogs or only my imagination. I cling to this belief, wanting nothing of whatever might live in those dank underground passages.

Will you wait for him to grow into a man?

"No," I say to the voice in the mirror, a sharp crack, a command that stays the invisible figure beyond the doorway. "Who are you? You're not him. Who am I speaking to?"

Cold, sick air blows in from the tunnel and caresses the candle flame.

You are speaking to yourself.

Unable to stand it any longer, I turn my head to look into the face that has been mocking me from the fringes, and with a start I see only my own face staring back—my own face, my own eyes, my own mouth, but all is strange and unfamiliar, like the face of a stranger. As if it isn't my face at all but only the house, replicating me.

"I am speaking to myself," I murmur, and then laugh wildly. Thank goodness Elizabeth and my mother are asleep and not here to witness my foolishness. And it will serve them right, I think spitefully, when they realize, at last, what Julian is. What he really *is*. Elizabeth will never believe, until she sees it with her own eyes, that she could create such a monster in her womb. Create something terrible out of her own flesh.

Unless, I think with a chill coming over me. Unless that is why the house is showing him to me—because I am the only one who can do the unthinkable. Unless I am to stop him from ever being born.

Can I do the unthinkable deed?

When a figure moves across the basement, I nearly jump out of my skin, thinking it is Julian, come at last, come to take care of his auntie—but it is only my mother. I laugh again, as we do so often when we are afraid.

"Jesus, Mother, you scared me. What are you doing up?"

I expect her to ask what I am doing sitting alone in the dark, laughing to myself; she does not respond but continues to the shelves, and I see in the candlelight that she is younger—not terribly younger, perhaps by fifteen years or so. It is not my mother. Or rather, it is an echo of her.

"What are you doing?" I ask, knowing she cannot hear me.

Taking my candle to light the way, I follow her to the shelves that house old dolls and boxes of dusty antiques, peeling away spider webs grown over the forgotten detritus. Holding up the light, I see that her face is haggard and drained, with hollow, red-rimmed eyes. This is from the time when she drank heavily.

Eventually she finds a small wooden jewelry box with a chain of pearls curled up in its velvet-lined interior. Lifting the tangled necklace, she takes something metallic from her pocket and slips it into the box. Just before she lays the pearls on top of it, I get a glimpse of rusted bronze.

Shutting the box, she stands on her toes and reaches up to slide it onto the highest shelf. Then, wiping dust from her hands, Agnes turns and stalks away.

Dread thrills my heart. What did she slide so delicately under that string of pearls so many years ago?

Because I am several inches shorter than my mother, I drag the wooden chair to the shelves and stand on it to peer over the highest one. As I do, the rickety legs tremble and rock beneath me. Lifting the candle reveals in that flickering glow a small jewelry box sitting at the far back of the shelf, flush against the wall and gray with years of accumulated dust and webs. I reach for it; the box feels sticky with grime.

Perhaps I will open this box and there will be nothing inside anymore—or perhaps I will find only my great-grandmother's pearl necklace, and I will be left to wonder at the mystery of it all. It feels somehow as if I have been waiting my whole life to open this little box, and I almost laugh again at my foolishness. Fear does make us irrational creatures. I vow to be less irrational, to be more sensible in the future.

Still standing on the chair, with the candle balanced on the shelf, I blow frenetic plumes of dust from the top of the carved wooden box and carefully open the lid, which creaks on its rusted hinges. Inside, the pearls gleam, untouched; gently, I pull them out in one long knotted strand and hold them up, away from the box.

Sitting in the black velvet lining, as if it has been waiting here just for me, is an old bronze key.

* * *

Perhaps they are like reflections, these echoes in the house. Reflections of what once was there, the house constructed of one great mirror so seamlessly incorporated with reality that we do not even see the edges or the backing but only the perfect image of the world echoed back at us. If so, my encounter with the mirror, with seeing a me that was not-me, reveals itself as a recursive anomaly; if I was attempting to shine a mirror onto a mirror, then I was creating an infinity mirror, and here I am, *mise en abyme*, placing myself into an abyss of reflections. If such is the case, and the reality of this house is a mirror, then it would stand to reason that all mirrors in this place are suspect, are wormholes to infinity, and are therefore not to be trusted. I shall have to be careful not to look directly into them while I brush my teeth.

Or, perhaps, shining a mirror onto another mirror will finally reveal the secrets of the house, solving the mystery of our lives. Like a key in a lock.

That I now have possession of the key mitigates my dread not at all, for the weight of it lies heavy in my pocket, and I can feel it there, waiting to be reunited with the lock. Even though I have never seen this key before, it is only too clear where it leads. All other doors in this house are fitted to the skeleton key that opens them all, all except one. The one that, supposedly, has never been opened.

But if it has never been opened—if it has been locked since time immemorial—then how did my mother come to possess this key? And did she use it?

And why did she hide it?

Before leaving the basement and after pocketing the key, I make sure to close the door leading to the tunnel, hesitating there to feel the cold rank air pass over me and to peer down its length as far as I can see, which isn't very far at all. Just far enough to make out the uneven ground patched with puddles and the roots that reach down through the earth like crooked tentacles from above.

It is almost two in the morning when I am finally back in bed. I leave the candle lit beside me and the mirror facedown, just in case.

* * *

My class the next morning proceeds in a groggy stupor. It is one of the introductory archaeology courses that does not involve fieldwork. You can tell, looking at the students, that they want to be *out there* doing things, digging in the earth like groundhogs, but instead they are trapped here in this little white box of a classroom, with me.

It is the kind of class where I set up the premise of finding a piece of clay pottery and ask them what sort of dating techniques they would use, and a student in the back replies, "I would start with buying her dinner." It is the kind of class where I try again after the laughter has died down and am met only with dull silent stares, two dozen pairs of eyes gazing blankly at me like chips of glass, waiting for me to answer my own question. And I fight with myself because I want to teach them, I want them to offer their ideas and their excitement, but I am also afraid of them, afraid of their unreadable condemnatory stares and the thickness of their boredom, which pours into the air with a physical presence. They are strange beings, fortuitously wrought in human form by the whims of nature.

When class is over, I sit briefly in the emptied classroom, thinking how different it looks with its unpeopled desks—how different everything is when those who are meant to be there have vacated. Then I make my way down the long corridor toward the exit, passing small clusters of students, rooms filling up for the next period of classes, colleagues who offer a polite, indifferent nod. I am nearly to the end of the hall and the double doors that will expel me into the late-morning sunlight when I see, to my left, just beside the bathrooms and the custodian's closet, a door that I have never noticed before, that does not match the others in this hallway. It is a large, heavy door of a dark wood with dizzying grain patterns that draw the eye to its bronze handle and lock.

There is no room number. When I put my hand against the wood, it feels cold, and when I put my ear against the wood, I hear nothing. I grasp the handle and try to turn it, but the door is locked.

And here is the bronze key, burning a hole in my pocket.

Perhaps, instead of unlocking the door and unleashing whatever lives inside, I should peer through the keyhole?

It is a large, old-fashioned keyhole, and I bend down and press my eye to it. Darkness within, but if I close my other eye and focus, I can just begin to make out a figure standing there, on the other side.

I stand up quickly, unnerved by the figure. I know it is impossible, but I wonder if my key will open this door. I consider taking it out, sliding it into the keyhole, stepping through . . . and where will I come out?

Footsteps pass behind me in the hallway. I ignore them.

Maybe Elizabeth is right. Maybe I am crazy.

Thinking this, I turn to leave the door behind me, and nearly step straight into one of my students, Valerie.

"Oh, sorry, Professor Wakefield," she says, catching her balance. She peers at me through thick glasses that magnify her eyes to insectile proportions. "I was actually looking for you. I hope you don't think I'm a snoop, but I heard you live near the Great Dismal Swamp."

My attention is torn in two—half to the door, half to her. The school is not in Shadydale, it is far outside that little town, in its own college world, and yet for a moment I recoil in horror, thinking she must be one of *them*, thinking that Shadydale has bled its boundaries over to the school and has come to spread its sickness here.

"Yes?" I say, my throat tight with dread that I may have to abandon my post here and find some other position to make ends meet, that it is no longer safe for me here with this Shadydaler finding me, pinning me to a corkboard, identifying me as *one of those Wakefields.*

"I've always been curious about the area. Have you followed any of the archaeological work done there? Or have *you* done any?"

"I'm afraid I haven't," I say, trying to swallow my heart. "Done any of my own work, that is. I have studied it, though. It is a fascinating place."

"It must be so interesting to live there," Valerie agrees. "Do you think it would be worth it to take a field trip? Or maybe an independent study? I'd really like to do some fieldwork."

"You want to go into the swamp?" What is she doing, I wonder; is she trying to distract me from what I have found? "It's dangerous. The swamp swallows people whole and doesn't even spit out their bones."

"Oh," she says, taking a small involuntary step back.

Briefly my mind flits to the possibilities of working with an apprentice in the field, the splendid conversations and the adventures we could have digging for small artifacts of forgotten civilizations, for Meriday's decomposing dolls, for Wind Walker's pipe, for the bones of the dead, the bones of children, the bones of those he's killed—

"Do you know what this door leads to?" I say instead.

"I don't know. I think there's a faculty bathroom at the other end of the hall, if that's what you're looking for."

"No." Suddenly the wide hallway feels oppressive, the fluorescent lights harsh against the dim corners, washing out people's faces and glaring strangely on their foreheads so that their eyes disappear into indistinct black pockets. There are no windows in this hallway, so we are enclosed, like the long narrow hallways of Wakefield Manor and its rooms draped with heavy curtains to keep out the light of the world.

"I'm sorry, but I have to go," I tell her, needing to get away from here. Surely my key would not have opened it anyway. This is not the same door. Reality and I haven't parted ways just yet; I am only mad north by northwest.

* * *

On the long drive home, I watch the countryside rush by and feel embraced by a state of calm. Now everything is opened up to me. How silly it was to fear that locked door, here with the sun beaming in through the windows. Next week, I will be wonderful with my students. I will be animated, I will engage them, and I will not be afraid of mysterious doors, because I will open the one at home and put it behind me. The thought brings me comfort.

How nice it is to drive, alone on the road. What a joy are the trees that stand so tall and proud even through their dying autumn, that lean this way and that to question who will inherit this earth of theirs, these trees that transcend time. What a joy is the day with its sun on the long dewy grass that hides multitudes of insects and other tiny creatures in its gently waving skin. I could stay out here all day and never tire of looking: the light, the sun. Why do we shut out life with curtains and shield ourselves from the marvel of the flowers that grow in their perfect golden spirals?

I almost consider passing up the turn that will lead me windingly to the house, passing it altogether so that I may simply keep driving, driving forever, but I do not because home draws me to it with a gravitational pull. I drive through the intricate iron gate with its fickle latch and come up to the house, observing it like a stranger to see what it looks like from the outside.

When you pull up, the house dwarfs you to insignificance. One can imagine it was once proud and beautiful, but now it is ill kept and fallen, bit by bit, into disrepair, into a great colossal wreck. I think one would not be surprised to discover that my mother and sister and I are all, in fact, ghosts, and that the place has actually been abandoned for years. That would explain the dusty windows, the thorny vines creeping over the facade, and the general air of gloom that presides over the land around it, which the house casts into shadow.

Autumn is especially apropos. Children who visit on Halloween come wanting to see the haunted house. They don't come for the candy, or if they do, the candy is a kind of prize, not to eat so much as to show where they have been. They will come riding up on their bicycles in zombie makeup or ghost sheets, and push and shove one another closer to the house as a testament to their bravado, through the front gate, until they are finally at the porch and cannot turn back because now they have committed themselves.

Elizabeth always loved trick-or-treating. She and her gaggle of friends would sprint out into the night in their costumes like a flock of hungry birds. My mother would likely be inside watching a black-and-white monster movie over a glass of wine.

As for me, I preferred to stay home. It gave me a thrill to creep to the front door and peek out at whoever stood on the stoop, quivering, their pillowcases outstretched like beggars. It pleased me to watch their faces contort in fear, faces that had previously eyeballed me with whispered looks and corner-eyed glances. Children who muttered nasty things about the strange girls who lived on the edge of the swamp, whose games I tried to join even as they snickered behind my back, or behind their books and magazines—whose snickers and smirks I would like to wipe right off their faces.

What a disappointment it must be when the person answering the door is not a disfigured monstrosity or a minion of the undead, but my smiling mother or little me. But it's the opening of the door that matters. You don't know who is on the other side; that's the thrill, the Parable of the Knocker. I could be anyone. Anyone at all.

One of these days, I'd like to give them a scare. I really would.

How would you like to see a real ghost, children?

No one is inside when I come home. I can sense it; the house has a quality of abandonment, the kind of feeling you get only in empty houses. It hollowly echoes my footsteps and my voice when I call out hello, only to hear my own self calling back and back and then silence.

Open the door, Sam, it seems to say.

I find them in the garden.

Mother is sitting in her favorite chair peeling a clementine while Elizabeth trots around, absurdly watering already-overgrown plants with a rusted watering can, despite the frequent rains we've had, the storms, the wetness that is always heavy in the air.

"Hello, dear, how was your day?" she says in a parody of wifely charm.

"It's only just past noon," I point out as a cloud creeps over the sun, dimming our world. Out in the swamp, the trees clothed in moss and hung with scarves of vines stand grotesque in the gray sea-like light, and angry little black birds dart across the pale sky like the shadows of souls fleeing hell. They scream at each other, and I remember the naked bird on the kitchen table. We are like birds, I think, like birds in the swamp.

In a moment, the sun returns, and everything is different again.

"What on earth are you doing?" I ask.

"Lizzie's watering the garden," my mother intones, as if this is not obvious, as she continues to peel her clementine, discarding shards of orange skin.

She hasn't gone near my filled-in holes, at least. From here I can see the mounds of overturned dirt beneath the red maple, fallen leaves already blowing over the grave.

"Someone's got to take care of this place," Elizabeth adds. "And, frankly, I'm getting bored sitting around all the time. Sitting around too much here can drive you crazy."

Open the door. The echo is following me, in my mind. Maybe I am crazy. *Open the door.*

"Look," says Agnes, and we all look.

The girls are playing again. Two little girls, bouncing a birdie on ancient tennis rackets that must have been rusting in the basement for years. The goal seems to be to keep the birdie in the air as long as possible. They laugh as it whips upward like a little rocket, bouncing and spinning, until it falls at Sam's feet. She signs an apology, but little Lizzie grins wickedly.

"You are banished from the kingdom," she says.

We watch, holding our breath. When we played at royalty in the old tower room, banishment meant climbing down, opening the basement door, and descending into the dungeon, there to stay for an hour in the dark. If you were lucky, the other wouldn't close the door behind you, trapping you behind it. I skirted the rules as often as I could—anything to avoid opening the door on the black maw of the basement and stepping through it to the other side.

Elizabeth turns around first, ignoring the memory, taking the watering can to the other end of the yard to drown the weeds there, turning her back on the girls. I watch as little Sam, instead of heading inside for the basement, takes off running toward the swamp, getting tinier and tinier, banished, banished from the kingdom.

Open the door, Sam.

* * *

I've left them outside and come up here alone to the end of the third-floor hallway, unable to put it off any longer, but unable, either, to do it. The closer I draw to the door down that cramped and narrow hall, the more terrible it seems. Standing here now, I am hardly able to lift the key, it is so heavy, and I cannot help but feel that something is simply *wrong* with this place, this room, this suffocating windowless hallway.

It is a door that should not be opened. What if it is meant to stay shut?

Shivering, I slide the key into the lock, and it clicks into place.

Open the door, Sam.

All right. I open the door.

9

The door opens.

The air smells like it has been shut up for a long time, like the breath of an ancient desiccated corpse. When I step inside, spider webs creep down and cling to my skin like sticky whispers, invisible in the fragile light from the hallway, which offers only enough for me to know if I might bump into one of the brooding funereal shapes that inhabit the room.

It is only a room, I think to myself. *Only a room that has been closed off for a very long time, like the abandoned wing of a hospital or a shuttered factory. There is nothing inherently bad about the room but that we have made it so, by locking it up for so long.* This is what I tell myself, even with my heart in my throat and the subconscious hint, from which I deliberately turn away, that there is something else to this place, that it is more than just a room, that what I *see* is not necessarily what is *there*.

If there ever was a light in here, I do not know how to find it, and it's unlikely still to work, so I feel my way across the darkness, my arms outstretched as far as they can extend, until I find the window and pull aside its heavy drapery.

Now the daylight can have its way with this place.

The tall, narrow window is so dusty that it lends a grayish quality to the sunlight.

In that light the color of winter, I can see the room now. The shapes are of roughhewn furniture, including a set of drawers and a table coated with dust. The ceiling here is unfinished; wooden beams crisscross overhead, spinning shadows for the spiders. Here and there the floor sags, made soft by rot; I see holes in the decayed wood; a dusty, cracked mirror sits along the back wall; a confetti of broken plaster gathers on the floor around a tattered old armchair, exposing the uneven slats of lath where the wallpaper has peeled away; and even along the rest of the walls, the ancient florid wallpaper of an infinitely repeating pattern clings barely, hangs down in yellowing strips.

Yet none of this truly conveys what the room *is*, how it *feels* when you step through the threshold. These details tell you of dust mites and neglect, but they do not explain the goose bumps chasing each other across my arms, or the sick feeling in the pit of my stomach, or the almost dizzying, magnetic impression of the air, charged not with electricity but some older, primal force, some undeniable strangeness that makes one's head feel thick and fuzzy.

Worse yet, there is a bed against the east wall, with a gross discolored mattress and a threadbare blanket that must have been white, once. I cannot imagine spending a night in this room.

Even standing here in the gray light observing the room is giving me a headache. The sick energy in the air makes me want to sit, but I refuse to go near that bed. It repels me like the wrong end of a magnet, and it seems to hold the indentation of forgotten souls on its surface. The infinity wallpaper makes me dizzy.

I have not mentioned this yet because I have been trying to ignore it, to convince myself it is only my imagination, but the more I stare, the more the things before me seem to warp and bend, as if I have taken some kind of hallucinogenic. It is almost, but not quite, like the time I tried mushrooms in college with my roommate and her boyfriend, and we danced out onto the quad at midnight while the stars pulsed with a great eternal heartbeat, and then, when we returned to the dorm, I felt feverish in the harsh light that made their eyes balloon strangely.

When I look around, everything seems normal at first, but the longer I allow my eyes to linger on any one spot, the more the warping creeps in from the edges of my vision, like a tunneling, as if trying to compress everything down to a single point.

It all becomes a bit too much, so I find my way to the table and sit heavily on a rickety chair. As I do, I hear a low groan, like a woman in pain, and it sets the back of my neck prickling.

The table is bare but for a dusty notebook that doesn't warrant too much interest, but I pick it up anyway and flip it open, wondering what sort of forgotten murmurs might have been etched in its pages. To my surprise (I'd half assumed the notebook would be blank, just another empty element of this soulless void, this nonplace), the pages are filled with sprawling handwriting.

As if the room left it here just for me!

An artifact for me to document.

I thumb through yellowed pages, mentally narrating what I will note down of this find. Five by eight inches, soft leather cover, worn binding, handwriting in black ink, most likely ballpoint pen. There is no name on the inside cover—the journal refuses to identify itself. When I flip to a random page, I find . . . Well, I'll let you read the entry for yourself:

Sometimes I wonder just when I began to lose my mind.

I've been looking at the shadows more closely ever since I came into this room. There seems to be more in the shadows here than anywhere else.

I have read that shadows are the absence of light, yet this seems wrong to me. Where no light exists, there are no shadows either. The shadow shows us not a physical shape that exists in reality but instead the place where light has been blocked. It shows us the inverse of that which we can see via visible light, in the form of a space that we cannot see that exists in the shape and semblance of the thing that is blocking the light. An absence and a presence.

And what if all we see are shadows? What does that tell us about the things we cannot see, the things that are somewhere above, blocking the light?

I cannot help but think it as I look around this room, lit only by the insufficient lamp that misses certain spaces or obscure corners that I cannot see, because the light cannot see them, and while the shadows themselves are not real *physical entities capable of existing on their own, there could, at the same time, be anything* within *those areas of non-sight, of nothingness.*

In a sense, the memories that move through this house are also shadows, cast by some sort of time-light. Like the shadows made physical in the aftermath of a nuclear bomb, shadows burnt into the ground with the force of the explosion. If light has enough force, then it can make shadows real, permanent.

Is that us? Are we only shadows made permanent? Are we any more real than the echoes that wander this house of shadows—this room of Nothing?

No, not so much nothing as beyond-all-things. But that isn't quite right either.

Humans have always had trouble understanding nothing. That is, the ness of no-thing, the nothing-ness, the concept of not-anything. And why is this? Because we live our lives in a world of Things: I am a Thing, you are a Thing, this house is a Thing, the grass the clouds the air we breathe—are all Things.

What do we know of 'no thing'?

The ancient Greeks had no concept of zero. The idea of it, the non-number, made no sense to them. They went about their lives refusing to use zero, even in practical ways, in mathematics and astronomy. It was an abomination. Unthinkable, unimaginable, beyond comprehension. Zero, the evil god perversely existing where it cannot exist.

In Sanskrit the word for zero, shunya, *comes from the concepts of void and emptiness. Arabs also used a word for empty, the circle they called* sifr. *Medieval leaders loathed zero. If God is everything that is, then what is everything that isn't?*

The Evil God Zero again, evil because there is no sense in it, because it breaks rules. We cannot conceive of the void any more than we can conceive of the infinite.

We cannot divide by zero. It is impossible. Try to divide by zero, and what will happen? Insanity. Physics breaks down, the world crumbles, the universe implodes.

Zero-dimensional space has no dimensions. Imagine that. It is a point, a singularity, like the center of a black hole.

Both a point and a void. No-space and all-space of no-thing.

The Zero is here in this room. This is where it comes through—where the nothingness comes from. Comes leaking out.

These philosophical musings on shadows stir something inside me, and it is all I can do to stave off thinking of *him*—the shadow himself. A nonentity who has yet to become itself, who can appear at any place, at any time, creeping through the long dark hallways of this house or perhaps standing in that corner right now, just behind me, the one I cannot see, watching *me* from some distant year.

Which reminds me, this feeling of being watched, of a class I once taught, late at night, in a classroom made cozy and small by the dark ruminating outside the window, pondering us as if we were a lone human outpost in a vast blank world, a refuge growing smaller with the encroaching night—the eyes of the students gleaming uncannily beneath the fluorescent ceiling, absorbing the light, drinking it, and me at the podium, trapped by the students and the outer dark, and the feeling of barrenness, hollowness, like a voice in a tin can echoing missives to no one.

The clank of a chain—I'm sure that's what I've heard. I turn around and catch a glimpse of a man chained to the bedpost, his mouth a rictus, and I nearly drop the notebook. Something creaks overhead, and I look up, but there is nothing there.

I cannot stay in this room any longer. The ceiling seems to keep getting higher, glimmering faintly as with stars. I take the journal with me and lock the door on my way out.

* * *

For the next few days, the journal consumes me. I carry it with me wherever I go, reading snatches of it between classes and over lunch. And then I cannot stop myself from pulling it out in class, too, the strange entries drawing me to them while my students are taking a quiz, and like a sneaky student myself, I read it secretly behind my desk.

The journal speaks to me, and this is what it says:

What lies at the heart of this room is what I have been trying to get at. I am working my way toward it. The no-time, the un-time.

My wife would know what I am trying to say, but I feel that I cannot talk to her. She is somehow far beyond me now, in the past or the future or in some other non-temporal sense. I have been keeping it from her, these dreamy midnight wanderings to this room, which draws me back. I can feel it during the day when I am away, my skin buzzing, needing to return. She must by now have noticed my distance, noticed that I get up and leave the bed cold at night, but she will want to know how I got in, how I found the key.

There was a pregnant girl in the house—I don't know who she was, but she paced the third-floor hallway, back and forth, as if in the midst of some dilemma. She kept looking at the door to this room, like she was afraid of it. I followed her to that room with all the old furniture—that storage room—where she pried up a loose old floorboard and dropped this key inside. And, wouldn't you know it, when I went in and pulled up the old floorboard, there it was.

But I am thinking, now, that maybe I shouldn't have opened the door.

The room seems to change, subtly, every time I enter it such that I cannot figure it out. When I first came in, it was no more than a closet, a bare little room from some other time that had no business being in this expansive house, as if it had wedged its way in where it wasn't originally in any sort of floorplan—and then it was as if it had grown with my being there, with a bed now that invited me to lie down in it and the walls having moved away to accommodate my expectations—and then it was a whole room grown where none had been! Yet it felt old and lived-in, as if it had been here all along but had merely shrunk over the ages because no one had been in it for so long, no one had watered it or nurtured it. Now I am onto something, yes, that is it, the reason it has been locked up all this time. Eventually if it had remained locked and unvisited it might have shrunk and disappeared entirely with no witness, until it was just a door that opened onto a blank wall. But it is too late, I am here, and now it is grown cavernous as a catacomb. Choked with dust and smelling faintly of rot, of the swamp, of burning, of ash.

And it was in this room grown vast and cancerous that I looked, and I saw it—the Zero. Like a hole burned through the world.

If you had seen what I have seen, you would know how impossible it is to look at the world the same way after, knowing it is filled with shadows, that reality lies somewhere beyond us still, or is merely cast on us by what never really existed in the first place, glimpsed through the hole that I have called the Zero, in the Never.

And now it has followed me out of the room, too, through the walls of the house. It's following me through the mirrors. I see it, from the corner of my eye, in the reflections—some vast dark nothingness behind the facade of this reality, and I cannot look directly at it, I cannot look any longer into any of the mirrors or I will see what no one should see and if it comes again—

if it comes again I should step through the circle

should I?

or failing that I can tie myself a Zero of my own to step through

oh god god help me

I can't tell what it means, only that the room—yes, the room drove this person mad. Perhaps I should dwell on who this might be, but I cannot bring myself to consider. It was someone who lived in the house. Someone with a wife. No, no, I won't think of that.

I am trying not to chew on this, listening to my students' pencils scratching at their papers, scratching away the void, and it makes my skin crawl. A slacker who did not study approaches me to turn in a blank sheet of paper. I slide it away from me, horrified, the nothingness crawling up my throat.

"Zero," I tell him, throwing the paper back in his dull, befuddled face. "Zero."

10

I carry the journal with me even at home, unable to let it go. I'm bending the soft cover in my hands when I walk past Elizabeth's room and hear her shuffling about inside, huffing in frustration over a box of wooden pieces.

She is trying to build a crib.

She has purchased one of those build-it-yourself contraptions. The pieces of wood and flapping pages of directions strew the floor while she sits on her bed, one leg crossed over the other, her foot jangling while she leans into her cell phone, texting furiously.

Most of Elizabeth's friends from our younger days have moved on to other places, and her other friends, later ones, haven't come out to visit. She must feel terribly alone, I think.

Her phone bleats again, insistently, and she makes a sound in the back of her throat while she types madly with her thumbs.

It is curious to see her glowering down at the phone as she texts; whenever I have seen her talk on the phone, she wears a smile to keep her words curving upward. It is funny to me, how we smile when we talk on the phone, even though the person on the other end cannot see our faces. Yet one can hear a smile just the same; there is no faking a smile in the voice without fitting your face to match, so we smile into the phone, hoping they will hear it.

She finally exhales with satisfaction, but the phone immediately begins to buzz again, and her face falls.

I enter and grab the phone from her. Elizabeth swears at me and reaches for it, but I hold it away from her and answer. "If you keep calling, you know she'll eventually just shut off her phone."

"Who—*Sam*?" Donovan's voice comes through the device. "What are you . . . ? No, she wouldn't do that. Liz can't live without her phone."

"She's been living just fine without *you*," I tell him. "Maybe she'll surprise you."

I can hear the exasperation in his voice: "Will you just put her on?"

I hold out the phone toward the cold statue of my sister, feeling a pang of sympathy for Don, since it seems entirely possible to me that Elizabeth, prone to exaggeration and intense exhibitions of emotion, particularly of the sort that would garner her some amount of pity, might be angry with him for very little reason at all, or for something so minor as to hardly register to the rest of us. Certainly I could be wrong, but as I stare into my sister's dispassionate eyes, her arms folded and refusing to take the phone, I have the urge to offer some sort of condolences to my brother-in-law.

During my time staying with them, there were nights when Elizabeth would work herself up over something or other while Don and I chuckled into our beers, sharing knowing glances over the tops of the bottles, until she managed to get Don sufficiently worked up himself that he lashed out with twice the cruelty. Once, he even broke his bottle against the wall. I can't remember why. Then he was yelling and she was crying, and nobody wanted to clean up the broken glass or the foamy puddle. When I bent down to pick up the pieces, they both shouted at me to stop, to stay out of their business, so I waited until they stormed off to bed to clean it up.

Then I would move restlessly about the house, peering out of windows, nervously checking the locks, too keyed up to sleep, until dawn peeked in through the curtains and I passed out on the couch. Having requested a substitute at the college for the remainder of the semester and relieved myself of my classes, unable to handle them in my state of constant nervousness, I would spend the days tidying up their house, thinking I was helping, until Don came home frazzled and told me I had organized the DVDs all wrong, and that he ought to work from home full-time, if only to stop me from changing over the whole house from the way he liked it.

There is something dawning in my brain, that whisper of revelation I have sometimes upon revisiting memories. What if it was him all along, and I just had it backward? What if it was him who started all the riling up, subtly goading Elizabeth until he had an excuse to boil his long-simmering temper, kept carefully at bay? The thought makes me ill with its ring of truth, and I find myself looking at my sister sideways, with new eyes.

On second thought, I decide I do not owe Don any condolences. I am still holding out the phone to Elizabeth when she finally snaps it from me and disconnects the call without a word.

"What did he do?" I ask her, thinking of broken bottles, of angry voices.

She makes a show of setting down her phone very precisely beside her, checking the screen for missed communications, and says at last, "Are you going to help me with this crib, or not?"

We ponder the instructions for several minutes until I lament, "Remember the days when instructions used to come with words?"

"Oh, but the pictures are so much easier," she says, pointing. "See? *Fit slot A into B using the F screws.*"

"No, that must be the textbook from high school sex ed."

"If it were, it would say *don't* first."

So it goes that Elizabeth deciphers the hieroglyphics on the page while I sit on the floor screwing pieces of wood together with great care and concentration, working slowly and deliberately. I may even reluctantly mention that we make a good team, with her ability to understand the instructions and my ability to construct the furniture.

"I forget you're actually good at this," Elizabeth admits, once I have gotten about a third of the crib built without much difficulty. "Remember when you decided to patch up that old canoe you found in the swamp?"

I laugh, having almost forgotten myself. I was fourteen when I found the abandoned canoe, the bottom largely rotted out from the damp, the oars splintered and stained. I spent over an hour dragging the thing back to the house like a prize, beaming with excitement when I finally deposited it on the wild grass. Elizabeth was less than impressed; she had come outside, taken a brief glance at the thing, and wrinkled her nose in disgust.

She didn't believe I could fix it enough to make it usable, but I found tools in the basement and bought some wood at the hardware store, and somehow I taught myself, through trial and error, how to patch up a canoe. By summer's end, I was taking it out onto the rivers through the swamp, and eventually Elizabeth's jealousy at my adventures bade her join me, where together we sailed along the darksome waters, sometimes pulling up the oars and simply letting ourselves drift. I believe that is where we spent the most time sharing secrets and desires, things we never would have shared with each other in the house. Secrets which, in the true fashion of a private refuge, never left the sacred swamp with us but disappeared into the air. I don't know how we managed not to use them against each other later, but things were different in the swamp than in the house, which would remember everything we divulged. I imagine that if we glided into those waters today, we might find our childhood secrets whispering through the air still, in a kind of magical remembrance.

I hardly remember what those secrets were, today. My secret fears, maybe, of time getting away from me, of people never taking me seriously, of failing to become what I truly wanted—to be a revered historian on the Great Dismal Swamp, to get my PhD and have my celebrated writings published by well-respected journals, to take eager grad students on archaeological explorations. I think of my student, Valerie, who wanted just this, and something sour curls up inside me. What were Elizabeth's canoe-secrets? I wish I could remember. Things that revealed her hidden vulnerabilities, her humanity, her true self.

I miss that old canoe.

"I remember," I say at last. "Maybe I should have been a carpenter."

"A carpenter from Carpenter," she murmurs, recalling the school we attended as children, Carpenter Elementary. We share a grin.

"Why do you suppose they called it that?"

She shrugs. "Who knows? Did they want us all to become carpenters?"

"Trying to bring good-paying, blue-collar jobs back to Virginia."

"Don't kid," she warns, though she is smiling. "There are probably still people in town who believe they're going to bring coal mining back."

"Oh, but it will be clean this time."

"If coal is clean, then I'm skinny."

"If you're skinny, then I must not even exist."

"If you don't exist, then I must be an only child."

"And if you're an only child," I add, "then you will have to build this crib on your own."

"Oh, but it's much more fun to order you around. No, not that one, *that* one," she says, pointing at the pieces. Like the wind suddenly leaving, deflating her, she sighs. "I expected Don would be the one to do this."

The happy mood deflates, too, although I am not yet ready to relinquish it. But she will not allow me to continue smiling and joking while she mourns, so I must turn my features frowningly at the floor, sorry for her, but sorry also for the turn to solemner things, when I was so enjoying myself, enjoying being with my sister and not worrying about dark things.

"Is he handy?"

"Not especially," she says. "Maybe it's better this way. Could you imagine him dealing with all these little pieces, the way he gets so irritated?"

I remember, yes, the kind of permanently frustrated energy he seemed to carry with him, as if things were never happening quickly enough or quite to his expectations.

"He's been much better about that lately," she continues, paging idly through the instructions. "Or, *had* been. At the start of the pregnancy, he downright *doted* on me." A sad smile has overtaken her face, and she is no longer looking at the instructions or me or the room but somewhere else. For a moment, I worry there will be tears, but she manages to keep them in check. "I don't know what happened."

She seems fragile despite her size—like she is made of glass, a Christmas bauble. And she is beautiful in her immensity.

I can imagine what happened: the reality of the child became a looming presence, impossible to ignore the larger she grew; suddenly it was no longer just Elizabeth but Elizabeth and a *baby*, and all the hormones and frustration and responsibility that came with it. And she wouldn't have wanted to hear his fears, I think, because she had fears of her own, so he bottled them inside bottles, maybe, until they burst. And this is all just speculation, of course—I might be completely wrong—but I imagine living with that kind of tension, and it makes me sorry for the terrible anxiety that must exist on the receiving end of it.

"Good riddance," I tell her. "Sounds like he hurt you." Even though it is a statement, it is rather more a question.

"So? Everyone hurts each other," she replies.

"Will you divorce him?"

She stares at me. "How can you *ask* me that?"

"Well, will you?"

She snaps, "I don't *know*."

"I think you should."

"What an awful thing to say."

I sigh. "Don't let him serve you with papers, if that's what he's going to do. You should serve *him*." I give her a wry smile. "It would serve him right."

She doesn't look so angry now, but contemplates the idea with her tongue just behind her teeth, like she is testing it out, seeing how it tastes. "Maybe you're right."

"Oh?"

"Maybe I will. Maybe I'll divorce him." Her eyes have become sharp, like shards of glass. "And I'll do everything on my own. A single mother." After the words are out, the moment of empowerment leaks away from her bright cheeks.

Neither of us knows what to say. As she looks around, perhaps for something to distract her from the conversation's turn, Elizabeth's eyes light on the journal that's been sitting beside me on the floor all this time. "What's that?"

I shuffle it behind me, like a secret. "Just an old journal I found."

"One of yours?" Her eyes gleam. "Come on, give me a taste. What deep thoughts did little Sam have as a child?"

"It's not mine."

"Oh." She deflates; I think she was eager for something juicy. "Whose is it, then?"

I pretend to concentrate on tightening a screw. I think I might know, but I cannot tell her, cannot voice it aloud, not until I'm absolutely sure. Someone who went mad, who stepped through a zero of his own making.

"I don't know. Just some old journal. I'm reading it for academic purposes."

"Well, that's thrilling."

I finish tightening the screw and move on to the next one. "Have you ever wondered what's inside the locked room?"

She frowns. "Sure, maybe. I guess I never really thought of it as, I don't know . . . existing, if that makes sense. I mean, I know there's a room in there, but it's like there isn't, really, at the same time, you know? It's just a door that doesn't open. You can almost pretend there's nothing behind it." She shrugs. "There's probably nothing worthwhile in there anyway, it's been shut up so long. I wouldn't want to go in there. Probably infested with spiders. No thank you." She glances again at the journal while I work. "Does that shed any light?"

I pick up the next piece of wood to affix to the base. "No," I tell her. "Not really."

I finish the crib in silence, and it looks strange, cold and white and empty. Because there is not enough room in here, we decide to move it into the nursery, and once we leave it there, it is as if it no longer exists. We forget about it, go on with our lives, the crib a passing moment like the passing moments in the swamp, something to think fondly of and promptly forget, as it is not useful, not functional, not yet.

Leaving the crib there reminds me of the canoe, long abandoned in the marsh, somewhere at the bottom of a river, rotted and grown over with algae perhaps, a home for fish.

When we were teenagers, Elizabeth and I, bored with the house and the land immediately surrounding it, began to venture farther and farther out into the swamp, escaping our lives. We became amateur explorers of the alien landscape.

There we were, one hot sticky summer. I remember the smell of bug spray, that sweet, sickly odor. In the summer, the swamp air is thick and foul. We rose early to go out, while morning mist still floated gently over the green water, which pulled us insistently forward, caressing the edges of the canoe. The sky was pink, and apart from the tugging water, the swamp felt very still, like it was just waking up. A settling peace came over me. The swamp was beautiful, calm.

Floating along, we were carried among the strange tentacles of the cypress. I never wanted to leave this place, where even the smell of bug spray became familiar, the perfume of the woodland made lovelier by it. Even with it, small flies and mosquitoes formed clouds above the water and flitted into our canoe. Elizabeth slapped them away.

"Where are we?" she asked. This was farther than we'd ever come. We had stolen into a small creek that branched off from the main waterway.

"I can't believe it," she added, when my only response was to shrug. "I can't believe you got us lost!"

"How is it my fault?"

She leaned over the side of the canoe, as if the depths of the water would tell her anything of where we were. We were far from home and now hours into the swamp, likely miles from anything resembling civilization—and the remoteness, the isolation, the thrill of it, actually excited me. I was too young to realize the acute danger we might be in, though, and I wouldn't tell Elizabeth. She was already too close to panicking. We had abandoned order and reason; we were in the wild. We floated in the reeds.

Elizabeth stood up, and the canoe rocked so much I gripped the sides as we shifted back and forth. "What are you doing?"

She looked around, as if a slightly higher vantage point would help her figure out the way to go. By now the water had become still and glassy beneath us.

"Well?"

"I don't see anything."

"What were you hoping to see?"

My nonchalant question irritated her. "Shut *up*, Sam!"

"Sorry. I wasn't aware you needed silence to see."

She cursed at me in sign language. In spite of the rudeness, I laughed. Apparently this was the wrong reaction to have, since her face turned red and tight-lipped with fury.

"You are insufferable," she spat. "What do you think of your good-luck charms now? How well have they worked for us?"

I fiddled with the dull pencil in my pocket, and a pencil eraser with a star carved into it, which called to mind good omens. In my other pocket was the wing feather of a great egret, long and white and soft. I had been carrying these talismans with me all summer as shielding, to ward off Mother's alcoholic bile and Elizabeth's searing glare. As of right now, my artifacts did not seem to be working very well, and I determined to find new ones as soon as we were home again, since these had lost their magic.

"You and your *stupid* good-luck charms," she continued, only half talking to me and half talking to the sky at large. "Since when did superstition ever save people lost in a swamp? That's what I get for coming out here, I guess."

And, just like that, I knew instinctively that our precious time together in the canoe, all those hours spent floating and daydreaming and murmuring gently to each other, conspiring and laughing, was over. We would never again return to the mystery of the swamp together, never again be intrepid explorers, partners; we would return home and resume being sisters who sniped at each other. The magic had been broken.

"I thought you liked coming out here," I said.

Elizabeth scoffed. "*Like* getting devoured by mosquitoes? *Like* smelling that swampy stench? *Like* getting lost and hot and sweaty and gross? I'm sorry, you must have me confused with someone else."

"I guess I have you confused with my sister."

"There's your problem," she mumbled, and out of spite, I deliberately shifted my weight from left to right to rock the boat. Elizabeth threw her hands out and bent her knees, as if she were surfing, and when the canoe began to settle she threw herself at me, pulling me up with her, and it took only a moment before the sudden movements tipped the canoe dangerously to one side, where it overturned and deposited us in the cold, slimy water with a splash.

We both emerged gasping and spitting and blinking the dirty water from our eyes. For a moment, I thought we were in sync and that once the shock passed, we would begin laughing. But Elizabeth was in no mood; her eyes fell on me, and they were quite vindictive. She paddled closer, grabbed my head, and pushed it under the water.

Now I was in the cool quiet, hearing only muffled rippling, and when I opened my stinging eyes I saw a world of murky green, reeds waving below me where the water got so dark I could barely see the bottom, specks of dust and whatever else floating past, sunlight shimmering the warmer, shallow waters just above me; and I was pinned in place by the weight of her hands pressing down on my head, unable to push up fully against them without leverage beneath me, suspended in the fishy green as my lungs started to hurt. I grabbed her wrists and tried to pry her hands away, but she held. My hair floated out in front of my face. I saw a fish with enormous silvery eyes dart past my feet. My lungs ached for air. When I flailed my arms, I heard the faint watery swish of their movement, but it was a calm sound despite my frantic fear. My lungs were burning.

After an eternity of green, the weight of her hands disappeared, and I shot upward, emerging with a crash as I dragged in heavy gasps of air, coughing, squinting through the water blurring my eyes, my hair plastered over my forehead.

"Come on," said Elizabeth, taking my hand and pulling me to the bank. I let go of her as soon as I could. A deep hurt welled inside me.

As we tried to turn over the canoe, we discovered it had sprung a leak; so much for my quality craftsmanship. It had lasted us almost a full year, at least, but now we watched as it quickly took in water, sinking, and we left it where it was.

We hiked in silence, until Elizabeth offered me a halfhearted apology that I pretended to accept. I didn't know how to tell her about the burn I felt in my heart, like the burn in my lungs, but lingering.

After half an hour, it became clear that we were hiking the wrong way; we were going deeper into the swamp. Now our roles had reversed: Elizabeth talked quietly, incessantly, about how we were going to find our way out soon, while I walked in moody silence, hanging my head to watch the uneven ground beneath my feet.

I wondered if Mother was getting worried. I wondered if she had noticed we had been gone nearly the whole day. It was summer, so the sun wouldn't set until later in the evening, but afternoon was already yawning on around us, the slant of the sun reminding me how little of the day yet remained in our grasp. Our feet slushed through the muck with sucking, sticky sounds.

"There. What's that?" Elizabeth said.

"What?"

"Up ahead."

We both paused to peer through the long, growing shadows between the trees. In the distance stood a small wooden shack.

"Maybe there's someone in there who can help us find our way out," she suggested. I nodded, but I was skeptical, as she must have been too, for the shack was of such shoddy construction that it looked as if it had been there for ages, that it might be abandoned to the wilds. The wood was discolored, water-rotted, and unevenly patched; vines crept along the sides of the little house. But it had a peaked roof and a front door and what looked like a boarded-up window, so we made our way dreamily toward it.

"Hello?" Elizabeth called out as we approached. Flies buzzed around us like static.

"I don't think anybody lives here," I whispered. The place exuded negativity, particularly the closed wooden door that concealed the interior of the shack. All of this seemed wrong. Why would someone build a shack way out in the middle of the swamp like this? We had come very far to get here. Surely there was no one who would, or could, live all the way out here in this remote place, deep in the swamp, so far from civilization.

All the thrill of our adventure had gone out of me. My clothes were still wet, and now they were cold, despite the warm humid air, and sticking unpleasantly to my skin, chafing; I was tired and hungry, and I just wanted to go home.

And I did *not* want to open that door.

It was too late, though. Elizabeth moved toward it, slogging through the thick heavy muck, and I wanted to warn her away, to turn and run from this terrible place, but I couldn't; I was rooted in place like a tree, thinking only that this was not right, this place was not right. My ears rang as she raised a fist to knock on the door.

At first, nothing happened, and I was glad of it. Elizabeth took a few steps back, clearly not wanting to be so close to the house, although not willing to voice her own fears.

Then, without warning, the door swung open with a creak.

Inside the doorway was an utter blackness unlike any I had seen before. It was not merely dark, the dark of a windowless interior; it was pitch, utterly without shape or light or form, inky and thick. A black hole. It was as if the interior of the shack did not really exist, or at least did not exist in this or any familiar dimension.

Elizabeth backed up quickly to stand beside me, unable to tear her eyes from the impossible black, the negative space inside.

Clouds gathered over the sky and began to drift in front of the sun, casting us in a dull gray light that prickled the hair on my arms.

Now a shape started to emerge from that doorway.

Just a silhouette, slowly revealing itself from the black, as if it were peeling away from the darkness bit by bit, and the thin gray light would only go so far as to light up the shape of a tall figure, a person who was about to step out of the doorway, a person who I did not want to step out of the doorway. The next thing the light touched was a pair of eyes, gleaming uncannily in the weird light, and all it took was the sight of those eyes for us to turn and bolt the way we'd come, running at full speed as if we were trying to outrun a fire licking its way toward us, running until our legs screamed and our sides pinched with pain, muddy water sloshing up at us in great dirty splashes, our shoes sticking, running, running back along the waterway, past the abandoned canoe, until we could not run anymore.

Who was it, coming out of the shack? The Swamp Witch? What would we have seen if we had waited a moment longer?

Darkness fell, surrounded us, and we were still lost. I don't like to think about that day, the day the magic broke, the day we lost the old canoe, because we spent that night in the swamp, shivering and afraid, huddled together for warmth without speaking. It was a long, dreadful night. The next morning, a police officer found us. When he saw us on the ground with our arms wrapped around our knees, he said into his radio, "Call off the search. I got 'em."

He and his partner, who appeared a moment later, picked us up and carried us home. We slept the rest of that day, bowls of soup appearing at our bedsides, Mother watching over us with a darkness that wouldn't leave her eyes.

I didn't really sleep, though. Every time I closed my eyes, I saw the figure emerging from the darkness, still out there, somewhere, in the swamp. And I cursed the day I'd found that rotten canoe.

* * *

I leave the canoe in the annals of history, and the crib in the loneliness of the nursery, and return to my room.

It is only when I am inside with the door closed that I feel I can safely open the journal again and lose myself in its pages, filled with dread but unable to stop reading. I wish I were back with Elizabeth laughing over the crib instructions, but instead I am sitting on my childhood bed with cloudy light peering in through the curtains behind me, watching the words scrawled across the page by a tremulous hand, in a handwriting that is almost familiar, somehow.

Woke up in the middle of the night but I don't know why.

How many times has this happened? How many times, waking up, and wondering, and feeling that there is something nearby that woke me but seeing nothing. I'll never get used to it.

I remember the first time it happened, years ago, that I really paid attention to it, in the way you only pay attention to ordinary things when they suddenly become unordinary.

Everything was dark and it must have been quiet because Aggie lay asleep and undisturbed beside me.

Whatever woke me, it was more a feeling in the air. An uneasiness that pulled me from sleep. This house, I'd guess. There's something in it that's wrong, but you can't tell *it's wrong, you only feel it. I see things, sometimes. Agnes has always told me it's normal here, to see things, but Agnes has always believed in ghosts. We've been living here for years and I still can't understand what it is about this house. What it* is, *really.*

The time when I woke up in the dark to the strange, crackling uneasiness, like a feeling of illness trapped in the air, I got up to check on the girls thinking I was having some sort of parental second sight which you hear about sometimes—parents who sense something is wrong with their children without any real-world indication.

I went to check on Sammy, all fine there, and Lizzie, sleeping with her arms akimbo and her hair in wild tangles over her face, her chest rising and falling in only that gentle, fragile way a child's chest does when they are sleeping.

Everyone was fine, so why that feeling? Why that static in the air? Why that sense that there was a presence, that there was someONE or someTHING else in the house, just out of sight? Lurking in all the mirrors, behind our reflections.

Since I was up, and could not, I think, go back to sleep anyway just then, I decided to check the other rooms. There are so many, in this house, and sometimes I forget what room I am in, and I find myself in a panic, thinking I've slipped through to another room, and another, and there are actually an infinite number of rooms in this house, and each time I open a door I will find myself in a room I have never visited before, and I will be lost forever.

In this way I found myself in the old nursery, where there should have been nothing; the furniture had been removed years ago, leaving a mostly barren space with that faded wallpaper, marked brown in places where furniture had once stood against it, an indented rectangle on the floor where the echo of a long-gone crib had sat, etc. But that night when I wandered into the nursery and turned on a small, dim lamp that was all we had left to light the useless room, I beheld a crib that should not have been there, with a gently turning mobile of strange creatures—an elephant with wings, a lion with horns, something like a cross between a moth and a katydid—and fearfully I approached this scene, thinking I might be hallucinating or dreaming awake.

And there, within the crib, lay a baby whose origin I could not claim to know, and the baby had its tiny fists curled up grasping its blanket, and its face was scrunched in dismay, its tiny mouth open and wailing silently into the void.

I wondered, briefly, if it was this baby's cries that had somehow awoken me. But that was nonsense, for I am completely deaf.

Yet it unnerved me to watch this baby screaming, and I had the urge to silence it even though I could not hear it, had that terrible urge that comes when you are contemplating the worst—what if I did the worst thing I could possibly do right now—and it makes you sick to think it, but you think it anyway. I thought, what would happen if I lay my hands around its throat and throttled the strange baby that should not be there until it vanished back to whatever abyss it had come from?

Instead I turned off the light and backed out of the room, unable to take my eyes from the dim hulking shape of the crib until I had turned the corner in the hallway. I went back to bed and crawled in beside Aggie, still asleep, and lay there imagining, and wondering.

The next morning I got up early and crept to the nursery to view it in broad daylight, but the room was just as empty as a tomb.

Maybe that was when I started going crazy?

* * *

I sit until the sun goes down for an early dusk, until the shadows creep out around me. Something heavy sits in my gut. I cannot bring myself to turn to the next page.

My father's journal.

How can I reconcile these ramblings with the man I knew? I never knew my father to be anything but sharp and keen, bright as reflected sunlight. All the marks of a mind that knows what it is, not one unraveling in the dark. I guess I didn't know him as an adult knows a person, but as a child looking up at the largeness and infallibility of a parent.

But was he truly mad, or did he catch a glimpse of something he wasn't supposed to see?

Am *I* mad?

Whatever was sitting heavy in my gut crawls up and up, into my throat, strangling me.

Am I?

And then, muffled by a multitude of walls and the softening effect of thick, old wallpaper, I hear a knock at the front door.

11

I ease the journal in among the other volumes on my bookshelf.

Three more heavy knocks, like the three knocks signaling the Devil in Beethoven's Fifth, reminding me of my tarot reading, and now I hesitate, wondering if *this* is the moment of change, if this is what my reading foresaw.

I wait for someone else to get the door, but Elizabeth is closed up in her room, silent, and I can hear my mother puttering about in the kitchen putting together dinner. She calls up to me, asking me to get the door, and reluctantly I go.

On the doorstep stands a young goateed man, perhaps in his twenties, wearing a camera around his neck and a tweed jacket too light for the season, a plaid shirt buttoned up to his chin, holding a trifold brochure in his hand like he isn't sure how it got there.

"Oh," he says, as a breeze staggers up behind him. "Good afternoon."

"Can I help you?"

"Can you help . . . oh," he says again, as if suddenly remembering the trifold. "Sorry to bother you, but if I could just have a few minutes of your time, I'd like to talk to you about our Lord and Savior." He seems more convinced of himself the more he talks.

"No thank you."

"Sam, who is it?" I hear my mother coming to the front of the house now, and I see her form emerge from down the hall.

"Just a Jehovah's Witness."

"Well," says the man, as Agnes approaches and looks him smartly up and down. "Well, I—"

"Don't be rude, Sam. Invite him in. I'm sorry . . . ?"

"Nathaniel," he says, sidestepping me to shake my mother's hand with a bit too much enthusiasm.

"Mom, he's just trying to sell us religion."

"Oh, I'm not trying to *sell*—"

"Come on into the sitting room." Agnes waves him toward the semidilapidated sofa, where he perches bemusedly on the edge of the time-faded cushion. "Can I fix you some tea?"

"Oh, I couldn't put you out."

"Nonsense."

Before she goes, she gives me a *look*—and if you are the daughter of a mother, you'll know what look I mean. A knowing smile budding behind her lips, like that of a cat on the prowl, suggests a shared recognition of the attractiveness of a potential mate for her young. I keep my face blank and give my head one slow shake, wondering what she could possibly be thinking.

Now I am alone with the Jehovah's Witness, standing with my arms crossed while he sits adjusting his glasses and clearing his throat several times over.

"May I ask you something?" he says. I'm of a mind to tell him no, but he doesn't wait for my response to ask, "How long have you lived in this fine old house?"

"All my life," I reply, surprised. Anyone in town would know that, after all.

Instead of recoiling in distaste, he smiles eagerly. "Well, it's certainly got character. A place like this, you ought to have your own historical society. Maybe a museum, give tours. Or a bed-and-breakfast! You ever think about that sort of thing?"

"And invite a bunch of strangers into our home?" My voice is filled with disgust, horror. "Why would anyone want to see a rotten old place like this, anyway?"

His eyes flicker around the room, and on his face is a hungry grin. "I bet you could make a pretty penny, enough for some renovations, at least, to restore this place to its former glory."

My hands find my hips. "What gives you the right?"

"Now, don't pitch a fit," he says benevolently, and I'd like to slap him. "It was only a suggestion."

"Well, it's a bad one." I lower my voice, keeping my ears attuned for the squeal of the kettle. "My mother would hate that. She doesn't need hucksters filling her head with stupid ideas. We don't need whatever you're selling."

"You're a delight, you know that?" He sits back, fiddling with the strap of his camera, looking anywhere but at me. "And I'm not *selling* anything."

"Tea," Agnes announces, coming in with two mugs. One she hands to the man, and the other she wraps in her hands to warm them.

"You didn't bring me any?" I ask.

"You can very well get it yourself, Sam. This man's company." She looks at him as he holds the mug, waiting for him to breathe in the lavender scent of the Earl Grey. "And we treat our company right around here. Besides, I'm always interested in having spiritual folks come around." She smiles, showing her teeth. I wonder if she was listening to our conversation from the kitchen.

Nathaniel leans over the steaming mug, and his glasses turn white and opaque. When he lifts his head, I can no longer see his eyes; he simply gazes out from two white disks.

"So, Nathaniel," says Agnes, as she takes a seat at the adjacent sofa. "Do you mind if I ask you some questions?"

"Not at all." He slurps the tea noisily. "Thank you for the tea, Mrs. . . . ?"

She lets the question dangle in the air like a loose thread. The stranger stares shrewdly, waiting for an answer or perhaps a confirmation. In either case, she does not give him the satisfaction.

"Agnes," she says, crossing one leg over the other. "Does it need lemon?"

"No, it's fine, thank you."

"Nathaniel, do you believe in ghosts?"

The tea chokes him on the way down, and he subdues a cough in the crook of his elbow. "Say again?"

"Ghosts, I said. Do you need to clean your ears out?"

"That's . . . that isn't . . . Look, I'm a skeptic when it comes to that sort of thing."

"You believe in the resurrection of Jesus but not ghosts?" I ask.

"Well, that's . . . the thing is . . ." He takes another sip of his tea.

My mother keeps her gaze fixed on him. "What made you decide to stop here today?"

As he fidgets, he looks at me from the corner of his eye, wanting to look at me but not, wanting me to help him regain control of the conversation. *You're on your own*, I want to tell him, but he keeps trying to look at me, so I ask how come I haven't seen him in town before.

"In town?" he says blankly. "Oh, you mean Shadydale? I'm from about forty miles west, as the crow flies."

"Legends travel that far?"

He sets down his mug, slides the camera strap from around his neck to hold the device in his lap, and shrugs. "Legends travel pretty far." Now he looks about the room, admiring it openly. "All right, so you got me. I'm not a believer—that's my parents' deal. They make me do this door-to-door stuff. I *am* a bit of an architecture aficionado, though. This house has been on my bucket list for *years*, but as it's a private residence, I never dreamed I would set foot inside. I was only stopping by to take pictures of the front, and, well, I thought I'd try my luck."

"I'm afraid I don't know very much about architecture," my mother drawls. "But I don't think I'm quite done talking about ghosts."

His smile falters. He looks at me again for help, but I offer him none. "If you'd just let me take a peek around, maybe snap a few photos for my blog, I'd happily get out of your hair. There's no need—"

"Nonsense," says Agnes. "Sit, enjoy your tea. We're only having a conversation. You know, we don't often get visitors out here. Most folks think to stay away. I can't imagine why." She smiles over her mug. "So forgive me, but I like to talk. While I have you here, I'd like to get your take on it. Do you feel any particular energy in this old house?"

"Well," he says with a shrug. "I don't know." He looks around. "I guess there is a kind of electricity in the air. Old wiring, you know. I've visited a number of nineteenth-century buildings that have the same problem, and I've blogged extensively about it for my column on East Coast Victorian architecture."

"Certainly, copper wiring is a conduit."

"I'm sorry?"

An elderly woman walks into the room, disrupting our conversation.

She is vaguely familiar to me, with white hair pulled neatly back into a bun, a pashmina wrapped around her plump shoulders, and a face marked by laugh lines.

"Hello," Nathaniel says to the new arrival, who, of course, ignores him.

"Sam," Agnes says, easy, nonchalant. "You remember your great-grandmother, Harriet?"

Oh yes, now I recognize her.

"Hello, ma'am," Nathaniel tries again, louder this time, as if the old woman is merely hard of hearing. She walks slowly, gingerly, about the room, touching potted plants that aren't there, straightening pictures on the wall that are already straight. We watch her perambulations with mild fascination.

"Is she . . . all right?" asks Nathaniel.

"Oh no, I'm afraid not," Agnes says lightly.

Nathaniel looks alarmed.

We continue to watch Harriet's slow, laborious movements around the room before she starts toward the couch on which Nathaniel is sitting. He moves over to make room for her, and through good fortune she sits in the vacated spot rather than on top of him. I've had this happen to me before, where an echo will occupy the same space as me for a moment or two, and while it doesn't physically *feel* like anything, it is an incredibly unsettling experience.

Harriet slumps back now, her breathing labored. What did she die of? A heart attack? Stroke? I can't quite recall.

My mother and I exchange a look. You know the one—I give her a quirk of my eyebrow, silently asking where this is going, and she retains that genteel smile-that-isn't-a-smile, her eyes glittering as if to say, *Watch, and you will see.*

"Ma'am, are you all right?" Nathaniel shouts in Harriet's ear.

Abruptly, she freezes, all her muscles strained taut, and her tremors become unnatural shaking as her eyes roll up to reveal the rheumy whites and her jaw clenches in a teeth-cracking grimace. Ah yes, it was a seizure. She was epileptic.

Nathaniel lifts his hands as if to grab her, but he won't bring them close enough to touch her seizing body. "What are you all doing? This woman needs medical attention!"

"Oh, it's too late for that, I'm afraid." Agnes gazes fondly at her grandmother. "Don't worry, it will be over soon."

She watches Harriet die like one who has watched many people die, and the look in her eyes disturbs even me. How much death has she seen in this house, after all?

When the seizure is over, Harriet slumps to the side, straight into Nathaniel, who shrieks as she passes through him and leaps to his feet, dropping his camera and turning to stare at the woman gone cold-eyed, one arm flung out above her head, which rests upon the spot where he was sitting. She is now still.

"What happened? What just happened?" Nathaniel cries out, patting his hands over his front as if to check that he is, indeed, solid.

"Now, Nathaniel," I tell him, smiling. "Don't pitch a fit."

Harriet remains too still after too much movement. Her mouth gapes and her eyes are infinity.

Agnes sighs. "Well, I do hate having a corpse on the couch."

"What is . . . *wrong* with you people?"

I laugh, then, pleased with it all, and with my mother especially. Perhaps having fun at this stranger's expense is cruel, but it is a delicious kind of cruelty, isn't it?

Finally, Harriet's paper-pale corpse flickers like a badly tuned television and disappears. Phantom laughter from another room drifts our way, unprovoked.

"What?" Nathaniel shouts, whirling around at the noise, and I find this reaction so comical that I laugh again.

"Are you quite sure, Nathaniel, that you do not believe in ghosts?" asks an amused Agnes as she sips her tea. "Why, didn't you know when you came here that this is a haunted house?"

At once, before he can make any attempt at a reply, a scream rends the air, and I think for a moment of the poor soul—Nathaniel's nerves must be frayed as far as they will go, and I almost want to tell the house to give it a rest now, we are done with the theatrics.

But I am on my feet just as fast as Nathaniel is stumbling toward the foyer, the forgotten brochure flying away in a flap of paper only to slide across the hardwood floor, scattering tumbleweeds of dust.

"You *people*," he keeps saying, like he can't believe us, like we have pulled some sort of mean-spirited prank on him. "You *people*!"

The scream, I realize, sounds familiar. Maybe it isn't an echo. Maybe it is happening right now.

Elizabeth.

Pushing him out of my way, I bound up the stairs to see about the scream, my feet taking me toward Elizabeth's room. My heart beats a frantic tattoo even as I tell myself it is merely an echo of some prior time, when someone screamed in obvious pain, the screaming like needles in my ears.

When I burst into Elizabeth's room, there she is, clutching her pregnant belly, blood soaking through her gray leggings. She has a sickly sheen to her skin and her hair sticks in sweaty tangles, her eyes embraced by dark rings.

Julian is trying to kill her from the inside out, I think wildly. He will tear his way out of her flesh, and he will keep tearing through flesh until I put a stop to him.

* * *

The ride to the hospital is a blur, even though I am the one driving.

Funny how that happens, isn't it? All those miles eaten up and forgotten in the whirlwind of thoughts, as if our brains can contain only so much at once and have to filter out the everyday motions of driving, signaling a turn, braking at red lights and stop signs.

All along I am wondering what happened.

Mother sits in the back seat with Elizabeth's head on her lap, and I cannot be bothered to worry about her, too, though she looks drawn and red-eyed in the rearview mirror, her left hand a clenched fist around the handle above the door.

I cannot be bothered to worry about my mother because my heart is clenched like a fist for my sister. After silently resenting her sudden chaotic appearance in the otherwise fairly peaceful life I had created back at home, after fuming at her refusal to listen to me regarding Julian, after being so dismissive of her, now, now I am feeling a kind of terror—not for Julian, although I cannot think of the implications if this is a late-term miscarriage, but the kind of terror that reminds me how desperately I need my sister to be all right.

* * *

Even when we are sitting in the waiting room while Elizabeth is taken for tests, with the dark falling softly out the windows like black snow and the gentle hum of air circulating through the building's vents, my mother clenches the armrests of her chair, her eyes closed and her face pinched like one fighting their way through the nausea of a roller coaster.

There isn't anything I can do, I think to myself. I have tried to take her hand from its death grip on the chair, but she refused to let go, swatting me away with her elbow, and I have tried to pat her on the shoulder, feeling ridiculous even as I did, but she shuddered away from the touch as if my hand burned with ice.

Her breath hums, wheezes in and out of her throat.

"Everything is going to be okay."

"I don't need you to tell me that," she says, struggling for air as if she were running a marathon.

"Then calm down. Just breathe."

"Don't you tell me what to do," she barks.

I almost laugh. As if she would stop breathing just to spite me.

"You're making me anxious," I tell her, wishing she would stop behaving like this and knowing it is unfair of me to wish such a thing.

"Ask them how much longer."

"I just asked them five minutes ago. They'll call us up when she's done."

My mother shakes her head. "This is ridiculous. I can't just sit here forever. I can't even *breathe.*"

"Of course you can," I snap, despising the sharpness in my voice. I ball my hands into fists and dig the nails into my palms. A few other people are in the waiting room, and they aren't looking at us yet, but they might be, out of the corners of their eyes, for all I can tell, and I just want to keep it that way. "You breathe every second of your life."

She lets go of the chair and bends over, hands on her stomach, and I grab her shoulder to pull her back up, to stop her from these hysterics, but she twists out of my grip, swaying, unstable, gasping, and dry-heaves twice before vomit comes up her convulsing throat.

When she straightens up again, she wipes the back of her hand over her mouth and fixes me with a glare that reminds me of my childhood. "You don't know," she says with a scratchy voice, and that is all she says.

Lucky for us, we are in a hospital, so she is given a sedative and a place to lie down, and then it's just me left to wander the lonely halls back and forth between my mother and my sister, down past the endless series of doors. I decide to sit in my sister's empty room, and what must be an hour passes as I wait for them to wheel her back. I look at the cold tile floor and the mirrored window that turns the falling dusk into a shadowy reflection of the room. I listen to nurses wheel the broken bodies in from down the hallway and wheel the empty gurneys back out to wherever they came from, in and out like the tide, until I can't stand it anymore and I get up to walk up and down the hallway.

Wheels creak and roll across the glossy tile floor. I can't remember what room I came from. All the doors are closed, and I cannot open them. I hurry back down the hall, toward the grinding wheels, just as a male nurse pushes a gurney into an open doorway, and there it is, the room, and there is Elizabeth, being moved to her bed.

The doctor follows shortly after, a stony-faced woman with her hair pulled back tight against her scalp. She offers her hand for a perfunctory shake and says I must be the sister.

"I suppose I must be," I say. "So what happened?"

"At first we assumed it was a placental abruption due to the pain and bleeding," she explains, "in which case, we would have performed an emergency cesarean. However," she continues, "that wasn't the case. The bleeding's stopped, and she's doing well. To be honest, there's nothing wrong with her."

"So . . . that's it?"

"That's it," she says with a shrug. "Just one of those things."

"Just one of those things."

"The body is a magnificent and mysterious thing." At last she smiles thinly. "Sometimes it does things we can't explain. But your sister is healthy, and everything looks good. This was just a minor fluke."

"What about Julian?" I ask.

"I'm sorry?"

"The baby."

She nods. "The baby is in good health. No problems, which is why we didn't induce. Better to let him come when he's ready. Now, we gave Elizabeth a little something, but I think she's mainly just exhausted from the ordeal, so we should let her get some rest. We'll keep her overnight for observation, and tomorrow, barring any complications, she should be able to go home." The smile returns, just slightly. "Good news, right?"

Good news, certainly, but why doesn't it feel like good news? Why does it feel like Julian is lurking in there, biding his time, waiting to burst free?

12

Like lonely islands in the darkness, streetlamps crawl past as I drive us home, spread out enough that their pools of light never touch. My mother in the passenger seat is partly dozing, groggy and dulled from the sedative. The darkness is broken; the silence, now, too.

"Mom."

"What is it, honey?"

I hesitate. I want to ask her about her experience this evening, about how she reacted to leaving the house for the first time in so long, but I can imagine how that conversation would go. *I am perfectly fine*, she would say, affronted that I would even suggest otherwise, and so directly. Perhaps it is best to approach such things sideways.

"I found the key."

"What key?"

"To the room at the end of the hall."

Agnes chews on this for a long moment before releasing a low, flat, "Oh."

I am driving slowly because I do not want to get home, not yet.

"I saw where you hid it."

"You did, did you?"

"I thought that room had been locked since—forever."

"It had been. Before. And it has been since."

"Are you going to tell me why you had it? Why you hid it?"

She is quiet for a long, long moment. "I would rather not."

Her non-answers are beginning to annoy me. "Come on, Mom."

The streetlamps glide toward us through the night, momentarily light up the car yellow, and then flee quickly behind us, retreating into the darkness. The moon is low and bearded with gauzy clouds. *This is a country road*, I think, for no real reason. *We are in the empty country dark.*

"You were so young, you and Lizzie," she says at last, carefully. "I hadn't thought it right, to tell you where he did it."

"You mean Dad?"

Neither of us looks at the other. I am watching the road roll toward us, and she too is staring straight ahead, the artificial light periodically flashing over us. Maybe it is easier, not to look.

Everyone knows my father hanged himself—because gossip travels fast in small towns—and even if my mother had wanted to keep it from me, there was no way she could silence the whispers. I always knew my father had hanged himself, but it never occurred to me to think beyond that, or even to imagine it. What it looked like. Where I was at the time. It was always just the words. It's not something you want to stop and really think about.

The silence in the car is incredible, heavy, absolute.

"He did it in that room. He'd found the key, somewhere, while cleaning up, I think—you know he always liked to keep things tidy. I'm not sure how he figured out it was for that room. He must have tried all the doors before he fitted it into the lock. Before then, he'd never seemed to *notice* the room. I'd told him once, early on, that it was just another room, one we kept closed, and that was that. He never asked, never mentioned it, never showed any interest whatsoever."

I can think of nothing to say, so I say nothing.

"I was no good afterward. I wanted to know *why.* I thought I might find some clue in there. I spent hours sitting in that wretched room, waiting for him to appear . . . *willing* him to appear."

"And did he?"

Before she speaks, I know the answer. My mother has that uncanny ability to draw specific memories from the house, to conjure up what she thinks she wants to see. I imagine my mother, desperate, pleading with the house to show her what she thought she wanted to see, using her witchy designs to make the house do her bidding, burning a lock of his hair, placing small tokens of his around her, until the house relented and revealed to her its secrets, as it always did.

"Yes."

The long quiet, again, as if our conversation exists only in the pools of light cast by the intermittent streetlamps.

"I watched him hang himself. Again . . . and again . . ." Her voice goes whisper-soft. "And again."

There she is, in my mind, watching the terrible act with morbid desperation, the endless repetition of it, and I feel something terrible inside me, in my throat.

"I drove myself mad, watching. And you know what I learned?" She waits a beat. "Nothing."

"So you hid the key."

She nods. "I couldn't have you girls wandering in there."

"Did you . . . did you ever find anything else in that room? Anything that might have explained why he did it?"

The corners of her mouth drag down. "I wish I had."

I am moments away from telling her about the journal, my mouth open to divulge his secret, thinking the answer she sought all those years ago must be within those yellowed pages—but the sight of home approaching just ahead stifles the words in my throat. It would only hurt her to reopen this wound. And what if there isn't a good reason, a real answer, hidden within those intricate writings after all? What if, seeing the madness playing out upon those pages, she plunges back into the weight of grief, knowing that something so terrible was lurking in her husband's mind all along, something she couldn't see?

I just want to protect her. I know what she's like when she breaks.

I roll down the window, and a cold wind unfurls through the car. She glances at me, but I say nothing. The cold air whips me awake, lifts my hair over my eyes.

In the end, I don't tell her. I pull through the wrought-iron gate and down the long driveway with tree roots disturbing the cracking pavement, toward the looming endless labyrinth of memories and rooms and locked doors.

* * *

Mother sleeps heavily tonight.

My thoughts are spinning, and I cannot sleep a wink. It is always like this, when the more I want to sleep, the more I convince myself to sleep, the less able I am, and I grow too hot for the covers so I cast them off, and my ear hurts pressed into the flat old pillow so I turn to my other side, and now I am too cold on that side so I pull the covers back up and stretch my legs out, pondering the end of the bed with my toes.

Outside I hear a rough-throated creak. It shrieks, pauses, shrieks again in a nerve-shuddering rhythm, as if to deliberately antagonize me. After a time I realize I am hearing the front gate buffeted back and forth on its rusted hinges by a bored, irritable wind.

Unable to take the incessant wails, I get up to go latch the gate shut.

Night meets me, cold, pushing me along the front drive, urging me away from the house. The sky must be overcast because there are no stars, only an oppressive dark, and the clouds breathing down on me. The wind incuriously whistles out the word *who* as it passes.

I wish the gate were closer. With the stars shut out, the only light comes from the hazy impression of moon blurring mysteriously behind thin clouds, and beyond that a dull flickering light on the front porch that I switched on as I came outside. My eyes adjust well enough, but the dark is unfriendly.

And in that unfriendly dark, the moon reveals someone standing on the other side of the gate.

The gate swings back, away from me, toward the faceless boy of twelve or thirteen who stands against the night. He grabs the rusted black edge of the iron gate, which must be biting cold to the touch, and pushes; it swings back my way, releasing a burdened groan.

The wind drags it back again, asking *who?* as it passes.

Julian pushes the gate toward me.

Slowly I begin to back up the driveway toward the house, my skin gone prickly with goose bumps and a sick chill, like that of a fever.

"Auntie?" he says.

I stop. His face is trained on me, the darkness of his eyes in my direction. I don't respond. Maybe he does not see me after all. It seems an irrational hope, but it is the only thing that makes sense.

"Auntie?" he says again.

My voice comes out low and rough. "Yes, Julian?"

"Let's play hide-and-seek."

"No," I say as I resume backing up, unable to turn my back on that faceless gaze.

"You better hide," he says. "I'm going to find you."

Then he puts his hands over his eyes and begins counting. "Twenty . . . nineteen . . ."

I turn and run.

Distantly I am aware of how absurd it is, to be running from a child like this, a child who isn't even really there (or is he?), but I can't stop thinking about the way he said he would find me, he is going to *find* me, and the wind is blowing frantically in my ears now, asking *WHO? WHOOO?* as I bolt for the house.

"Sixteen . . . fifteen . . ." His voice recedes, almost inaudible beyond the roar in my ears.

I reach the front door, pull it open, throw myself inside, and close it behind me.

The sudden silence and utter dark make it all feel unreal. My heart thunders in my ears. I lock the door.

Go to bed, I tell myself. *Go to bed, forget this happened, and in the morning you'll feel awfully silly, won't you?*

Instead, I peer around the curtain to see out the window. From here, I can't quite make out the gate, even with the porch light still on. My breathing is annoyingly loud. I wait, searching out movement in the stillness, for a moment that seems painfully long.

Maybe he has gone, I think.

Then I see the shape of him moving slowly up the driveway toward the house. My heart leaps and I flick the switch to turn off the porch light, realizing belatedly that he will know I am standing here when he sees the light go out, realizing also belatedly that now I cannot see him out there, cannot watch his progress to the front door, cannot know how close he is, knowing that at every moment he is closer still, and even though the door is locked, I drop the curtain and back away.

All the house seems strange and unfamiliar to me. I have to feel my way blindly from the foyer into the sitting room, where I trip over something hard and land roughly on my knees. The offending object is Nathaniel's camera. He must have left it when he ran from here. I pick it up and pull the strap around my neck to carry with me.

Just when I think I have passed into the dining room, I realize I am actually in the library, and I've not a clue how I got there. Panic rises in me, reminding me of the time I became lost in the dark as a child, running through the house in a frantic bid to find my way and finding, instead, tucked away in a corner of the library, the old woman in the chair, the old woman with Xs for eyes, who froze me fearfully while her gnarled fingers trembled as she lifted them into the air, who chuckled behind closed lips, who vanished when I threw on the light. It is as if the house must mutate in the dark, changing and transforming itself when it cannot be seen. As if it becomes malleable, uncertain.

I hear the front door click and swing open.

Maybe it is Julian making the house like this, making it shift into different shapes. Maybe Julian is like a tumor, a cancer, driving the house insane.

The twisting in my gut tells me to hide. Whatever happens, I don't want him to find me.

There is nowhere to hide in this room. The walls are lined with bookcases, and the only furniture is a set of ancient moth-eaten chairs and a chaise lounge. It's possible I could elude him by slinking along the towering bookcases, making sure there is always one between me and him, but eventually he would find me. In the foyer, I can hear his footfalls creaking slowly across the floor, and I pad on silent cat feet, carefully distributing my weight so as not to make a sound.

Now I am in front of a door where I do not think there was one before—or maybe only the memory of a door, the house remembering something that once was here but is no longer. Can I open the door if it is only a memory? And where would it lead? Into memoryscape, dreamland, the impossible space between dimensions?

I push it open, and it is solid under my palm—real, then. And within a descending blackness, releasing an abyssal cold. I am at the door to the basement, though I cannot fathom how I've gotten here. I am turned around, and it so unsettles me that I feel on the verge of panic at every moment, thinking I may never find my way out of this rat's maze. At least, not until dawn, which seems so very far away.

Julian is much closer than the sun.

No, I do not want to go into the basement, but I can hear him following me through the rooms as he rustles through hiding spots—the shift of a curtain, the opening of a large cabinet, the tossing of blankets off couches—all done in methodical silence rather than the boisterous animation one might expect of a child playing hide-and-seek.

Away from the basement door, I move on, across to the billiards room inhabited by a very old pool table, never used even though sometimes you can hear the faint clicking of balls when you walk past. Now three-quarters of the balls are missing, and there are only two sad lonely cues left, splintered and long forgotten, against the wall to watch over the green domain of the table. At the other end of the room are another sitting area, a china cabinet, and a small card table.

Shall I hide beneath the pool table? That is a terrible spot, as there is no real cover—but does it matter, in this kind of darkness? I could simply stand in the corner and I doubt he would find me, for he wouldn't be able to see. Though now, as I think it, I am getting the strange sensation that perhaps he has the capacity to see in the dark. Certainly it is absurd, but I cannot shake the idea, and as I stumble around the room, seeing it only in my mind's eye, from memory, I slam my hip into the corner of the pool table and let out a yelp of pain and surprise.

As soon as I do, I freeze, listening.

At first I do not hear anything. Then, footsteps, moving quickly now toward the billiards room. I stumble and feel my way to the next room, thinking how ridiculous it is that there should be so many rooms with so many names and functions, so many layouts I have had to memorize, and for what? So that I can get lost in my own house as it pushes me from one room to the next, daring me to forget, forget where I am, until I am locked in a black hole with no escape?

I make my way to the back of the house, through the kitchen, and now I am in the laundry room, a cold concrete space that seems to lack the warmth of the rest of the house. This is it, I think, and for a moment I contemplate climbing into the washing machine, but the thought of locking myself in that tiny space unhinges me and I instead ensconce myself in the linen closet, which unfortunately has slats in the doors and only so much room that I must stand right up against the doors when they are closed. From the dingy window, the moon washes gray over the little room.

Just then I hear several sharp clacks, something bouncing and rolling across the floor. A white orb, like a flash-frozen blind cow's eye, rolls into the laundry room and eventually comes to a stop. It is the cue ball.

The laundry room door, which I left ajar, creaks open a little more, and the shadow steps in.

"I'm going to find you," he says.

He is holding one of the two remaining pool cues, its dull tip pointed up and the heavier end below. When the light approaches his face, it seems to blur even further until it is no more than a strange white oval.

Julian jabs the cue into a pile of laundry like a javelin and uses it to lift up the crumpled shirts. He comes around to the washing machine and taps the cue against it, three small hard taps with increasing force.

He starts laughing as he hits various objects, laughing at nothing.

I could tackle him, I think. I could burst from this closet and throw myself upon him, wrestle the pool cue free—

But what if he is stronger than his size suggests? What if I am not fast enough, or not strong enough? I am small, yes, perhaps not small enough to be bested by a twelve-year-old, but who is to say?

At last he approaches the closet. He brings the cue up and drags it down the slats, making a staccato sound.

"Auntie," he whispers into the slats. "Are you in there?"

He can hear my breathing. He must know I am here, even if he cannot see me through the slats of the dark closet, where the moon doesn't penetrate.

Then, bringing his mouth up close to the nearest opening: "Found you."

He rips open the closet doors as I lift the camera and hit the shutter, and a bright flash sears the air but does not seem to slow him; he swings the pool cue wide and hard. The stick connects with my shoulder and I cry out at the sting, fold over to my knees on the floor, the camera swinging around my neck. He hits me again on the small of my back; the force nearly puts me flat on my stomach, but I manage to crawl forward, away from the blows as he laughs above me, and reach out for the cue ball. As I do, he lunges forward, stomping where my fingers were only a moment ago, trying to stomp them like he did to those frogs, to that bird, and laughing. When he steps back, I reach out again, swiftly this time.

Before he can bring the stick down on me, I turn over and heave the ball at him like a shot put. To my amazement, it passes through him as if he were no more than smoke, then passes through the window with a great shattering crash. Julian disappears before his laughter does.

The cold moon creeps in upon me through the hole in the window as I lie panting on the floor, feeling a red sting in the places where he hit me.

From upstairs, I hear my mother call out groggily, "Sam? Sam? What was that?"

I crawl to my feet and look out the broken window. Outside, the cue ball sits in the dewy grass among the glittering shards of glass.

* * *

"I'm sorry about the window."

Agnes waves a dismissive hand, but I can see she is thinking about her bank account and making some calculations. "At worst, we have cardboard and duct tape. I think there's an old tarp around here somewhere."

A red welt has erupted on my shoulder, and it hurts when I move it; I try not to let on as I crouch in the damp grass, picking up shards of glass by the light from inside the laundry room. Mother initially told me to leave it until morning, but I find something cathartic about picking up the glass. It focuses my attention away from the bruises growing on my back.

"Why did you throw the ball?" Agnes asks. Her voice is nonchalant, but there is something more beneath it, covered over with carefulness.

I cannot keep it inside me any longer. The secret is clawing its way out. What if Julian hurts my mother, too? She has to know about him.

"He frightened me," I say at last.

"Who did?"

"Julian."

I prick my finger on a shard of glass and put it in my mouth as blood bubbles to the surface. "I've seen him," I continue, not looking at her. "I've seen him everywhere." I think of the small crawling thing in the hallway, the boy pulling feathers off a bird, the one who chases me through the house, these many incarnations of him.

When I finally look up at her, I see shock on her face. Shock, but not the disbelieving kind.

"Why didn't you tell me?"

"I didn't want you to worry." I turn back to the work of picking up the glass. "There's something wrong with him."

The moon comes out and lights the pieces of glass into beautiful shining things. How strange that something so sharp and dangerous could be so beautiful, like stars crashed into the ground. I remind myself to be careful.

"What do you mean?"

"He's going to kill a little girl," I tell her, wishing this revelation felt like a weight off my chest rather than a deep, sinking feeling in my gut, as if speaking it aloud has made it more real, as if the act of sharing reality has cemented its true form. I hear my mother suck in her breath. "And . . . others, too, I think. I don't know how many. There's something . . . inhuman about him. Even as a boy."

My mother appears to be speechless. A long moment passes. "Well, that can't be," she mumbles at last, shaking her head.

I resume my cleaning while she stands where she is, lost in thought, and we are left with the sound of the locusts buzzing low and mellow, owls adding their spectral moans to the song of the swamp. The night is cold, and the dew on the grass is half-frozen, making it increasingly difficult for me to differentiate between glass and ice. My fingers, gone white and numb, grow clumsy and stiff. They stop feeling like my fingers.

"Let's finish this in the morning," says my mother with a hand on my shoulder, pulling me up.

"But what about Julian?"

Her eyes are sharp as the shards of glass scattering the ground. "What *about* him?"

I gape at her, wondering how my mother can just tuck away the thought of her grandson murdering children—tuck it away with whatever else lives under the blanket of wine she used to pull over her brain, the way she had to learn to tuck away the sight of her husband hanging himself.

"Don't you *care*?" I snap, thinking of all those times she ignored us as children, turning away from my nightmares of the old woman with Xs for eyes, becoming a ghost of herself while Elizabeth and I got lost in the swamp. My heart feels laden with rot.

"There are more important things," she says. "Lizzie is in the hospital right now."

"Yeah, because of *him*!"

"It's no use making yourself sick over it now." She turns to go back into the house. "We will deal with Julian when the time comes. We will make everything right." Wind whistles through the gaping, jagged hole in the window, and she pauses beside it. "Put some tarp over this, will you? Best keep out the chill."

She disappears into the house and, presumably, up to bed. I do as she asks—what else can I do?—but even when I return to my own room, sleep eludes me. I gaze wide awake through the dark, imagining Julian creeping up the stairs, Julian twisting the handle of my bedroom door, Julian hovering somewhere in the shadowy corners of my room, watching me sleep, and I find I can hardly close my eyes. The welt on my shoulder stings when I remember where it came from.

I go to the bathroom to splash water on my face, and when I raise my head, I think I see him, or some dark shape, behind my own reflection.

My father said something was following him through the mirrors. I rub my arms, my skin prickling over with goose bumps. I back out of the bathroom, unable to turn from the mirror until I can safely step out of its grasp.

Perhaps there is more in his journal that will help me understand. I go back to my room for it, but before I grab it, my eyes alight on the old brass key hanging on a small hook. Maybe instead of telling me, he can show me.

Do I want to see what my mother saw?

I take the key and let my feet carry me up the creaking stairs, around the soft sagging spots where the floorboards have rotted, to that narrowing of the third floor hall that gives one a sense of the walls closing in.

I have already placed the key in the lock when I notice a piece of paper on the floor, stuck partially under thc door. It is a child's drawing, filled with trees, and frogs leaping out of the swamp—leaping, in motion, but dead, their eyes covered over with Xs, closing them forever from what they cannot see.

I take a step back, considering the drawing.

This is Julian's room, isn't it?

The back of my neck prickles. I feel the sensation that I am not alone. Someone is behind me, perhaps whoever I thought I glimpsed in the bathroom mirror.

When I turn, expecting Julian, expecting whatever dark shape lurks on the other side of our own reflections, I see August Wakefield holding a gun.

13

At the sight of the gun, I freeze. I feel a ghost of the gun on the back of my neck, my mugger's weight on top of me, the cold ground pressing into my cheek.

"We are not your slaves," comes a voice from behind me, and I turn, put my back against the wall, and see Jonah and Meriday standing in front of the locked door. Jonah has his hands up in a pacifying gesture. Meriday is clinging to his side, hiding partially behind him as he shields her from August. "Your father was paying us. We cannot continue to work for you without pay. You must understand."

"My father isn't here anymore," says August. The barrel of the long gun trembles.

"And we are sorry for your loss," says Jonah.

"It is because of thee." August's face is twisted in a rictus of anger and grief. "First mother, then Constance." He shakes his head. "But my father was weak. I am not like him. I am the master of this house now, and it is time I set it to rights."

"Please," Meriday murmurs into her father's side. Her hands cling to the fabric of his shirt, twisting it in her fists.

"Go on," says August. I am horrified by the look on his face. He always seemed a bit rash to me, and more hard-hearted than his father, but he has managed to keep his temper in check beneath a veneer of righteous calm. That all seems gone now. Here in its place is a darkness that lives in some men, waiting dormant for the kind of grief that will set it free.

"No." Jonah lowers his hands and stands his ground.

"Get in!" August shouts. "You *will* obey me. I will not have thee traipsing around my house, as if I am not in charge of it. You will do as I say, or I will report thee to the authorities. Insolent swine! I'm sure your master would be glad to have his property returned to him."

For a long, tense moment, I think that Jonah will not back down; I think that August, in this vicious, wild state, will aim the gun at his face and fire. But at last Jonah turns, and I see that the door to the locked room is standing open. Placing his hands on Meriday's shoulders, he guides her into the dark room at the insistence of August's gun.

I follow them.

August lights a lantern with the gun still propped under his arm, aimed at Jonah. By the flickering orange glow, he fixes chains to the bedpost and forces Jonah to close the free end around his ankle.

"When you are ready to obey me," he says, "I will let thee out."

"I will *never* obey you," Jonah snarls. "I will rot before I call you master."

"Please," Meriday tries again, her voice small. Though she isn't chained, she still clings to her father's side. The lantern light gleams in her wide eyes.

August ignores her. When he leaves, he takes the lantern with him, plunging the room into darkness. Meriday gasps at the sudden loss of light.

I am here, too, in this darkness. My heart skips a beat as I listen to the grinding sound of August locking the door, his footsteps receding. Jonah's and Meriday's voices murmur softly in the dark. How long will August leave them here? I wonder, my heart crawling further up my throat. I try to find the window, but it isn't here. When the window appears, I am not sure, but at the moment this is a windowless room. The room has not grown it yet. And they are trapped in the dark, in this amorphous negative space that seems larger by the day, large enough that they hardly dare ungrasp their hands to find where the room ends.

But I am not locked in. I feel my way back to the door and let myself out, closing it behind me and releasing a long, slow breath of relief. In spite of my escaping, horror churns in my gut. I stand outside the door, hoping August will return and let them out.

It is difficult to tell the passage of time when you are watching a memory. After a while, I hear Jonah and Meriday pounding on the door to be let out, begging, screaming. And I think they have been in there for a long, long time.

What is it that this room is hiding? My father killed himself in it. Jonah and Meriday were held prisoner. Julian will live here, too.

There is an evil in this room.

Just as I am finally backing away from the door, I see August return and release Meriday. I do not know how long it has been, but she comes out haunted. Her eyes are vacant, unfocused. When light spills into the room, Jonah holds up his hand over his eyes, which look blind and lost.

Instead of leaving, I wait and watch.

Meriday has been given tasks. Perhaps August let her out so she could tend to the house. She returns to give Jonah food and clean the bedpan, and she looks older now.

How much time has passed? Weeks? Months?

Years?

And I understand, now, all the glimpses I've seen of her and August in the house. Now they make sense.

Because fate is cruel, and because they had no one left in the world but each other, during the course of these years, Meriday and August grew close. I've seen their cordial, clipped conversations give way to familiarity. I've seen them in the evenings, sitting beside the fire while August reads, or teaches Meriday to read and write. I've seen her look at him with fondness—but a fondness conflicted with fear, with disgust. Imagine what it must do to her to have to be in August's company and pretend that her father isn't upstairs rotting away.

Eventually, Meriday became pregnant.

I never knew what to make of it. I've seen glimpses of her growing belly. She was so young, a teenager, but beautiful, glowing with pride, imbued with the gift of creation.

Meriday gave birth to a son who was fortuitously pale—pale enough to pass as white. She named him Lucius.

I know he was able to live as a white man for the whole of his life—that he never told anyone who his mother was. I know, because Lucius was my great-great-grandfather.

I wish I could go back in time and kill August. *Julian*, I think, *you killed the wrong Wakefield.* He was an evil man, and hasn't the world had enough of evil men?

As I leave this hallway behind for my own room, I think of Clementine when she came limping stiffly out of the swamp, dripping with muddy water, her skin sodden, her eyes gleaming like reflected fire. I think of her final words to Meriday: *I will protect you from what will happen to you. If you come with me, we can stop it.*

Clementine, who could see the future, must have known what would happen between her daughter and August, must have seen Meriday's attempts at refusal, the consent she was obliged to give, for to refuse him might have meant death or imprisonment. It was the same fear Clementine had carried with her from John Garrow's plantation, the thing she was trying to save Meriday from all along.

But she must have known, too, that Meriday would give birth, and that her son would have children, and on and on, and eventually, somewhere down the line, a boy would be born, a boy unlike any other, a boy who could see Clementine for what she really was.

* * *

Safely back in my own room with the door shut, I pull out my father's journal and open it to the desperate pencil scratches of its final entries. By this point he has been scribbling circles, spirals, zeros, onto the paper, filling them in with so much pressure that the page bubbles on the other side, at several points making holes with the sharp pencil tip. These holes in the paper, for some reason, concern me the most.

Will he tell me what he saw in the locked room? Can I comprehend what is really in there, what Jonah experienced when he was locked inside? What did my father see that so broke him, that made him commit the ultimate final act of his life?

Do I really want to know?

* * *

Please don't think me a coward, Aggie.

I have been watching myself in this room. He is deliberate in his movements, but there is something in his eyes, something—would I see it, if I looked in the mirror right now? He is showing me what to do. He has been showing me the answer, all this time.

I think I will follow.

He—I—this version of myself—

~~*how can I be me if I am also him? who is he if I am me?*~~

I watch him, me, with a rash of stubble and bloodshot eyes, wearing my blue flannel and black jeans—~~*where are these clothes right now? In the laundry?—*~~*fasten a rope around one of the beams in the ceiling. Where did he get the rope? In the basement. Yes, there is a rope down there, now I remember. Why is there a rope down there? Is it there for me/him, for this moment?*

Once the rope is tied tight and proper, he sets the wooden chair that I am sitting on right now underneath. ~~*Is the chair in two places? Am I?*~~

What are you doing, I wondered, the first time I saw. What am I *doing? But I couldn't sign to him because he cannot see me, I can only see me. Him.*

And then I watched him put the rope around his neck—it is tied into a circle, a zero—and step off the chair. Me. I have watched myself do this. And I asked, why? *And the next time I asked,* why? Why? Why?

And the tenth time, and the twentieth time, and the hundredth time.

And he kept doing it. And I kept watching.

I watched him struggle when the rope pulls taut. It doesn't break his neck; he's not high enough, but he cannot get any higher. There is no way to create a larger drop. So he chokes, swinging, kicking, clawing. ~~*My*~~ *His eyes bulge, as when you squeeze on the end of an underinflated balloon.* ~~*His*~~ *My face goes red.*

It is awful. It is grotesque.

How can I watch this and keep coming back? I am fascinated. I cannot help it. How could I not *watch this? It's the same every time because it is only one time, I think, so many times and only one time, after all.*

Why did he do it? I wonder.

And the more I wonder, the more I cannot understand, the more I understand, the more I will never know, the more I feel I know, what is it, why do I do it, is he telling me something? Where is he going? Where has he gone, once it is done and he hangs swinging in the air, staring and not seeing me. Where is he. Where am I.

Maybe he went through the Zero. Logically, I think, that could be the case. If he went through the Zero, then maybe he is in some other place right now, and maybe he has found the truth.

I have to follow through. I will follow.

I have just realized, they're not in the laundry, after all. I am wearing my blue flannel and black jeans today. I haven't shaved.

And there is the rope.

I will follow.

* * *

I close the journal and push it away from me, that sick feeling that lodged itself in my gut earlier tonight crawling around in the back of my throat.

Was it fate?

Did he do it because he was always going to do it, because it was his choice, or because he saw that it would happen? Is it fate that dictates what will happen to us, or do we? And if we do, does that mean whatever will happen will still happen as a result of us, of our choices and actions, or is there a possibility to change the outcome once you know it? Does observation allow us to change reality? Or is there nothing at all that we can do to change what will someday occur?

All of this is to say: should I kill my nephew?

PART FOUR

THE KING OF CUPS

14

Home, again. Elizabeth is back and resting. The color has returned to her face, and she is happily barking orders at me to fetch her a glass of water or a fresh pillow, so it seems she is doing just fine. Mother has been fussing over her more than usual, with checklists for when the baby comes and instructions for how to clothe, how to change, how to feed. She puts a hand against her belly and stares into her face. "You're feeling all right?" she says, her voice hard, only half a question. And then, "Sing to him. He can hear you."

Elizabeth eyes her suspiciously, leaning back to distribute her weight, hands planted against her hips. She frowns as if trying to think of a song.

Mother leans down, her face close to the bulb of Elizabeth's belly button protruding against her lilac maternity shirt, and softly sings, "*Oh my darling . . . oh my darling . . .*"

I have to turn away.

A sour note lingers at the back of her desperate song.

Maybe she thinks if we get everything right, he will be fine. If we only love him, and care for him, he will be a normal boy. Maybe she thinks this is her second chance.

But all the love in the world won't save a boy without a soul.

When I went through the pictures from Nathaniel's camera, I found the one I had snapped from the laundry room closet. Where Julian should have been, right in front, flash lit, there was only the empty room. I don't know why I thought he might appear in the photograph, why I thought I could make him tangible. It wouldn't have proven anything to Elizabeth.

All moves apace for a day or two, with little interruption from the house. The world has renewed its regular rhythms, and I find myself floating through them like a leaf in a stream, pulled along by the current of time with glimpses here and there of passing moments like fish darting by.

I try not to think of my father, or Jonah, or Julian. I have reached a point where if I think of these things, my heart will begin sinking like a stone and anchor me in the bottommost depths of the river, stuck in one dark place while I watch time flow past above me, unable to partake of its cool movements.

But every time I look at Elizabeth, I think of Julian. "He could kill you," I tell her, wondering if it isn't too late, thinking of the yellowing bruises on my back. He could kill us all, at any time. We might never see it coming.

"I appreciate your concern," she says, "But this isn't the nineteenth century. I'm not likely to die in childbirth."

"I don't think you understand."

"Leave me alone, Sam."

Perhaps when she is at the top of the stairs, I can sneak up behind her and give her a push. I imagine her tumbling head over heels like a rag doll, the corners of steps jarring into tender flesh. No heartbeat. Having to carry that dead thing inside her womb for another week or two, then pushing it out, laboring to deliver a corpse into the world.

I shudder. Perhaps not.

But what if I nick her, just a bit, with a rusty blade, and she gets an infection, and that infection travels to the fetus, and . . . ?

I imagine creeping up on her in the dark with an antique knife raised, and Elizabeth waking to find me there, a murderous phantasm come for her child. Samantha Wakefield, Killer of Infants, is what they will call me. And the people of Shadydale will whisper out of the corners of their mouths and tell the tale of the Mad Wakefields, insane killers all, with death in their blood.

No, there must be a better way. I spend my time brooding over the problem, waiting for inspiration, thrilled with terrible thoughts.

And then one morning, as I am grading papers, sipping coffee and pleased to be commenting with my lucky blue pen, there is a knock at the door.

I stop cold, dropping the pen midway through my sentence, angry that I have been interrupted. My heart thuds unhappily.

Elizabeth, who lounges on the couch opposite me here in the drawing room, absently flips the page of the magazine balanced on her enormous belly. "Be a dear and get that?" she says without looking up.

The knocking returns, a relentless rapping.

"What if it's another Jehovah's Witness?"

"Then thank him kindly for stopping and tear his brochure to shreds," she says mildly, carelessly, and I wish she were the one to get up and check the door.

The essay will have to wait. I go to the door, and the knocking dies away as wood is pulled from knuckles.

Standing there, disheveled and desperate-eyed but trying to hide these things beneath a veneer of self-control, is—

"Donovan?"

A sweep of brown hair curls over his stubbled face.

"Sam," he says brusquely, brushing me aside and looking around the foyer as if he will see Elizabeth hiding just behind the empty vase. "Where is she?"

"Don?" Elizabeth's voice calls distantly from the drawing room.

"What are you doing here?" I ask.

He looks at me strangely. "Your mother called me."

"Is that Don?" Elizabeth calls again.

He takes a step forward, toward his wife's elusive voice, but I move to block him. "Who said you could come inside?"

I am reminded of those easy evenings at their house, of being grateful to have his buffer between me and my sister and our tendency to get into little spats, but now I feel I must defend her from him. Don looks at me incredulously, as if he cannot believe I am trying to block him from entering.

Then, from the other end of the foyer, her voice softer now that she has approached, Elizabeth says, "Let him in."

Grudgingly, I step aside. Elizabeth watches him blankly, her hair pulled away from her face only halfheartedly. Donovan moves forward but stops shy of touching her, even though his hands are outstretched.

"Are you all right?"

"I'm fine," she says without inflection. "And so is Julian. Is that all?"

He glances at me with a look that asks me to leave them alone, but I refuse to move. The front door is still open, inviting him to exit and inviting in the frigid winter air.

"Lizzie," he says. "Can we talk?"

Silence lingers like smoke, subduing the foyer in its somnolence. Elizabeth stares at her husband with eyes beset by purpled bags, and the wind shivers her hair over her face. Finally, when the silence has grown so pregnant I expect it will burst at any moment, Elizabeth says, "Sam, would you close the door already? You're letting in the cold."

Shutting the door feels like defeat. I will be closing him in here with us instead of pushing him back outside where he belongs. "Are you sure?" I ask, my hand on the door.

"Yes."

"But what about—?"

"Sam, close the door."

All right. I close the door.

* * *

It requires a certain amount of convincing for me to leave the drawing room and allow the two of them to talk, although I do not go far, instead electing to eavesdrop from the hallway. My mother, after appearing and disappearing again, keeps away, mumbling to herself all the things she has to be getting on with.

If I keep my ear to the door, I can just hear them.

"Come home with me," says Don.

"Come *home* with you?"

"I'm your husband."

"For how much longer, I wonder?"

"We made vows, didn't we?"

"Yes," she says, sounding wistful. "We did."

They sit in silence for a moment, or perhaps they are continuing the conversation with their eyes. I've seen the way Don looks at her—he can put on a gaze with such intensity that I would be uncomfortable to have its sights turned on me, but it is a gaze that must be flattering to Elizabeth, must make her feel special.

"You can't take care of that baby all by yourself," he says at last.

"I'm not all by myself," Elizabeth counters, but her voice no longer sounds quite so sure of itself. Don has a way of making her falter.

"Lizzie." His voice is earnest, gentle, as he can be, sometimes. "This isn't the way. You know this isn't want you want."

"No," she says, like the coldness of space. "It isn't."

"Our child should grow up in the best environment we can provide him. Do you really think this is it?" Elizabeth makes a noncommittal noise I can't decipher from my limited perspective. "He's my son too, you know."

"I thought you didn't want him."

His sigh is heavy, weighted with regret. "Of course I want him. He's my goddamned son, for Christ's sake. I just want to do things the right way. And I love you, but you don't always know what's best."

Don's words echo in my mind, and I think of the other times he has wanted things done the *right* way: when I organized their books wrong and he knocked them to the floor; when someone at work had an error in their code and he berated them over the phone; when Don himself discovered he had overcooked our chicken breasts for dinner, stabbed his fork into the tough white meat, and pushed the plate away, disgusted. Threw it away, uneaten. What will happen, I wonder, when he decides they are not raising their son in completely the *right way*?

The next pause is so long that I wonder if they've fallen asleep, or engaged in a staring contest, or if time has frozen and I will find they have become statues. I peek around the corner, through the sliver of the open door, and I see a slice of the scene, the two of them sitting there.

"What are you doing?"

I jump and turn around.

My mother is standing behind me with her lips pursed and her eyebrows raised. She looks from me to the door, then finally pushes it open and barges into the room; when we enter, both Don and Liz are staring in our direction, their marble eyes shiny and expectant.

Now with an audience, Elizabeth sits up straighter and looks back at Don. "All right," she says. "But I'm not coming home. I'm all settled in. You can stay here if you like." She glances at my mother for confirmation, and Agnes nods.

"Okay," says Donovan uncertainly, looking around the room at the ornate mantelpiece, the burnt-out fireplace, the moth-eaten sofa, the age-worn curtains, the stained carpet, the anachronistic bronze floor lamps with dusty shades, the antiquity and gloom. He stands and kisses Elizabeth on the forehead.

She allows this and says, "You won't stay in my room, though."

"What? You're giving me the couch?"

"Oh, no need for that. We have plenty of spare rooms," my mother chimes in.

And that's how Donovan Hill came to stay with us.

* * *

I have been tasked with changing the bedsheets in the Rose Room, where Don will be staying for the foreseeable future. The other spare bedrooms have sunk so far into disarray that it would take weeks to make them livable again, and while their doors have not been locked, they have been shut up for quite some time—long enough that these rooms have been colonized by spiders and dust mites and who knows what else besides.

The Rose Room, at least, may be made passably comfortable with a bit of sprucing up.

Although I have pulled open the drapes as far as they will go, the room seems impervious to light. Dust hangs heavy in the air, saturated by the cloying pink of the walls and floor. As I yank off the sheets and turn to beat the dust from them, to scatter the gray motes dizzyingly into the air where they will settle again at random, perhaps only to spite Donovan, to provoke some latent allergy, I hear, from just behind me, the wheeze of a consumptive inhale.

The sheet billows back down to the floor when I freeze, listening for the sounds of illness and decay that haunt this room: the death rattle of Frances Wakefield.

Behind me I feel a presence, the feeling when you know someone is watching you, such an intensely revolting feeling that you must turn around and double-check, even when you know you are alone—

I try not to. I take a few steps away from the bed, thinking I will escape this room, but the feeling compels me so, and when I am almost at the door I turn around and see a shape on the bed.

My heart wobbles with the shock of it. Even though I am used to the way this house works, one can never really get used to the sudden appearance of a figure where it hadn't been only a moment ago.

The shape lies beneath a woven blanket, a relic from the past that doesn't belong beneath the sheets I just stripped from the bed.

I step closer.

The figure reveals her face: an emaciated death mask with sunken pockets for eyes and chapped, gaping lips. Her lank hair lies plastered to her skin. From between those parted lips she draws a wet, labored breath.

Her glassy eyes, made delirious by disease, stare blankly at the ceiling, in some other realm halfway between the world of the living and the world of the dead.

"Frances?" I murmur.

She coughs convulsively, without even the strength to turn her head, and her eyes roll in their sockets like scattered pool balls. I watch in horror as blood bursts from between her lips, splattering her face and the blanket before sinking back down into her throat. Her breath is a wet gurgle.

One likes to think of death as a peaceful thing, a relief from suffering. A quiet slipping away.

But there is no one here to turn Frances's head, and no relief from the choking.

Her body fights desperately to draw in air but can only suck blood back into those corrupted lungs, and the sound of her drowning in her own blood is terrible, like sucking the dregs of a milk shake through a straw, and she asphyxiates where she lies, her eyes rolling back in her head as her chest shudders, shudders, and it goes on and on—

Until finally she is still.

Slowly I creep around to her side, the sole mourner at her deathbed.

Oh Frances, I think. But at least she wasn't entirely alone, at the end. There was someone there to watch her, after all, from across the span of time, even if she didn't know it.

And yet, now there is a dead body in this bed, and how am I to change the sheets while staring at her too-still flesh, her glassy eyes, her bloodied frozen mouth? I turn to get the fresh sheets, shuddering with the thought of working around her, wishing almost for the haunted sounds of her dying instead, thinking I may as well give up and wait until later, but luckily, when I turn back to the bed, it is just as empty and pristine as I left it, without so much as an indentation to indicate the death of the bedridden woman. Though that faint odor of illness remains in the air, Frances Wakefield is gone.

Tonight, Donovan will sleep where she died.

* * *

And the lone wind blows, wheezing its way inside. It's a cold night, with frost creeping across the windowpane.

As if it's any surprise to you, I cannot sleep—insomnia, my persistent companion, keeps me bleary-eyed awake, watching the clock tick its way to dawn. So off I go, to wander through the house in the dark, marking my way through time as I wait for sleep or for morning. Perhaps I will rearrange the furniture several inches to the right.

In the parlor, I find a figure sitting on the sofa. Hulking. A dark shape. I switch on the light.

"Donovan?" Tiny fingers of dread ease away from the pressure in my gut. "What are you doing up?"

He has been sitting in the dark, sitting and staring at nothing, with a strange smile on his face as if he is trying to work out a riddle.

"I heard something," he says.

That off-putting smile does not leave his face. I feel I must tiptoe, unsure if that smile will crack into something else.

"This house makes noises sometimes," I say, carefully. These old houses groan and sigh at night, like restless creatures. "It's an old house. I'm surprised Elizabeth didn't tell you about it."

"She never talks about this place." Then he shakes his head, still smiling without a hint of good humor. "I was trying to sleep, when I heard someone coughing. But there was no one there." He shakes his head again. "Isn't that funny?" By the way he says it, he doesn't think it's funny. Not at all.

"It's funny how much Liz doesn't talk about," I say, sitting down and rubbing my arms against the chill in the room. "She must not talk much about us, I guess."

"Oh, no. She talks about you. A lot. Sam this, Sam that."

"Really?"

"Are you surprised?" He looks at me. "You're her best friend."

As I mull this over, a deep shivering cold invades me, and I cannot keep still. Donovan is in a T-shirt but sitting stiffly, uncomfortable.

"Is it cold in here?"

He nods. "Must be a draft coming from somewhere."

I grab an old throw with unraveling threads to pull around my shoulders as I stand, and we go off through the first level of the house to find where the cold is coming from. It's a bit like a scavenger hunt—is the door open? No, not that. How about a window? No, windows are shut and latched. Is the heater working? Yes, it is pumping out that stale, dry heat that smells faintly of gas.

"Where in holy hell are we?" Donovan mutters angrily after walking into a chair in the dark. "This place is a goddamned rat's maze. Who built this house?"

"Mad Catherine," I reply.

"Mad Catherine?"

"Circa 1800. Catherine's husband, Arthur Wakefield, had become remarkably prosperous from lumber trade based out of the Great Dismal Swamp, and—" I pause and eyeball him. "You want the whole story?"

Don pulls back a curtain, checking to make sure the windows are shut. "Sure, why not."

"Well, she begged him to build her a grand mansion. Now, Arthur was more than a little prudent with his wealth, so he bought this marshy land on the edge of the swamp for dirt cheap. It wasn't the ideal place to build, however, and they had a good deal of trouble framing the house on the soft soil. It took a while to get the building under way, but they did, eventually. Arthur was too stubborn to sell and move elsewhere. Anyway, he was only halfheartedly overseeing the construction, since he was otherwise preoccupied with his booming business. Not much was getting done."

Don's yelp interrupts me.

He's barked his shin on the edge of the coffee table in the drawing room. I turn on the light so we can get our bearings, and when his eyes catch the offending furniture, he delivers a swift kick to its splintered leg, juddering the table across the hardwood floor with a squeal. It slides, stops crooked. I glare at him.

"Can you fix that?"

He blinks around at the room, ignoring me. Oil paintings hang in brass frames around the walls, most of them portraits of unsmiling ancestors. "So which one of these is them?"

"Catherine isn't in here. They destroyed her portrait after all the trouble." I slide the coffee table back into place, fix the bunched-up rug it ran into at the corner, and turn for the doorway yawning into the black hall. "Come on. The draft isn't coming from in here."

He passes me into the hall, then seems to realize he doesn't know where he's going and slows, letting me guide us along.

"Trouble?"

"That came later, after Catherine decided to step up and take charge. Supposedly she was a bit of a taskmaster. She worked the men round the clock. They built and they built, and even when the house was finished, she decided to keep on building. Maybe she liked the power and she didn't want to relinquish that position and go back to being a housewife, caring for her three small children. She kept coming up with new additions, adding on layers like an onion, and so the construction stretched on for years, the house built piecemeal. That's why the layout is so confusing. Once you start adding things, the original plans don't make sense anymore."

It is getting colder now—an arctic breeze insinuates itself through the coarsely woven throw blanket I wear like a cape.

"Her husband just let her do that?"

"He was preoccupied with work. Or maybe he didn't care." I shrug. "Or maybe he did, but she overruled him."

Don laughs—a mean sound. "Right," he says. "So what about the trouble, then?"

"Over the course of the construction, which lasted for some eighteen years, three men died," I tell him.

"Damn," he says, sounding impressed. "What happened?"

"One was crushed by falling timber, which broke his back but didn't immediately kill him, because the ground was so soft; instead, it pushed his face into the earth until he suffocated, or drowned, in the wet soil. The next death, however, was what really set Catherine off."

"Set her off how?" Don asks, and I am pleased by the interest in his voice. It is a story I don't often get to tell.

"They were adding on the third level, which hadn't been planned in the original blueprints, and one of the men came down the stairs babbling about how they shouldn't have built here, that they'd gone too far. It seemed obvious—they already knew this was bad land to build on, being so wet and soft and prone to flooding. But the man insisted there was another reason. He suggested that in all their building, they had hammered a hole through the world. Then, according to the accounts of the other men, he took up his hammer and bashed his own brains in."

Don looks at me with a measure of amused disbelief. "Gruesome."

"Yes."

We wend our way through the darkness, turning and turning until the cold hits with a bitter, shark-tooth bite, and I push open the door to the laundry room. My breath exhales as a faint mist in the moonlight.

Here is the culprit: the tarp I taped over the broken window has blown aside, flapping gently and letting in the outdoors through the gaping, jagged hole in the glass. Winter air frosts the tiny room.

"That'll be it," says Don.

"Well done, detective."

"What happened?" He approaches the window to inspect it. "Didn't anybody ever tell you not to play ball in the house?"

"My mother and I can get very rowdy."

He pulls the tarp back over the window and fixes the tape securely in place. "Should hold for now. I'd better measure this window, go get a new pane. Can't just leave it like this through the winter. Jesus, what would you people do without me?"

I ignore the question. "I'm sure my mother would appreciate that."

He finishes pressing the tape into place.

Satisfied, I turn to leave, but Don grabs me by the wrist, forcibly keeping me in place. His grip digs into my bones. He is too close; I can smell his stale breath. "You didn't explain why they destroyed her portrait. Why they called her Mad Catherine."

I twist my wrist free and hold it to my chest with my other hand. He doesn't seem at all bothered or contrite. I think if I try to walk away now, he'll grab me again, harder this time. Don is used to getting what he wants.

"After the man killed himself with the hammer, Catherine became convinced that they *had* opened something up during the endless construction. She claimed she started seeing the dead man around the house, still working, like he didn't realize he was dead, and in order to get away from his ghost, she had them continue building in a frenzy, a confusion of rooms and doorways and halls to befuddle his spirit so that he would get lost and go away. No one could reach her at this point, not even Arthur."

I start to back out of the room, relieved when Don doesn't reach for me again. He follows me out.

"That's why you call her Mad Catherine?"

"Well, that," I continue as we walk back slowly toward the main staircase, "and because, after all that, she claimed the house had taken over its own construction: it started mutating, without the builders lifting a finger. She claimed that doorways would spring up out of nowhere, leading to strange places, and that rooms would grow and shrink on their own. Construction finally petered off, while Mad Catherine roamed the halls of her insane mansion—her life's work, as it were. There were only a few workers left doing some finishing touches, painting and such, and Mad Catherine had started to blame them for what they had done. In a fit of rage, she grabbed one man's head and pushed it down into a bucket of paint, and she drowned him in it."

"Jesus. And she got away with it?"

"Oh no," I assure him. "She was hanged for it. The Wakefields were quite despised and became reclusive after that, particularly Catherine's son Everett, who rejected society and turned to Quakerism. It was a famous trial, fraught with drama. You can read about it if you look up the old defunct papers from around here. I don't believe the town has ever really forgotten."

Don is frowning, now, as he looks up the staircase with distaste.

Feeling as though I've regained the upper hand, I smile. "They say you can still see Mad Catherine wandering the halls at night by the light of a single candle, and that the house rearranges itself in her wake, wherever she walks."

I have no candle, and the staircase looms above me in the dark. Donovan hesitates at its base, and I hope I have unsettled him. Turning to offer a devious grin over my shoulder, I give my cape throw a theatrical flourish, imagining, for a moment, that I am Mad Catherine, and that the house will mutate behind me as I go up the stairs, that I am in control of this place and that it can do me no harm, for I am its master.

"Good night."

15

Shall I slip a bit of arsenic into her orange juice? Oh, not enough to kill *her,* although it would likely be enough to make her a bit ill.

Shall I arrange a precarious tumble of books from a high shelf in the library to fall, somehow, onto her waiting protuberant belly?

Now, of course, I don't have just Elizabeth to worry about, but Don, too, and how he will react if something should happen to his child. In another few days, the weather will turn, and it will seem as if Don has always lived here. Already he has made himself quite at home, busybodying around the house, asking about the door on the third floor that he found stuck when he tried to wrench it open.

"Oh, that room is locked," my mother told him nonchalantly.

"How come?"

"I don't suppose I know," she replied. "It always has been, and we don't have the key."

"I bet I could bust it down for you."

"I bet you will *not,*" she warned him.

When he pressed for a reason, I asked why we should need to get into that spare room. Certainly Don does not need to insert his presence into every corner of the house. Let some secrets lie. "Is this place not large enough for you as it is?"

His face was wry and daring. "Actually, it is sensible to close off any rooms you don't use, especially in big old houses like this one. It'll conserve heat in the winter, and I hear we're due for an unusually cold one this year. Even with four of us here, I bet you could shut up half of this house and still have more than enough space to get lost in." He looked around, then, warily, as if he did not trust this rambling old mansion with its creaking floorboards and ancient, groaning pipes. He was right, of course; he shouldn't trust it.

But he looked at it as if it were a beast to conquer and make his own. I didn't like it.

Luckily, he was to find reason to leave the house soon enough when Elizabeth asked how he would work, if he was staying here—the commute would take hours if he went into the office. Don had been working from home several days a week when I was living with them; it seems one needs only the right sort of equipment for his work, creating medical databases or something of that nature—I've never really asked. It's all ones and zeros to me.

"I can set up my rig in any of these rooms," he replied.

"But there's no internet."

After my mother shot down the possibility of him calling the cable company to install wireless, he looked aghast. "Well," he said at last, "I'm sure I can get *something* done if I bring my laptop somewhere with a connection. There's got to be someplace in town I could work."

Mother claimed she didn't want to pay for internet service, but I know it was rather that she feared the intrusion of all that electrical energy from the outside world crackling invisibly through the air, bringing its charged, negative vibes into her domain. She would be able to feel it, she confided in me once, crawling along her skin like insects.

I wonder what would happen if this house were connected to the internet. Could we digitally download its memories? Could it travel through the cloud and bring in a host of memories from elsewhere, all the history of the world uploaded from the internet into this one unnatural space, a mansion out of time? Would it break the fabric of space-time? Perhaps it is best if we keep things as they are, as they have always been.

On his way out the door to go find a place to get some work done, Don leans into Elizabeth, pressing his rough stubbled face against hers. She dutifully kisses him back, but her body is leaning away from him even as he leans into her.

When she notices me looking, she puts on a smile and holds it until the door is closed behind him.

"This is what you wanted, isn't it?" I say. "Having Donovan back, one happy family?"

"Oh." She pauses as if thinking it over. "Yes, of course. It's exactly what I wanted."

But I see her smile fade as she walks away.

* * *

I am in a dream.

In the dream, I wander the house like a stranger in a place as unfamiliar as a distant eldritch castle in Europe, growing and stretching and spreading cancerously across a naked landscape, sprouting warrens of crooked corridors and secret rooms that bloom here and there like fireworks out of an abyss. I go about wide-eyed in this oppressively vast arrangement of rooms and hallways, while a heavy dread sits low in my chest.

Everything seems backward, as if I have stepped through the reflection in a mirror. Perhaps I have. Oh God, I think, I forgot—I had intended to smash the mirrors, hadn't I?

A hallway extends from me, dark and muted, and I cannot for the life of me think of where it goes. From down its unknown length comes a faint bubbling sound, like the frantic percolations of a coffeepot, but higher in pitch.

What is down this hallway?

Part of me wants to turn around and go back the way I've come, but I cannot remember any longer what lies behind me either, and so I am trapped between a mystery that was and a mystery that has yet to be, terrorized by the unknown on either side. The longer I stand there, torn between dark worlds, the more familiar the boiling sound becomes, until I recognize it as the phantom giggling of a child.

I strain to see in the dark, wishing I had brought with me a candle or a flashlight on this nighttime dream-jaunt.

Deep in the darkness at the far end of the hallway, if indeed the hallway has an end at all, a silhouette appears by the minutest of degrees, as if from nothing, blooming out of the Never into our own dimension to take a peek.

I am reminded of the phantom I used to see as a child, the Nothing Man. The shadowed shape with nothing inside but a seething, sucking darkness, as if it were sucking in the light around it. As if there were nothing there at all, which is what Elizabeth used to tell me when I complained of seeing him standing at the top of the stairs, blocking my way.

"Sammy's making up stories again," she would tell Mother, who would in turn tell me there was no Nothing Man, just as there was no woman with Xs for eyes—that the house showed only *memories*, not fantasies, and certainly not nightmares. Surely what I claimed to see was only that: a nightmare made manifest.

Now I'm not so sure. I didn't believe them then, and I don't know that I do now. But then again, I am in a dream, after all. This isn't the Nothing Man, though; this shape is smaller. A Nothing Boy. A boy without a face.

I feel along the wall for the light switch, knowing that it must be somewhere nearby, frantic for its light as the realization swarms over me like a scourge of mosquitoes—the Nothing Boy, the Nothing Man.

The future is all around us.

The laughter burbles out of the shadow again like boiling water, like hot muddy swamp water gushing out from between his teeth and through the tender black holes where baby teeth have fallen out, submerged creepers dangling from his open laughing mouth—

My spidering fingers snag the switch, and yellow light floods the hallway.

There is no one there.

But on the floor, leading off down the hall and around the corner that gave birth to the disembodied laughter, is a trail of wet, muddy child's footprints. I step carefully around the wet patches soaking into the diseased wooden floorboards, toward the end of the hallway where it makes a sharp turn, sensing that someone is standing just around that corner. Somewhere around the edge comes the low creak of a floorboard, the sound of shifting weight. My heart lurches into my throat.

Carefully I ease myself to the edge and hesitate there, feeling the presence just on the other side of the wall, the breathing, and it is only when I turn the corner and see the man standing there that I realize I am not dreaming at all.

I am awake. I have been awake this whole time.

"Don?"

"Sam?" His eyes are frantic as he grabs me by the shoulders. "Where are we?"

"What do you mean?"

Sweat rings the arms of his gray shirt. "This house is a fucking maze," he mutters, almost to himself. He lets go of me and steps away, hands fishing in his pockets. "Doesn't make any sense."

"What are you doing?"

He pulls out a pack of cigarettes, slides one free, and sticks it in the corner of his mouth, unlit. "I can't find the door. Just these hallways—two, three miles long. Shapes and shadows moving around, like there are other people here. Did you lock the front door?" He doesn't wait for my answer. "I went through so many rooms. There can't be this many. A hundred. Maybe more." He flicks a lighter a few times against the trembling cigarette.

"Can you not smoke in here?"

The cigarette catches the flame. "You're playing some kind of trick," he snaps. "You're playing me, aren't you? Trying to fool me with that bullshit story about Mad Catherine. What's really going on here?" He starts laughing, that terrible laugh of his, which manifests in a cloud of smoke. "You don't have a candle, do you?"

"No," I tell him, knowing he isn't asking if I am Mad Catherine changing the house around me by the light of a candle flame. "Can you put that out?"

"Funny how we keep meeting like this," he continues, ignoring me still. "What's your problem? Always sneaking around, following me."

"You're the one sneaking around."

"You know how fucked up my eye was after you blindsided me? Took weeks to get back to normal." He pulls his cigarette from his mouth and points it at me, his own talisman of power. "Think you can just get away with that? And whatever shit you're trying to pull on me now?"

I glare into his dark eyes, refusing to blink.

Finally, I say, "For the last time, will you put that out?"

His gaze turns to the cigarette in his hand, contemplating it as ash flakes off and disperses. Before I can stop him, he takes my hand, turns it over, and presses the burning tip of the cigarette into my palm. I sharply inhale.

A moment of searing pain—his grip is too strong for me to pull away—and then it's over, just a black circle on raw skin that I curl my fist around protectively.

I open my mouth to shout, to berate him, begging my voice not to warble, my eyes not to tear, but he beats me to the punch.

"Just be glad it wasn't your eye."

He turns, and he's gone.

* * *

It isn't so bad. Now that I've rinsed off the ash, all that's left is an angry red mark buried in the grooves of my palm, echoing vaguely the ache of the burn. The skin there is smooth and taut. It will probably scar.

We're even now, I suppose.

Even so, I want to get back at him. I glare into the mirror, wanting to smash it to pieces, then to take one of those pieces, one with a nice sharp edge, and slash his throat—

I shut off the water, stray drops plinking down from the rusting faucet. Afraid I will see August Wakefield with a gun behind me, I avoid looking at the mirror as I dry my hands, taking care not to drag the rough fibers over the tender spot on my palm. Terrible men, all around me.

Something ought to be done about them.

* * *

I leave for work early the next morning so I won't see him on my way out, and I manage to avoid him after I return, too, taking my dinner into the parlor under the pretense of needing to grade while I eat. My eyes stare blankly through my students' quizzes; in the silence, the only sound is my fork clinking against the plate and the old clock ticking quietly on the mantel. It seems to slow and quicken, as if it can't quite keep the right pace.

After I've finished and lingered longer than necessary, I go to rinse my plate in the kitchen, which is dark and empty by now. I freeze for a moment, listening to see if I can tell where everyone has gone. Voices further down the hall. Footsteps, light, right behind me—

I turn to find my mother.

"Have you finished your work?" she asks, sipping a glass of wine that I'd swear has been glued to her hand.

"Not quite." I glance behind me, toward the hall, trying to gauge where the voices are coming from. "Where is everyone?"

Refilling her glass, she tosses casually over her shoulder, "Don is fixing the window in the laundry room. Isn't that nice of him?"

I cross my arms, curling my hands into fists and gently fingering the sore spot on my palm. "I thought you didn't like Don."

"He's making himself useful." She turns from the counter and looks at me, glass in hand. "Fixing what *you* broke. And he's doing it out of his own pocket."

"Well, if that isn't some fucking chivalry."

"Samantha," she snaps at my language. I pull a face. "Anyway, it's nice to see the two of them talking again. This seems like the right thing for them. I think they can make this work."

"Seriously?" I can't keep the incredulity from spilling out in my voice. "So you're playing matchmaker? Is that why you called him up, so that he could come in and take care of things—so that Elizabeth wouldn't be your problem anymore?"

Her lips form a tight line. "I just want what's best for her—and Julian. The boy needs a father in his life."

Don is a terrible man, I want to tell her, but her eyes are two dark flints, sharp as arrowheads, and suddenly I am nine, frightened in my own house, and my mother is barking at me to leave her alone, the reek of alcohol on her breath.

"You really think having a father around will make a difference?" I ask tightly.

The lines in her face deepen, shadowed by the overhead light, which throws darkness under her eyes. "Would it have made a difference for you?"

My gut clenches, as it does each time I remember that my mother is capable of cruelty, too. I slink against the wall to let her pass, then wander down the hall myself toward the laundry room.

Inside, Don is toiling away, measuring and fixing the glass into place with the biting cold whipping in at him, while Elizabeth sits folding a pile of towels. A scene of such ordinary domesticity, you would hardly know it's happening in a haunted house.

"Come on," Don grumbles as he tries to fit the glass pane into its new home, a task that doesn't look all that difficult. I'm sure I could have accomplished this in half the time he's taken, but there is something painstaking, meticulous about the way he works, like a surgeon at his craft. Because the window is not yet sealed tight, frozen air slithers into the room, shivering my bones as I hover in the doorway. I peer around the edge of it, keeping myself out of sight.

"Are you *sure* it doesn't fit?" asks Elizabeth.

He sets down the glass and picks up a tape measure, pulling out the yellow tongue and holding it along the window frame. He makes a noise in the back of his throat as if it's irritated with phlegm, then casts the tape measure aside, where it slurps up the yellow tongue into its round body with a sound like a zipper.

Moving with slow heaviness, Elizabeth gets up, squats, and picks up the tape measure. Once she has made it back to standing, Don snatches the tape measure and remeasures the frame, something I get the sense he has already done several times now.

"I don't think measuring it again will give you a different answer."

"You sure about that?" he says, thumbing the measurement and shaking his head, holding it up for Elizabeth to see. "This is impossible. See? It keeps changing. It won't just stay one length."

She reaches out again for the tape measure, but he slaps her hand away. Throwing her hands into the air, she turns, goes back to the towels. "If you don't want my help, fine. Just get that pane into the frame already, before we freeze to death."

"I told you," Don snarls, "it doesn't *fit*. It needs to be done properly. You can't just jam it in there and expect it to work."

The chill of the room reaches out toward me. I want to close the door on them, but then Elizabeth says, quietly, "Do you want this to work?"

I have been eavesdropping too long. I turn, take a step to disappear down the hallway, but the floor groans under my foot, and they both snap their heads up to stare at me in the doorway.

Don's eyes are dark, unreadable; Elizabeth has a hand on her belly.

"Everything going okay?" I ask nonchalantly, as if I'd only just stopped by to check on them.

Don's eyes flick to his wife, then to the window, beyond which the black night looms. "Fine," he grits out, picking up the glass pane by its razor edges to slide it into the jamb. This time, it fits. He steps back, staring at it, his eye twitching.

A sigh of relief escapes Elizabeth, and she sits back down.

"All right," I say, turning again to leave—only when I do, I am frozen by the boy standing at the other end of the hallway, blocking my path.

Though his face is a pale blur and his mouth nothing but a thin black snarl and his eyes just two empty pits, a terrible familiarity washes over me—not just the familiarity of having seen him so many times, now, in this house, but the familiarity that comes when you've just looked upon a child's father and then at the child itself, and seen the resemblance there.

Even though I cannot see his face, that resemblance feels uncanny—the temper, the violence simmering just beneath the surface. I look from one to the other—Donovan's back is to me as he rechecks the window, running a hand over the edge, and for a moment I consider imploring him to turn around, to come look upon his son, but the words choke up in my throat—and I feel as if I am caught between two mirrors, and I wonder just how much Julian is his father's son.

Outside, it starts to snow.

16

All those eyes gaze up at me, here at the front of the classroom, like the eyes of Shadydale all turned at once in my direction, fixing me with their stony gaze, the white corners of their eyes vanishing into vast pupils like black holes. Frost creeps across the windows and trees bend over the walkways, limbs laden with snow. It is a colder winter than we're used to. All the weathermen are in a tizzy over it, predicting *snowmageddon* all down the East Coast.

A hot coffee sounds so pleasant and lovely on a chill day such as today, but I cannot bring myself to stop at the diner in town, where I know Don will be sitting hunched over his laptop in the corner booth, a strange out-of-place fixture, an uprooted artifact.

In the study of archaeology, context is what gives artifacts meaning. No matter the site, every artifact found has a relationship to the situation, the time period, and to the other artifacts nearby. That is why each artifact must be properly documented before it can be removed. Once an artifact is removed from its precise location without prior documentation, it has been removed from its context, and it no longer has any identifiable scientific value; its meaning is lost forever. Without context, you have objects with no clear relationship to one another or to the situation, and without those relationships, you have no patterns—just random chaos.

This house is an archaeological nightmare: people and objects and sounds appearing and disappearing at whim, with no rhyme or reason, with no intelligible context unless one has already studied deeply the history of the site. And it isn't as if the memories can be precisely documented either, as I have discovered with Nathaniel's camera. I can keep notes in my journal, which I have been doing for many years, as you know, but even those notes must be biased by my own hand. All I can do is try to identify and document the context, to desperately try to make sense of the patterns and form them into a coherent narrative. I am, if anything, a pattern seeker, and where no pattern clearly exists, I will try to find one, or form one, or make one up.

As an archaeologist, I am trying to make sense of the context in which Donovan appears in this tale. I consider ghosts and memories of the house's inhabitants to be artifacts just as much as anything else, requiring documentation, so I suppose I have come to consider human beings artifacts in their own right. And as you know, artifacts require context.

What is the location in which he has appeared? What is his relationship to that location, and to the other artifacts (or people) present? Your assignment will be to write a report in which you find the pattern, and then explain the meaning of that pattern.

* * *

In the evening, we find Don tearing apart the Rose Room. Elizabeth and I were paging idly through books—by some unspoken agreement we have been spending more time in the same room as each other lately—when we heard the racket going on up here, so we threw each other a look before hurrying to Don's room.

Pillows and blankets have been dashed to the floor in a frenzy as he rips open the floral curtains, yanks them shut again where they dance and sway before falling still, pulls open empty drawers, grunts, and leaves them hanging there like gaping, hungry mouths.

Elizabeth folds her arms and raises her eyebrows at the scene of destruction. "Looking for something?"

Don whirls around like a feral cat startled by human presence, his body taut and lithe and ready to pounce. "What are you playing at?"

"I don't know what you mean."

His arms rise and fall to encompass the room. "There's someone coughing in here!" His eyes dart from me to Elizabeth, daring us to reveal our secrets.

A sad uncertainty comes over Elizabeth; her stance is no longer wry and charming but worried, defeated. "If you're going to go around tearing up my mother's house, maybe you shouldn't be here."

He steps closer, towering over her. He shaved yesterday, I believe, but stubble is again growing over his cheeks, roughening his hard-eyed face. "Shouldn't *be* here?"

I think this is the moment—in the slump of her shoulders and the way she picks at her cuticles—when I realize that Elizabeth has begun to regret her decision to admit Donovan into the house. It is not like it was when it was just the three of us; having him here is like inviting in an unpredictable stranger. At least that is how it feels to me; it must be so much different for Elizabeth, since this is the man she has lived with for years, her partner. And yet she shies away from him as he passes us out into the hallway, shies away from his touch as if afraid he will turn those ravaging hands tearing up the room onto *her* and tear her up, too.

* * *

As we straightened up the room after Donovan destroyed it, I found a curious artifact—a letter wedged deep in the bottommost crevices of a little-used drawer, yellowed and curled at the edges. I am surprised the paper has lasted this long, but a mother's love, I suppose, can last an eternity. I will add this to my records.

To my dearest,

Forgive me, my son, for you will not see me again. Yet I know you will do well without me. You have your whole life ahead, and all the world is open to you. You are going to have opportunities I could never have imagined, and I am so glad for this even though it brings me pain. I know your father will look after you well, for he loves you, and you are nearly a man, ready to look after your own self. While I do not believe any child ever truly stops needing his mother, you will do better without me. I know it. We can only live a half-life, each of us, in our present circumstances. I can never truly be your mother; you can never fully be free of where you come from. But once I am gone, you will be. You will be able to be a white man, and I do not know any greater freedom than that.

Now I am returning to the one place that I have ever felt free, the one place that I feel I can call home, as strange as that may seem, for I only lived there a few short weeks when I was a child. In some ways all my experiences there seem like a dream, and at the same time, feel more real to me than anything else in this life. Yet do not despair, my son: this way, we will both be free.

Even though I am not there, I will always be with you. Think of your dear mother, but only in the quiet spaces, when you are alone and away from the burdens of who you must be, from now on, and how you must present yourself to the world. Think of me when your heart is sore and the world seems cruel. And think of me when your heart is full, too—for I will be there with you in your joy. And even though you must never tell a soul who your mother is, remember always who you truly are, at those times when you are able to be exactly your own wonderful, beautiful self.

With love great enough to fill an ocean,
M.

I carefully fold the old, yellowed paper and take it with me. Whatever became of Meriday? What happened to her when she went back to the swamp? Did she find her own mother?

I slip the letter between the pages of the notebook in which I've written down all my notes about Meriday, Jonah, Clementine, and the Wakefields of that time. Another artifact to add to the puzzle—the last one, perhaps. The end of their story, even if it ends in a question mark.

Poor Lucius, I think. For, despite all his good fortune and the depth of his mother's love, he still had to grow up with August Wakefield for a father.

* * *

Winter in Virginia is never what you expect it will be.

Up in the Blue Ridge and Appalachian mountains, you could be freezing to death in a snowed-in cabin, but closer to the coast, the ocean keeps our winters typically mild, save a nor'easter or two. Things get quiet in winter, as if the blanket of snow has muffled all living beings; the insects hush, and the lonely wind blows through dead trees. Winter is a time for the quiet—for aloof wind and soft flakes and the low crackle of flames in the fireplace, and the quiet shadows they cast on the walls, shadows that cavort silently behind you.

In our childhood winter days, Elizabeth used to bury me in snow the way you'd bury someone in sand at the beach, packing it up to my neck until I couldn't move. Once, she left me there for half an hour, and when I came inside my lips were blue and my mother scorched my throat with hot tea.

In a winter like this one, even the primordial swamp crystallizes with the cold. But in all my life, to tell the truth, I can't remember a winter quite like this one.

Already the snow whirling outside is climbing up the windows. Campus has been closed due to the blizzard, classes canceled; and I am marooned here in the house, with nowhere to go, with the rest of the world slowly dissolving beyond the white and the white and the endless white building up around the house. Campus is a distant blur. Shadydale is erased. Even the roads are gone, buried, and the cars in the driveway, so encrusted with tumorous growths of ice, will not budge. Don goes out again and again to take a hammer to the sheet of ice that has grown over his windshield, and I wince with each blow, thinking he will crack straight through the glass. A bucket of hot water melts the worst of it, but the tires will need to be dug out; they are glued to the frozen gravel. We are trapped in a house filled with ghosts.

Little Liz and little Sam scamper through the house, appearing and disappearing as ephemerally as steam from a teakettle. In the library, I look for a book to read and find instead my mother sitting in that old blue armchair with a half-empty bottle of wine—no, it isn't now-Agnes but another Agnes, and she cannot see me, though I do not think she can see anything, as she stares blankly into the distance. Perhaps she can see my father hanging himself again and again, somewhere deep in her mind. And then I find her, again, this time in her reading room, with a watered-down highball, and I can smell the memory of bourbon as she shuffles her cards methodically. And I find her, again, in the dining room, snapping at little Liz to go to bed, to put Sam to bed, and it is midnight on the mantel as she goes to pour herself another. And I find her, again, sitting beside the cold ashes of the vacant fireplace, sipping on a glass of red. I pause to contemplate this memory, all these sad memories, wondering if the house is trying to tell me something, if only I could decipher its code.

At last, my mother looks up at me and says, "Are you just going to stand there and stare?"

"Oh," I say with a jolt. "I thought you were . . ."

She does not ask me to finish. Instead, she holds up the bottle of wine at her feet, and I nod and go to find myself a glass, thinking that when I return I should really tell her to get a fire going, for the room is gloomy and chill without it on this darkening afternoon.

When I step into the hallway, though, I hear the ghostly echo of someone calling my sister's name from somewhere else in the house. His voice rings out hollowly and dies away as I turn the corner, nearly running into Elizabeth herself.

She hisses at me as I open my mouth and pulls me into the next room, standing near the door to listen.

"What are you doing?"

"Don's looking for me," she replies, still peering out into the hallway.

I frown. "Should I tell him where you are?"

"No," she says. "Why would you do that?"

Don's voice echoes emptily down the hallway, closer now.

I look around; we are in the den. I grab a chair for her to sit down, and she gratefully lowers herself. She sucks in a sharp breath, but before I can even ask, she waves me away and says, "It's nothing."

"If you don't want Don here, why don't you just tell him to go?"

His voice reverberates down the hallway, and I look questioningly at her.

Elizabeth stretches out her legs and leans back, trying to get comfortable. "For one, none of us are going anywhere—he still hasn't managed to get the car out."

Before she can get to her second point, a shadow falls over the room as Donovan steps into the doorway.

"There you are!"

Elizabeth smiles weakly. "Here I am."

"I've been looking all over for you." He takes a heavy step toward us, the floorboards groaning beneath his weight, and Elizabeth cringes. He stops. "Why are you avoiding me?"

"I'm not avoiding you," she says. "It's just a big house."

Don looks at me, and I cross my arms. The ghost of a cigarette burn haunts my palm, even though it's healed and doesn't actually hurt. He turns back to Liz and speaks as if I am not in the room at all.

"You know, when you told me your weird sister was going to stay with us a while, I didn't say one word about it. I made her feel right at home. I went out of my way to be nice to her. And now I'm here, and you're all acting like I'm some uninvited guest."

I realize he's holding a tool in his hand, a metal crowbar it looks like, and I wonder where he got it, and I wonder what he will do with it.

"You know, where I'm from, we have a little something called hospitality." He fiddles with the crowbar, and I see Elizabeth's eyes dart toward it. "A little something called gratitude." He throws the crowbar down by Elizabeth's feet, where it clatters and rings metallically. "I just wanted to tell you that you put together that crib all wrong. *All* wrong. I've taken it apart. I'll have to fix it." As he turns to leave, he looks back over his shoulder and spits out, "You're welcome."

Elizabeth and I share a look. Her lips are pressed together; her face is white and shiny. I want to tell her I will help her get rid of Don. I want to tell her I will protect her. But these sound like such silly things to say, so I don't say anything at all.

I make a mental note not to go near the nursery, if Don is in there destroying the crib I built. I won't go near the Rose Room anymore, either. The rooms I am avoiding are starting to add up. I wonder if he has seen any children in the nursery, running around, playing.

A few months ago, before Elizabeth showed up in the rain, when the house was still quiet with only Agnes and me tiptoeing around it, I saw little Liz and little Sam playing house in the nursery; the same room that so frightened my father when he woke up that night years ago to find, in his eternal silence, a baby crying in a mysterious crib. We never spent much time in there as kids, but it must have seemed the right spot to play house that day, with muted sunlight streaming in through the window onto the tacky yellow wallpaper.

Little Liz and little Sam were playing house. The elder wore a ratty old apron several sizes too large for her, and carried a rolling pin she'd found in the kitchen. She was the mother. She was nine.

Little Sam didn't have any props but the picture book she carried in with her, and she was made to sit on the floor. She was the baby. She was seven.

When Liz noticed the book, she said, "Babies don't read," and took it away.

"Hey!"

"Babies don't talk, either."

Playing along, Sam simulated a baby crying and reached out for the book, which Elizabeth held just out of her grasp.

"You can have it when you're older."

"When will that be?"

"Quiet, Sam! You're a baby!"

Sam crawled around on the floor while Liz pretended to cook in an imaginary kitchen, moving the rolling pin back and forth over the air and humming to herself. "The cookies are almost done," she said. "Do you want some cookies, Sam?"

Sam nodded, for she could not speak. She was only a baby.

Liz handed her the imaginary cookies. "I'm going to be the best mom ever." She was too young to notice the irony of the statement as she pretended to give cookies to a pretend infant, but I notice it when I watch the scene, and it makes me laugh.

Breaking her role, Sam pouted, "But Mom is the best mom ever."

The look Liz gave her little sister was too old, too wise, a look noticed only when revisiting the memory many years later, when you start to see someone for who they really are and not who you perceive them to be. "Eat your cookie, Sam."

Sam pretended to eat her cookie, looking a little disappointed that it wasn't a real cookie, but not complaining, at least, because it was easier to play her role than it was to set off Lizzie's temper, and it would be better for everyone if she just acquiesced so that Lizzie would like her and want her around.

And that's when the crying started.

At first, Liz and Sam were delighted by the disembodied echo of a baby crying, because it was the nursery and they were playing house and why shouldn't there be some realistic sound effects? Elizabeth clapped her hands and looked around, but it was only the sound of it, no baby to be seen. For a time they danced around the room looking for the baby, calling *come out, come out, little baby*, but nothing happened, and the crying rose to a wail, and an adult watching this scene might start to wonder what baby they were hearing, what time period it was coming from, who would neglect the child so completely as to leave it crying, crying, crying.

Sam put her hands over her ears and rocked back and forth and began to cry. "Make it stop," she begged her sister, still believing that because Liz was two years older, she had some sort of power over these situations that Sam did not yet possess.

Lizzie did not seem as bothered, and as she watched Sam's discomfort, she giggled.

When Sam had had enough, she got up off the floor to leave the room, but Liz slammed the door shut on her, blocking her way.

"I want to go," said Sam. "Let me out!"

Liz pushed her back, telling her, "You can't leave. We're not done playing yet."

To block out the awful, incessant wailing of the invisible baby, little Sam slapped her hands over her ears, hating the sound, hating how loud it was, the way it crawled under her skin. But little Liz grabbed her thin, fragile wrists and pulled her hands away from her ears, forcing her to listen.

"You're a bad mother!" Sam shrieked, trying to wriggle free from her older sister's grasp.

Frowning, Liz let go; Sam, still squirming, toppled onto her side on the floor.

"*I'm* going to be a good mother," Liz said, her voice so low that Sam could hardly hear it over the crying. "Now sit down and eat your cookies, Sam."

Tears snaking down her cheeks, Sam crossed her legs and dutifully pretended to eat imaginary cookies while the baby's wails echoed around them.

I shudder when I revisit the memory, hearing the ghost of the crying baby in my mind, and I wonder what sort of parent has left this child alone—and I wonder whether the child will grow up and remember, in a subconscious part of the brain, this neglect.

The wounds of youth never really leave us, I suppose. There's no leaving it all behind because, even as adults, we're still playing. And we're not done playing yet.

* * *

The Atlantic is closer in my dreams, lapping up all the land between here and the coast, licking at the edge of the swamp as if testing the water. And the water is cold and gray and churning with furious whitecaps that roll in and roll in on an endless loop. And somewhere out in the middle of that vast gray ocean, underneath a colorless winter sky circled by crows, floats a throne like a lone island, buffeted and beset by waves but unmoving, immovable. And on that throne is a man, plagued on all sides by the relentless madness of the sea. Gray himself, with his eyes reflecting the dull gray waters, he is both familiar and changed, like a broken reflection.

It is Don and Not-Don, and looking at him hurts my eyes, as if he is slowly dissolving into not darkness or shadow, not exactly, but nothing at all. A nothingness that has come leaking out, as my father said, leaking out from the cracks in the world and replicated in every mirror of the house.

He holds a rusting bronze chalice in one hand, filled with some unnamable liquid. Whatever camera my eyes have become in this dream, I try to zoom it in on the cup, to see what is inside it—I want to know what the liquid is—but I can't. He is too far away on his throne in the ocean, too far away to see what is in his cup.

* * *

When I wake, I can't stop seeing Not-Don behind me in the bathroom mirror as I splash water on my face. Not-Don, or some other dark shape—it's hard to tell when I can't look at it straight on without it disappearing. I close my eyes on the mirror, trying to control my breathing, forcing myself not to snap them open to try to catch whatever is there. I tell myself there isn't anything there. It is only my reflection.

But when I open my eyes, I wonder—is it *really* my reflection? Are those my eyes, gleaming in the yellowish light? Is that my mouth, almost curling up, with the ghost of a knowing smile?

Or is it only the house imitating me?

I slam my fist against the mirror; it rattles in its frame, my reflection jittering. I find myself disappointed when it doesn't shatter or crack. To rectify this, I pick up the soap holder—a heavy, shallow dish—and slam it into the mirror, which has the desired effect: cracks spider-web from the point of impact, which gouges a hole where shards break off and fall.

At once I drop the soap dish and step back, staring appalled into my fractured reflection. How will I explain this to my mother? First the window, now this.

Unless I can convince her it was someone else. Someone who has just arrived, who shouldn't be here. The King of Cups.

I think of the sort of father he will be, and it frightens me.

Is *he* the reason Julian will turn out this way?

Staring into my cracked reflection, I press my thumb into the smooth spot on my palm, filled with dawning horror.

I must get Don out of this house and away from Julian. That is the answer staring me in the face.

But how? I've waited too long to tell them about the cigarette burn—with the wound healed over, would they even believe me? At once I imagine them all lined up before me, telling me perhaps *I* should be the one to leave, after all, if I cannot get along with anyone in this house. And just like that, Elizabeth and Don will have taken over and kicked me out, once again, into the dark. Even my mother, I think, wouldn't be sad to see me go.

But this is *my* house.

My face, still wet and broken into a thousand jagged pieces like a Picasso painting, glowers back at me, my eyes hidden in the empty hollow where the shards fell out.

I will keep everyone out of this house who does not belong—Don, the Shadydalers, the witch, whatever evil has leaked in. I will keep them all out until it is only us: my mother, my sister, and me.

And I realize my father's mistake: he didn't think to break the mirrors.

I have to stop whatever is leaking out through them. Whatever is behind our reflections, whatever is imitating us in the mirrors, whatever might be able to slip into our world through them. There isn't any other way. It must be done, and now is the time to do it, before I lose my nerve. My reflection's dislocated jaw twists into a grin.

First I make my way to the den and find the crowbar that Donovan left. Then I do my light-footed leap around the endless halls in the endless house, twirling with my baton, finding a disused bathroom here, a full-length mirror there, shattering as I go. The shattering is lovely, and I laugh. I haven't had such a good time with my insomnia in ages. Will they wake, I wonder? No, the house is my friend; it cushions the blows in its velvet folds of drapery. I am alone with the shattering. Even when I steal into Elizabeth's room for her vanity, she does not wake, I am a ghost, and I give it the most delicate of taps, cracking it like a nut. Now we will not get trapped on the other side! Now we cannot fall into an infinity mirror with endless reflections of ourselves—now it will just be us!

* * *

The next morning, I allow myself to sleep in, sleeping more deeply and blackly than I can remember, and it isn't my own nervous mind that wakes me but the sound of shouting.

"Who else would have done this?" my sister is yelling from down the hall. I creep awake to them and find my mother, teary-eyed on her knees, picking glass from the floor outside the bathroom.

"Why would *I* do this?" Don snaps back.

"I don't know! Isn't it funny, though, that everything is fine until you show up, and now all the mirrors are broken?"

"That's some bullshit."

Elizabeth disappears around the corner and returns with the crowbar, throwing it to the floor like Don did yesterday. I must have left it there when I finished last night. They both look at it for a moment, and I think, with some amusement, that she shouldn't have moved it without documenting its precise location first—now it is without context.

"This is *our* home," she says. "You don't see us marching around with crowbars to destroy things!"

"What have I destroyed? I fixed your window. I'm fixing your crib. I'm fixing things here because *you* can't keep them together." He turns away from her angrily and sees me coming down the hall. "Ask your sister, then. She's the one who broke the window."

"Oh please, Sam didn't do this."

"Well *I* didn't." Don's eyes are locked on me as I approach. "Sam?"

Without looking at me, Elizabeth snaps, "You don't have to answer him, Sam."

I look from one to the other with wide eyes, trying to hide the smile bursting free beneath my face. This will do it, I think. This will get rid of him. Elizabeth's anger is glorious.

My mother hisses and pulls back her hand from the floor. Don and Liz both hover over her worriedly, but she waves them away. "All these beautiful mirrors," she laments, wiping blood on her fraying bathrobe.

"Someone must have broken in," suggests Don.

"Just to break the mirrors?" Elizabeth scoffs.

"Maybe it was a ghost," I say.

Elizabeth glowers at me. Don frowns, as if he is not sure whether my suggestion is sincere or not.

The rage is dying away; I want to call it back, but it's no use. We can sustain such righteous anger for only so long. "Maybe it wasn't Don," Elizabeth concedes.

I want to slap her.

"Thank you," he says, without any real gratitude. "I don't like being falsely accused."

"But maybe it *was*," she adds pointedly. "Either way, it doesn't matter right now. We just need to get this cleaned up. We can't have broken glass all over the house."

Not being fully absolved puts a pall on Donovan's face, but he says nothing more. Silent with fury, he stalks away, eventually returning with a dustpan. Elizabeth stares at my mother until she gets to her feet, allowing Don to take over the cleaning, which he does, exuding such an air of frustration and brooding that we can all feel it from several feet away.

My mood sours. I haven't gotten rid of the beast at all. I've only poked him with a stick.

17

It is day two of our incarceration, and Donovan is in the nursery.

Elizabeth has taken to the drawing room, separating herself from her husband by as many floors and walls as she can. My mother tut-tuts over her, propping pillows behind her back and rubbing her feet with lavender. When she gets up, she puts a hand on Elizabeth's belly and murmurs, "We'll see you soon." I see the worry hiding in her eyes, even if Elizabeth doesn't.

Snow whirls up around the windows, frosts the edges of the panes, and the wind rattles them, pounding to be let in. I've pulled some of the shutters, telling the wind to *stay out, stay out there where you belong, we don't want you in here*, but the cold gets in all the same, from the cracks under the doors and invisible crevices that allow the outside world to leak inside, little by little. Where is it coming in? Don already fixed the hole in the laundry room window. We should be sealed shut, locked away from the cold.

To avoid going stir-crazy, I have gone all over the house to covertly admire my handiwork, pleased with all the cracked mirrors and their fractured reflections, and the ones that have shattered right out of their frames. It calms me to see them broken. Now nothing, truly, can get in.

From upstairs, the house echoes with the sounds of banging, hammering, building. The pieces of the crib Elizabeth and I built have been broken down and scattered across the floor as Donovan reassembles it to his liking, vigorously shaking the slats to be sure they are sturdy enough to withstand his assault.

"Is he still up there?" Elizabeth asks me when the sounds die down. We listen for footsteps creaking down the stairs, for the whirr of a power drill—for his voice, shouting at shadows.

Reverting to the silence of sign language, I ask her if she would like me to go check. She throws me a quick negative.

Conversing like this, speaking without speaking, makes me feel like we are conspiring together. If we always spoke in sign, the house would be silent as the grave. My mother would surely approve. That way, we would never hear echoes of ourselves calling out, talking, laughing, bickering. How lovely it would be, to embrace the quiet without that fearful jolt that comes when a voice whispers just behind your ear or wakes you from your bed with a start. Here the air is infected with small, strange, unbelonging noises such that even the quiet is uncomfortably met, such that my sister has set her teeth on edge, wanting to remain quietly out of mind of her husband while abhorring the very quiet she must inhabit, the very quiet that characterized our childhood with my mother shutting off the radio whenever she ambled past, and snapping the strings off little Lizzie's guitar, and grabbing her arm to stop her racing, stomping down the hallway after me.

I sign, *Should I ask him to leave?*

Elizabeth gives it a moment's thought. *He won't go*, she signs at last—clumsily, haltingly, returning to a half-forgotten language from her youth. Her hands are like question marks, asking me if these are the right shapes.

But you don't want him here, I sign back, marveling at how quickly my fingers remember their old tongue.

Elizabeth shrugs dismissively.

You don't want him around your son, I try again. She frowns, trying to decipher my code, then purses her lips together. *He is a bad influence*, my fingers draw in the air. *He is a bad influence on J-U-L-I-A-N*. We haven't made a sign for his name, so I have to spell it out.

Then maybe we should just stay away from him, I sign at last, when it is clear that Elizabeth will not respond to my assessment. *It is a big house*.

My sister shrugs again, an acquiescent or indifferent shrug. Then she says, out loud, perhaps having tired of going two minutes without hearing her own voice, tired of the ambiguity of an unspoken conversation, or perhaps because she wants me to hear it said: "You're worrying too much again. Stop that."

Does Elizabeth ever worry? Of course she does; don't be silly. She simply doesn't let it control her, I think. She doesn't hunch her back protectively against the side-eye given her by the Shadydalers in town; she doesn't perform small rituals like checking the locks three times before bed, or grabbing the oven dial to be sure it's in the off position, or fretfully picking the dirt out from under her fingernails; she doesn't carry around small amulets for good luck; she doesn't crouch at the end of the hallway with a candle in her hand, waiting for the beast to come slouching through his home.

Instead, she smiles and laughs a little too loudly and raises her voice over whatever is going on in her head, and she doesn't look at the snow creeping up the windows, darkening the early-afternoon room to something akin to twilight. She doesn't watch the snow burying us here, and she doesn't get up to check how high it is now, how many inches have fallen.

And she doesn't flinch, as I do, when the lights blink off as one, and leave us in this gray purgatorial dusk like television static. When my mother finds us, she mutters about the finicky old wiring, and she flips light switches on and off as if the rapid clicking will ignite them. "Sam, help me get a fire going."

With the firewood we had stashed away ages ago hauled over to the fireplace, my mother manages to light a spark while I crank open the flue.

In the distance, Don's voice comes to us, shouting about the power, that he needs light to finish the crib, and I hear him stomping down to the basement where he thinks he will find the breaker, and where he will indeed find the breaker, but he will also discover that flipping it will do no good, as the power isn't looking to come back on anytime soon. Snarling, he stomps back up to the nursery, where he will have to finish his work in the dull gray light of the winter storm.

We sit around the crackling fire looking at each other as we listen. Eventually, my mother says carefully, "Has he always had such a temper?"

Elizabeth looks around the room as if she hasn't seen it before a million times, anywhere but at our mother. Eventually she sighs. "Don't act surprised. I know you never liked him."

"Well," says Mother, her mouth gaping. She closes it, having lost whatever it was she was going to say.

Elizabeth's eyes have locked on to the fire now. "I'm not sure why you called him here in the first place."

"I just want you to be happy."

"Yes," Elizabeth says to the fire, her voice bitter. "Look how happy we are." I notice that her eyes are wet, bulbous with unshed tears.

We sit for a moment in silence.

"Why did you leave him, anyway?" I ask.

Elizabeth glares at me. "I told you." Her voice is rough, biting like the winter wind. "We had a fight."

The pop of the fire spitting a stray spark makes us jump. The room feels too close, closed in; the snow entombs us like primitive peoples sitting around a fire in a cave, telling the stories of our ancestors. Telling the same stories, again and again.

"Well," says my mother, rubbing her legs. "Charades?"

Elizabeth shakes her head as she stares into the fire. Her eyes are very wide, as if she is trying to stop them from spilling over, as if, should she only make them wide enough, they will become like two bowls holding in the excess liquid. And finally, perhaps because she is doing such a good job stopping her eyes from spilling, she cannot any longer stop her mouth from spilling out the truth.

"He hit me."

"What?"

Elizabeth drags her eyes to my mother and then to me. "That's why I left, if you must know."

The silence that rings in the wake of her pronouncement is heavy and cancerous. My mother rockets to her feet but then doesn't seem to know where to go, so she stands there gaping. "How *could* he?"

"We were arguing. We'd been arguing a lot. Sometimes he grabbed me too hard. This time, he just . . . it went a bit farther."

My mother shakes her head and strides over to the telephone. "That's it."

"Mother," Elizabeth says again, tired, exasperated.

"It's not right." She picks up the phone and puts it to her ear, though who she would call I'm not sure, then drops it back down and turns to us. "Phone lines are down."

When I finally find my cell phone, which I have left up in my bedroom, as it hardly gets any use, I find the battery giving its last gasps, and with that remaining seven percent, I hold it up to find a signal. The one bar that was there flickers out to nothing, and it seems no matter where I walk around the endless dismal hallways, I cannot find it again. When I return to my mother's expectant stare, I shake my head.

Without any power to charge it, I have to watch as the battery winds down to nothing.

"If he won't leave, then we will," my mother decides. "We'll get a hotel room in town."

She nods to herself, and I feel a great respect for my mother, knowing as I do how ill it will make her to leave the house. But as Liz begins sluggishly gathering her things and I follow my mother to the foyer, a feeling of dread aches in my heart. She swings open the front door, and we find a drift of snow creeping halfway up the car, locking it in place, and a blustering whirlwind of thick flakes filling the air.

"Jesus," she murmurs, but I am not surprised. I have been watching the snow from the windows, watching the wind sweep it into great drifts against the house.

We shut the door.

"Hold on," says Elizabeth, who is searching her pockets and frowning. "Where's my phone?" After twenty minutes of fruitless searching, Elizabeth growing more and more frantic as we open drawers and unearth couch cushions, we have to admit it is missing. Our last vital connection to the outside world.

Biting back tears of frustration, Elizabeth finally goes to the staircase and shouts up for Don. My mother and I hiss at her, as we've no desire to invite him down to us, but it is too late; he has heard her call, and we hear his footsteps groaning on the stairs before we see him emerging from the shadows at the top.

"Do you know where my phone is?" she asks.

"Have you misplaced it?" he says, heading to the kitchen, compelling us to trail along after him as he pours himself a glass of water from the tap. "You should keep better track of your things."

"Thank you for the unsolicited advice. Have you seen it?"

Don shakes his head. "What do you need it for?" he says, and his voice is strange—a false attempt at levity. "Who are you trying to call?"

Elizabeth sucks her teeth and breathes slowly as if through frustration or pain. "Why does it matter?" she spits out impatiently.

His empty glass slams down on the table. "It matters if you're trying to call a lawyer to divorce me, or the police to kick me out, as if I'm some stranger and not the father of your own son!" With one step he is directly in front of Elizabeth, and my mother has opened her mouth wide as if to call him out but does not know what to say.

Then he pulls Elizabeth's cell phone from his pocket and smashes it on the floor, where the glass screen cracks and bits of the plastic case skitter off across the tiles. He crunches his heel into it, and the screen flashes erratically before going dark. "There! There's your phone."

Elizabeth's face is a mask of fury and horror, and behind Donovan my mother has pulled the cork from a nearly used up bottle of wine and is emptying its contents into a glass. A dribble of red runs down the length of the bottle and leaves a spot on the kitchen table. I cannot believe she is pouring herself a drink right now and am almost ready to shout her down, her and Don both, to ask why she needs to retreat into her own little world when anything goes wrong, why she can't stay out here with the rest of us, why she can't *help* us, for goodness' sake, her own daughters, and I think I might be even more angry at my mother than I am at Donovan.

But Don is pulling Elizabeth closer to him, laying a hand possessively on her belly.

"Take your hands off me," Elizabeth growls.

He doesn't move. "I'll put my hands wherever I like."

Then my mother smashes him over the head with the business end of her empty wine bottle.

* * *

Is this the rope my father used to hang himself?

It is all I can think about as I tie Don's hands behind his back, around the back of the old wooden dining chair.

Elizabeth's arms are wrapped around her belly, and her face is pinched and white. My mother shuffles back to the table with hands wet from washing and a sterilized needle. I bend down to secure Donovan's ankles to the legs of the chair.

A cut bleeds sluggishly over his brow from when he went down, hitting his head against the sharp edge of the kitchen counter; there is more dark, tacky blood matting the hair on the back of his head from the wine bottle. My mother stands over him and begins stitching him up.

"What are we going to do with him?" I wonder aloud when he rouses, groaning, trying to pull his head from my mother's needle as she gives him a sharp rebuke to hold still. When she is finished, she steps back, and though it has been many years since my mother has stitched up a wound, her work is excellent—tight, small, even little stitches that hold the gaping cut closed. He'll hardly scar, I think.

He hangs his head, tugs on his restraints, and then his groan turns into a low, guttural laugh. "Are you serious?" he murmurs. "You're insane. You're all insane." Then he laughs again, that strange awful laugh.

"It's for your own good," Elizabeth tells him. "And for Julian's."

He looks at her, a trail of unwiped blood snaking slowly from his forehead down the side of his nose. "You won't keep me from my son."

Elizabeth steps back, away from him, and hisses as if burned.

"Come back here," Don commands, but she keeps drifting backward until she has left the room. My mother and I exchange a look and follow her into the hallway, with Don calling behind us, yelling for us to come back.

We find Liz bending over and breathing heavily, making a high keening sound in the back of her throat.

"What is it?" I ask, alarmed by her obvious pain.

My mother's eyes flare. "You're having contractions?"

After several long minutes, the wave passes on. Liz, one hand clamped over her belly, looks at my mother with her lips still pressed tightly together and nods. "I've been having them all day," she manages to get out. "But it's not time yet, it's not time yet! He isn't due for another week. I'm not ready." Her voice rises almost hysterically, as if convincing us will convince Julian to stay put.

Beyond the window, the light-gray sky darkens to a deeper gray. An early night is falling.

"As soon as the snow lets up, we'll get out of here," I chatter mindlessly. "We'll dig out the car. We'll take you to the hospital."

But my words fall silently as the snow, cold and without meaning. We may not be able to wait that long.

As my mother helps Elizabeth into the sitting room, I hurry back to the darkening kitchen, where Don is groaning and pulling at the rope, and down the glass of wine my mother poured in one long gulp. How long will it be before Julian urgently begs to be born? How long will it be before Don manages to break free from his flimsy restraints? I admit, I am no expert at tying knots.

He looks up at me. "I'll kill you for this."

I set down the glass and back away, leaving him in the growing shadows of the kitchen.

Back in the sitting room, my mother has stoked the fire back to blazing, and it throws its light and shadow and warmth around the walls, closing us in with the flickering glow while Elizabeth groans through another contraction. They are coming more quickly now, and lasting longer. Despite the fire, there is a chill of expectant tension in the air.

When the contraction passes, Elizabeth looks up to where I stand, panting; then her eyes drift behind me, and she frowns.

"Who is that?"

I turn to look.

A faceless boy stands in the shadows—but no, he is not quite faceless, not anymore. Already some detail has begun to etch itself across the blank white egg of him, carving an expectant grin filled with teeth that have the slightest of gaps between them, sharpening his prominent nose into the very shape of Donovan Hill's, leaving only his eyes like two black pits that have yet to decide what they will be, like the chthonic sockets of a grinning skull.

Julian, are you ready to be born?

I turn back to Elizabeth to tell her who it is, to introduce her to her son, but she gasps in surprise before I can get a word out.

And then her water breaks.

PART FIVE

THE NEVER

18

In some other realm, we would not be who we are. My father would not have killed himself. Elizabeth would be a ballerina who moonlights as a punk rock guitarist. My mother would be happily tending to patients in her bygone medical career, the way she did when I was young and our father stayed home to watch us, back in those days when she would return with a smiling glow—you know the kind, the one you see in teachers after a rewarding student breakthrough and in artists who have just finished a painting, the glow of fulfillment that comes only from doing what you love. Perhaps I would be a renowned archaeologist, with a full professorship at the university where I adjunct now and funding to take expeditions into the swamp, to find the remains of Meriday, wherever she went when she disappeared back into the only place that ever felt like home to her.

Perhaps we would not be here, snowed into a haunted house with a devil tied to a chair and Elizabeth moaning through her contractions.

Panting through a wave of pain, she grabs me by the wrist. "I don't want him here," she grits out.

I look helplessly at my mother, who shakes her head. "We'll have to deliver him," she murmurs, and then goes off decisively.

"I don't think there's anything we can do about that," I tell my sister. "He's coming."

"Not Julian," she hisses through clenched teeth. "I don't want Don here. Don't tell him. I don't want him with me. I don't want him with the baby."

I let her cling to me, not wanting to tell her that it is too late—sooner or later, Don will be able to get himself out of my knots; we cannot keep him tied to that chair forever. And when he does get free, he will want to be there for the birth of his son. No matter where we go in this house, he will find us.

Where can we go that he won't find us?

"Oh," I say out loud, staring into the shadows in which Julian disappeared when Elizabeth's water broke, leaving only a trace of childish laughter floating on the light that leapt across the room from the seething fire.

"Spit it out," Elizabeth snaps.

"I have an idea," I tell her, just as my mother comes back into the room with an armful of towels. I stand up from where I have been crouching beside Elizabeth, my knees popping.

* * *

When I was eleven and waifish, I used to fit myself into tiny nooks and crannies when I didn't want to be found. I had secret little spots in the narrow crevices behind doors and the empty cupboards in the kitchen, back in the days when my mother wasn't good about keeping food around and you'd be more likely to find dead flies and ancient rusted cans in the cabinets than anything else. I could tuck myself into my little dark space and while away the afternoon as Elizabeth frantically called my name, fearing she had lost me somewhere, and my mother would tell her to stop shouting.

When I got too big for my little hiding spots, I had to start looking for other places where no one would find me when I didn't want to be found. That's how I came to be more and more curious about the locked room at the end of the third floor hall. When I was fourteen and inventive, I stole some bobby pins from my sister's dresser where they lay scattered amongst tangled jewelry and a menagerie of makeup, and I used them to try to pick the lock.

After half an hour of careful clicking and poking, the door was just as locked as it had always been, but I was stubborn. It took three more attempts over the following weeks before I finally gave up—although I kept the bobby pins, just in case.

Giving up was more of a relief than anything, actually. The longer I sat there poking and clicking, the deeper my uneasiness grew and the more I wanted to get away from the door and escape back down the long dark hallway, back down to a more welcome part of the house that wasn't so closed up and dusty, with a smell like wet old carpet and rotted floorboards. As much as I wanted to open the door, I'm not sure what I would have done had my unpracticed lock picking actually worked; I'm not sure I would have wanted to open the door and see what lived on the other side of it, if anything indeed lived there at all.

It would have been an excellent hiding place, though, if I had managed to get it open, and if I had plucked up the courage to step inside its shuttered recesses. My sister never would have thought to come looking for me up there—and neither would my mother, for that matter, had she any inclination to put down her drink and come find me at all. I could have lived up there for years without them knowing, while they lived below and wondered whatever had happened to poor missing Samantha, and why food kept mysteriously disappearing from the kitchen, and why they could occasionally hear the odd flush of a toilet, although perhaps it was only a memory of the past.

So of course Don would never think to come find us all the way up here at the end of the narrow hall. After all, he thinks this door is locked.

As soon as the key is in my hand, I freeze up.

It is a terrible idea. All the awful things that have happened there—our father's suicide, Jonah's captivity—how can anything good possibly come of the place? All the evil that lives there, that has leaked out and infected the house . . .

But where else can we go where Donovan will not be able to get to us? It is the one room he cannot get into, the one place that will shield us from him.

Besides, I might have fixed it when I smashed the mirrors. I cling to the thought that I might have broken the connection to the evil that has plagued this house ever since Mad Catherine's workers cracked a hole in the world. If I did, then maybe it is just a room now. Maybe it will be okay.

* * *

Getting Elizabeth up the stairs proves an arduous task. We have to stop every few steps so that she can lean on one of us and catch her breath or grit her teeth against a contraction that elicits a low animal sound from the back of her throat. When I ask her if she is ready to move on again, she snarls at me to be patient.

As I fit the key in the lock, Elizabeth doesn't even ask me how I came upon it, she is so focused on keeping herself together. The door opens with a primordial creak and shows us the way into the darkness.

My mother looks on without stepping inside, her face pinched and pale. "I'm not sure about this, Samantha." Her eyes find me. She does not want to say aloud what we both know about this room, not in front of Elizabeth.

"Do you know anywhere else where Don won't be able to get to us?"

When after a moment she does not respond, it becomes clear that she has no better suggestion; and it becomes clear, too, that she hasn't set foot in this room since she spent all those hours watching my father kill himself. That image must be pasted onto the back of her eyelids now, must float ethereally before her when she looks in here, seared onto the scene like an image burned into the screen of an old television after it's been frozen too long. I give her a little nudge.

"It will be okay."

I can still hear him shouting for us, his voice echoing distantly.

Elizabeth groans, and we help her into the room, where the shadows entangle us in their musty, suffocating embrace.

We wait in the darkness as my mother goes to find the candles she hid away in her reading room after the last time the power went out. Were I to pull open the moth-eaten curtains, outside we would find only the encroaching night and the clouds too thick to let in a breath of the moon; and when my mother returns, she places the candles all around the room, dozens of them.

The room is as I remember it: wallpaper peeling like rotten flesh from the walls; undefined grime covering the blackened, creaking floor; the gross, stained mattress, the sight of which makes my heart rise into my throat; the beams of the unfinished ceiling where the creaking of a distant rope echoes dimly from the past; the rusted chains I see peeking out from under the bed, chains that must have held Jonah here; and all about that strange unreality, as if what I am seeing now isn't really what is here at all, but only what the room has stitched over itself, like a kind of mask, to show us. The candle-light bends strangely over the room's ancient cobwebbed fixtures, falling over a reality that is shaped quite differently than the one we inhabit.

My heart plummets when I see a tall oval mirror standing resolutely at the back of the room. It isn't quite broken enough for my liking, although it bears a spider web of cracks on its splintered face. But I wonder—then how did this one break? I didn't smash this one to pieces with the rest. Someone else did.

There isn't any time to wonder about it now.

Throwing a clean sheet over the bed to hide the hideous mattress, my mother helps Elizabeth find a comfortable position, takes her hand, and mimics her breathing. "Sam, get a heating pad and fill some bottles with fresh water."

Gratefully I creep out of the room, the sounds of Elizabeth's moans chasing me out, down the stairs. I pad about on deft, silent feet, trying not to make a sound, and when I fly down the stairs, I leap catlike over the steps I know would complain. I feel like a ghost, able to leap and hurry from place to place with utter silence. On the dining room floor, I find a discarded cork, and I put it in my pocket for good luck. It is still faintly purple with wine, and I think this will have to do. I haven't any time to find a better charm. It soaks up the stain like it will hopefully soak up other invisible toxins floating on the air.

I will have to go into the kitchen to fill the bottles, but a terrible foreboding has filled me. All is quiet now. Has Don given up shouting for us? I feel an urgent need to make sure my knots are still secure, that they aren't starting to come loose, that Don isn't sawing away at the last fraying threads of rope. I step quietly up to the doorway and peer inside.

The chair is empty. The ropes are unwound snakes on the floor.

I back away from the doorway, panic rising in my throat, wondering where he has gone. He could be anywhere in the house. I could turn around and find him just behind me; he might be waiting on the stairs; he might be just behind a door, ready to reach out and grab me as I pass.

Quickly as I can, I find some bottles to fill from the tap and fly like a bird back up the stairs, oddly grateful now for the sanctuary of the locked room. The door clicks behind me, and in the flickering candlelight, Elizabeth screams.

* * *

It goes on for hours.

My mother keeps track of dilation while I allow Elizabeth to clutch my hand, squeezing it so tightly when the contractions come on hard and fast and strong that I fear she might crack my bones in her fist. Her face shines with sweat in the candles' glow, and her hair is plastered to her face.

"Get him out, get him out," she sobs when the pain comes on.

I have never seen her like this before. She is like a force of nature, like a storm, and all the energy in the room is concentrated around her; she is a great planet so dense that it bends space-time around it; her womb is a locked room, but it is about to unlock.

"Water," she gasps, so I pour small sips of water into her mouth until she pushes me away agitatedly. "Why is it so *hot*?"

"Liz, it's freezing in here."

With the room closed up and so far from the heating source in the house, it feels dangerously cold in here, although Liz's pain seems to radiate and heat the air around her. The touch of her skin is hot as an infection.

Frost clouds the window, out which I have looked periodically to watch the drifts of snow below, to look away from the room that makes me dizzy when I try to focus my eyes; the snow has mostly stopped falling by now, just light flurries whizzing to and fro, but too late, indeed, for us to dig our way out through the front door, free the car, and get to the hospital.

"Tell me about him," she hisses, talking to distract herself.

I hesitate. Did she believe me about him after all? Has she believed me this whole time, only pretending not to—clinging to normalcy? "What do you want me to say?"

"Say anything," she snaps, her voice a fury of clenched pain. "For god's sake."

I think. "He likes animals."

Her fury turns into a sob. "This isn't how I wanted it to be."

"I know, honey," says my mother, petting Elizabeth's untamed hair away from her slick face. "But pretty soon you'll get to hold your baby boy in your arms and none of this will matter."

She glances up at me, and I know she is thinking what I am thinking: what we know about that baby boy and the child he will become. Perhaps it is the habit the room has of shifting minutely around us, but I feel nauseated of a sudden, and I want Elizabeth to clench her legs together and not let him out into the world at all.

Somewhere above us is the maddening creak of a heavy weight swinging on a rope.

I do not know how many hours it has been; the candles have melted almost all the way down to their bases, dripping wax into puddles and expelling thin smoke that obfuscates the room, which smells of burning, rancid sweat, dust, and the faint pervasive musk of the swamp, so strong you could just about taste its bitterness.

Elizabeth's low, familiar birthing groan turns into a throaty wail, and my mother checks below the sheet she has thrown over my sister's legs and looks at me. "It's time."

Elizabeth's scream echoes around the room, and I imagine the waves of it ringing out into the swamp, filling the swamp with the terrible sound of her labor—but it isn't the swamp we have to worry about hearing.

All this time I have imagined Don somewhere below, pacing from room to room in search of his wife, finding, perhaps, strange ghosts who are not there, and strange memories that are not his. But now heavy footsteps pound their way up the stairs and creak down our long narrow hallway; he has heard, and he has found us.

"Liz!" he shouts through the door, which rattles and shakes as he works the knob, but remains mercifully locked. I never thought I would be so relieved to be locked in this dark, festering place. "*Open this door!*"

My mother kneels on the floor at the end of the bed, instructing Elizabeth to breathe, propping her up with her knees bent. "Push," she commands, her voice low and calm against the sounds of pounding as Donovan beats his fists to be let in.

Elizabeth makes a hideous sound through her clenched teeth, her face turning red, and then collapses on her elbows, panting. "I can't. I can't."

"Yes, you can. You're doing great, honey," says my mother, and I do not know how she can sound so calm with Donovan beating his way in and Elizabeth screaming and the baby coming—it's too much even for me as I crouch beside my sister, letting her hold my hand but unable to do much more than that, staring wide-eyed and frozen as the room seems to close in around us, then stretch as if into a yawning abyss. The air crackles with static. I want to scratch my skin off. I want to get out of here. Were I a spider, I imagine I might crawl up the walls on my eight spindly legs and spin myself a web to watch and wait. The room blurs at the edges, like its veneer is wearing thin.

In the recesses of the room, which seems larger than it did only moments ago, stands the cracked mirror. I try not to look at it, but I cannot help it; the surface is odd, reflecting nothing.

"Let me in!" Don shouts from the other side of the door, which bangs and rattles like a thing alive. "Let me in!"

Elizabeth gives another push, throws back her head, and screams—this time because she sees the man hanging from the ceiling.

"Don't look up," Agnes tells her softly. "Don't look up." She continues murmuring odd nonsense, telling us that the baby has started to crown. I remind Elizabeth to breathe, but I have to look away, feeling dizzy. I remind myself to breathe. I don't look up at the dead man swinging from the rope. I don't want to see my father hanging above us. It's too horrible to contemplate.

Elizabeth's cries mingle with the echo of Jonah's and Meriday's—cries to escape, to be let out, a rising crescendo of wails.

"Don't look."

But it's not my mother's voice this time—it is Jonah in chains, on the floor a few feet from the bed, his pupils blown wide as black holes. "Don't look at it. It's where she came through. You look, and you'll see. You don't want to see." He is wasted, his clothes worn to rags. He has been here a long time. "That's where death is. The death of time. Ain't no time in here."

He's told Meriday not to look, but I am not Meriday. I look behind him, into the depths of the room, at the mirror. And I know, with dreadful certainty, that this is where he does not want me to look.

But the more I look, the stranger the mirror appears. I try to focus my eyes on it, and it blurs and gapes open like a wound.

The crack has split and widened. It is a darker shadow than the dark. It is like charcoal, like a hole burned into the molecules of the air, like a long black slit slowly dilating, opening up. A primal, empty, sucking dark.

"What is that?" I murmur, but no one else is paying attention—Elizabeth pushes and my mother nods and offers small inane encouragements, both of them trying to ignore the bang of the door as Donovan pounds at it—and I look back again, unable to draw myself from it. Darkness there, unlike any darkness I have ever seen, or perhaps like a darkness I saw, once, long ago.

As the darkness opens up, deep inside I can almost make out two small pinpricks of light, a reflection of our candles, and the darkness gives birth to itself, and its edges peel like a flame burning a hole through a piece of paper as it spreads beyond the mirror's frame.

I ought to smash it before it spreads any further, but I cannot move. Elizabeth is clutching my hand too tightly.

"*Push!*"

Elizabeth's face is red, her muscles taut. She strains her whole body to get him out.

"Open this door, dammit!" Don shouts, rattling the doorknob.

I want to get out of here.

If I wander to the far reaches of the room, I think I may not find my way back. I think I could just keep going and going eternally into that everlasting dark, finding myself in an increasingly strange and unfamiliar world, a place that is somehow both contained within the house and also much larger, much vaster, and much older than the house. And whichever new direction I turned in, I would see floating before me, mysterious as death, that gently smoldering hole. All around, the room is like outer space, with our candles like stars shining in the distance I left behind. And somewhere, here, in the dark, live primordial entities from before the birth of the universe, and far-future enigmas I could never hope to understand. I go around and around, and the geometry makes no sense—I may wander here for weeks. The darkness inhabits the mind, and time becomes illusion. But always, always, that black hole following me, as if it exists in all places at once, even though that cannot be.

But so it is, and as I look around, the light begins to bend strangely, the way the distant light of stars and galaxies bends around objects with high gravitational fields, light bending around a black hole and in doing so revealing its shape but also unnaturally curving the galaxies that lie behind it, warping them into twisted shapes so that the way they look is nothing like the way they *are*. I see the light bending in the room around that singularity of the endless hole—and everything, everything is bending outward from this central point, this moment that has fractured the world and sent its ripples outward like a stone dropping into a pond, distending the room and all that lies beyond it, the edge of the earth, the curve of a pregnant belly.

Oh, I have gone mad, haven't I?

When the room snaps back and I wake up from my weeks-long reverie, Elizabeth is saying that something is wrong, while Agnes reassures her and tells her to keep pushing. Liz says she can't, she can't, and the door rattles madly on its hinges with sharp, deafening bangs like some great beast beating its fists.

Liz pulls my hand closer to her. "No, no, something is wrong," she pants, her eyes beseeching me to go check, to make sure our mother is not lying to us. I nod, gently pull my hand free, and go to the end of the bed to peer beneath the white sheet.

The child's bloody head has emerged, but I see a soft wormlike cord wrapped around its neck twice, like a noose—I gasp involuntarily, and Liz begs me to tell her what is wrong.

For a moment, I consider not saying a word. It would be fitting, perhaps, for the child to strangle itself upon exiting the womb, in which case the future the house showed me could not come to pass. Then I start to say, "The umbilical cord—"

My mother hisses at me as she reaches to gently slide the cord up over the infant's head. "See? No big deal," she says. "Happens all the time."

And then the rest of the baby slides out, crying as he waves his tiny fists, and my mother wraps him in a towel and hands him to an exhausted, delirious Elizabeth. Agnes bends down to kiss her daughter on her sweat-slicked forehead and murmurs, "You did it."

For a moment, Don's banging and yelling fades into the distance as we all look at what Elizabeth has birthed into the world.

Elizabeth gives something like a cross between a laugh and a sob as she brings the baby's face up to hers, gazing upon it with wonder.

"Hello, Julian," she whispers, staring at him as if she cannot believe he is real, and in this moment, something in my own heart breaks.

How can this small helpless child become a monster? It is unthinkable. This tiny creature does not know evil—knows only love and comfort and perhaps that terrifying moment when he was expelled from the womb. But how could he ever be what the house has told me he must be? How could I ever think to harm him—my nephew, only minutes old, not having yet opened his eyes to the world?

My mother discreetly cuts and ties the traitorous umbilical cord that tried to strangle him, and for a moment, in the faint glow of the candles imparting their soft warmth to the chill, dark room, its ghosts having vanished for the moment, it seems to me that everything will be all right, that there is nothing to worry about after all.

Then, its lock giving way under repeated assault, the door finally bangs open and swings away from Donovan Hill, who steps into the room and says, “Give me my son.”

19

"I've been looking all over this damned place for you," says Donovan, his eyes locked on Elizabeth still clutching the small bundle to herself, a bundle that has started to cry, shrieking into the void.

The stitched-up wound on Don's forehead looks crusty and black, stark against the pallor of his haggard face. His eyes dart from me to my mother to Elizabeth, haunted eyes.

"She doesn't want you here," says my mother. "Please leave."

He takes a step toward her, staring her down with disgust. "Not without my son."

"I don't think Julian is safe with you," Elizabeth admits, holding the child close. He is beginning to quiet down, calming in his mother's arms. "We can talk about this later, but for now, please—"

"Not safe with *me*?" Donovan laughs cruelly. "You hit me over the head with a wine bottle and tied me to a fucking chair!"

Elizabeth looks as if she wants to respond, but instead she frowns and reaches down between her legs. Blood has begun to soak through the sheet over her lap, and when my mother gently lifts it up, we see a larger spreading stain on the bed.

"It's okay," says Agnes. "We just need to stop the bleeding."

"Give him to me." Don reaches for the baby, but Elizabeth yanks the bundle away from his grasping arms, telling him no. He manages to get his hands on the towel and tries to wrest the child from her, and they struggle momentarily for possession of Julian; Don bumps into the table near the bed, overturning several candles, which sputter and roll and eventually come to rest on the floor, where they burn out.

My mother hurries up behind Don and tries to pull him off of Elizabeth, but he slaps her away like a fly; she goes sprawling on the floor with a hand on her shocked face. I slide over to her on my knees to help her up, but I realize, too late, that opting to help my mother regain her feet means I have given Donovan time to pry the baby from Elizabeth's fingers while she yells at him to give Julian back, not to touch him.

"Stop, stop it!" Agnes shouts at them both as she wads up a spare towel to staunch the flow of blood, looking worried. Though Elizabeth is heated and still shouting at Don, I can feel in my bones that she is bleeding too much; her skin is pale, hollow, and I can feel too her energy waning, the way, I suspect, my mother can feel the energy of a place. Perhaps I have inherited her peculiar sensitivity, passed down the line of Wakefields living in such an acutely sensitive place.

Don steps away from them both, leaving Elizabeth sobbing quietly as she falls back onto her limp pillow, utterly spent. He backs away from the bed and his bleeding wife, and when he turns around, he sees what I have seen, what Jonah told me not to look at.

"What is that?" he murmurs.

I look, and I see what he sees: the back of his head in the mirror, as if it's forgotten how to reflect properly. But no—it isn't the back of Don's head. It is my father, standing in front of the mirror.

He turns, looks back at the room, a terrible knowing in his eyes. He shakes his head. I want to reach out for him, but I know if I did my hand would pass through empty air.

"Who the hell are you?" says Don, though the bravado has gone from his voice; he doesn't seem to know what to make of this man, and I suspect he has begun to realize that the people he may see in this house are not always there. He hesitates where he stands. The baby complains in his arms, calling out, perhaps, to its mother with those high-pitched pitiful shrieks, but he ignores it.

Behind me, my mother is distracted by cleaning Elizabeth, and I think she must not see her husband here. I almost tell her to look. But then my father rears back his fist and punches the mirror, the cracks erupting from the impact. He pulls his knuckles away, bloody.

"Hey," Don snaps. "I said who the hell are you?"

Distantly, I hear my mother murmur, "This isn't right," followed by quiet reassurances, as if to make up for her small slip—but it isn't right, none of this is right, and I don't think there is anything I can do to make it right.

Don steps toward the man before him.

"He can't hear you."

He hesitates, turns to me. "What?"

"He's deaf."

My father steps away from the mirror and nods, as if he's done it, as if he has fixed everything.

But he hasn't. He's only opened it up.

The cracked mirror melts into that dark hole again, reaching out into this world.

"The Zero," I murmur, recalling my father's name for it.

He reopened it, just like Mad Catherine's workers, who maybe weren't even the first ones to open it back then.

Don doesn't seem to understand what he is seeing. Holding Julian in one arm, he reaches out his free hand toward the surface of the mirror, the Zero, as if to test it with his fingers, and the closer he gets the more he becomes distorted from my perspective, moving slowly, liquidly, his very skin warbling, Julian's cries taking on an eerie note like sound warped by the Doppler effect, and I wonder, if they do step through, where will they come out on the other side? Donovan is so enraptured that he is paying no attention to the child in his arms.

In one quick movement, I snatch the baby from him and run.

* * *

This house is a labyrinth.

On the third floor, after I turn the corner of the crooked hallway, I duck briefly into the room that was once my hiding place—the room used for storage, filled with unmatched furniture and strange old things like dressmaker dummies, a full-length mirror (broken now), an antique wardrobe, sofas and chairs covered with dusty white sheets, and the out-of-tune piano. I look around frantically for a place to hide—inside the wardrobe? No, the door is rusted shut. Beneath one of the sheets? No, I could not stand there, still, indefinitely, hoping not to be found. After a moment, when I hear his voice call out from down the hallway, knowing he is in pursuit, I decide to leave this forgotten place and flee down the stairs instead, to the second level, which is where I lose my bearings.

The twists and turns I think will take me to the east side of the mansion instead curve back in on themselves and deposit me in a place that does not look familiar at all. One moment I am in the reading room, where a ghost of my young mother is holding a séance, surrounded by cold candles that do not flicker; and I am in the Rose Room, where a shape lies beneath a white shroud on the bed, a shape I can only hope will not rise up and prove itself to be something more than the long-forgotten form of Frances Wakefield; and then, inexplicably, as I back away into the hall, I find myself on the first level of the house.

Perhaps I am wrong, I think as I hurry down the hallway, clutching a softly cooing Julian to my breast the way I imagine a mother might clutch her child, but the farther I go, the more sure I am that this is one of the hallways on the main level—and, indeed, when I come to the four-way intersection of identical halls, I know this to be true. Yet I did not descend any stairs; or did I, automatically, the way one sometimes forgets the act of brushing one's teeth, even though one tastes the echo of mint and knows it has been done?

Each way down the four-way cross, the dark halls shoot off into an abyss. The old wood of the floor creaks and groans where I step, and the dark-paneled walls, briefly dotted with dormant cobwebbed sconces, I see more with my memory's eye than with my actual eyes, for the dark here is near absolute without windows to guide me, without electricity lighting the sconces. Which way shall I turn? I hear Donovan's footsteps on the ceiling above as he rummages through the second floor looking for me. I must act before he comes down—but suddenly I am paralyzed with choice.

The hallway to the north will lead me back to the front of the house, to the foyer and the main staircase; to the east lies the billiards room, and the dining room, and the kitchen; west, I will find the den, the parlor, the sitting room; and the hall that takes me south will lead me to the library, the basement, and the back of the house.

The only problem is that I cannot tell which way is which. My heart thudding in my throat, I convince myself it is only the dark that is confusing me—anyone would get lost at this intersection, even one who has lived here all her life, who has found her way in the dark countless times before through touch and memory and spatial intuition, perhaps by feeling the magnetic field of the earth, like a bird.

Wrapped up tight, Julian nevertheless manages to wriggle free his tiny arms as if to punctuate the cries that build from his throat. I try to shush him as I tuck his arms back in, but he cries anyway, to spite me. Then I wonder if I should leave his arms free, his fists flailing, and I realize how very little I am prepared to care for an infant, how little I know about this whole mystery of life. The weight of it is abrupt and appalling.

"Sam!" Donovan's voice echoes down to me. "What are you doing? Where are you?"

Perhaps I ought to give him up to his father. I am not the child's parent; Julian does not belong to me. And why not give him up to the future, at that? It isn't my responsibility to stop the future in its tracks. I can give him up, yes—I can leave this place—I can let whatever happens to him happen.

But he is not yet the child who smashed the frogs and cut Constance Wakefield down. He is a small infant in my arms, fragile with precious life. There is a magic here beyond what I thought I knew, beyond my mother's tarot cards, beyond even the house's sad talent for recalling not life but merely echoes of it. I bounce him gently in my arms, which calms him some.

Down the hall I pass a ghastly vision—the hulking shadow of Donovan, brooding and pacing.

My heart is so far up my throat I think I may vomit, but when he turns my way to pace back in the other direction, his hate-filled eyes pass blankly over me and Julian, gazing past us, and I know this is the Donovan of several hours before, pacing as he wracks his brain wondering where we have gone, losing himself, yes, losing himself utterly in the house. I sidle past as he stalks farther down the hall.

I think I have gone east, to the billiards room, but I am wrong again; I've turned unwittingly north, to the foyer and the base of the main staircase and the front door. Above I hear Don moving toward the stairs, and I shush Julian, whose small mewling sounds may yet give us away as I crouch in the dark. Does he know we are down here?

He calls out, his voice ringing through the foyer. "Stop this, Sam. Give me my son!"

An instinctual drive to escape impels me to dash for the front door and yank it open toward cold freedom—only to be met, of course, with those mounds of snow closing us in, and the bitter darkness beyond. I cannot go out there.

Don's footsteps pound down the staircase behind me, and I turn again to run blindly down another hall, east or west it hardly matters. My running has begun to jostle Julian enough that his wails echo behind me like a sonic trail, calling Donovan to us even as I run away.

I am in the parlor; I am in the drawing room; I am floating along the hidden staircases, believing myself to be ascending, but realizing instead that I am going down; I am stealing through the cobbled back corridor that serves no purpose but to provide a secret byway around the house; I am at the base of the rickety spiral staircase that leads up to the tower room at the top of the turret, where I once looked out as a girl, seeing all the way across the tops of the trees in the swamp for miles; I am turning, turning, and all the while Mad Catherine changes the house around me as I go, as the shadows reach out to snatch Julian from my arms.

Along the way, I pass more visions—there is August, cold and terrible, rearing up to beat Meriday. There is no time to dive around them, so I pass directly through, a strange chill dousing my bones, the sensation of passing through a memory that isn't mine.

In the library, I slow, feeling momentarily safe amid the towering shelves of books, which I imagine will protect me like a magic shield.

If I do not make a sound, if Julian remains quiet, Don will not think to look in here. The clouds must have parted, as a faint white glow comes in the window, moonlight bouncing off snow. It lends a silvery quality to the bookshelves. Somewhere in here is an armchair; I will find it, I will sit, and I will think of what to do.

I am creeping through the library delicately as I can, bouncing Julian in my arms to keep him calm, when drifting through the darkness comes a huffing sound, breathy laughter puffing through someone's nose.

I am not alone.

The skin of my neck crawls with morbid recognition, but I resist, I resist, until I come around the side of a bookshelf and see the figure sitting in the corner of the room. It is her, the old woman, and she is laughing to herself, though she cannot open her mouth for her lips are glued shut, and she cannot open her eyes for her lids are glued shut, and over those lids someone has drawn in black marker the Xs that denote a cartoon's death. She cannot see; she cannot talk. She can only sit in her wheelchair and laugh to herself, a horrible knowing laugh I recognize again, but I tell myself that recognition is only because I have seen this ghost before, I have seen her about the house ever since I was a child. She is just as real as Julian.

She cannot even push herself to a different spot in the room, for her fingers are broken, crooked and bent, just as I remember them. She is so familiar.

"Who are you?" I whisper, knowing she cannot answer and thinking, *no, why did I ask that, I do not want to know.*

The sight of her untethers my nerves, and I back away from her slowly as the clouds roll over the moon and cast her in shadow.

When I try to go up the hidden staircase from the library, I find myself somehow emerging back onto the main level of the house, in a room that looks unfamiliar to me. Can it be there are rooms in this house that I do not know, that I have never set foot in? When I exit the room, I leave behind me a man drowning in a bucket of white paint, struggling against the invisible force holding him down, paint splashing out onto the floor around him.

In the parlor, I finally have to stop, sinking to the floor with a stitch in my side and trying to calm an increasingly agitated Julian. The window reveals again the faint glimmering of starlight; at last the snow has stopped, and the clouds have shuffled off. Across from me, glinting dully in the moonglow, stands a broken mirror with jagged shards still clinging to the frame, reflecting bits and pieces of us. I pry free a dagger of glass, jostling Julian enough to elicit a complaint, just as the approaching footsteps slow and stop at the parlor's entrance.

Crouching low to the floor, I swing upward as Donovan comes through the doorway, but he easily sidesteps the blow as if he knew exactly what I was going to do. The glass slices impotently through the air, its edges biting into my palm.

"What are you trying to do, Sam?" Donovan asks.

"Stay back," I tell him, holding up the shard in one hand while holding Julian precariously to my chest with the other, casting about for an escape route. Isn't there a small trapdoor somewhere in here that should take me into the hidden hallway and back out to the drawing room? But I search the walls, finding nothing.

"You're out of your damned mind. Now give me my son."

I back away from him, cornered; then, knocking aside the tall mirror so that it falls with a crash, momentarily separating us, I find the opening there, a low dark doorway, and I duck inside.

I feel my way through the blind dark and stumble instead into the dining room, which is not where I thought I would be, which has never held an entrance into the hidden hallway, and I am so shocked and lost that my eyes prickle with tears.

Then Donovan is there, grabbing me from behind, his hands yanking roughly at my clothes, twisting me around to face him—and as I do, I slice the air with the shard. This time it slashes his face, and he spins around, catching himself, while I gape, frozen. The arm holding Julian is growing tired as he seems to get heavier and heavier, and I have to drop the shard in order to hold him with both arms. A searing, bloody line marks my palm.

Donovan straightens and snarls at me, blood on his teeth. The glass sliced through his nose and lips, and his forehead wound has split open again and weeps down his face.

"You going to finish the job this time?" he asks, spitting blood on the floor. "Didn't manage to take me down last time, so you're trying again? You fucking women. You think everything belongs to you."

I back away from him. "Don, stop. You're out of control."

"I am the only one here *in* control!" he bursts out.

"What if I told you that you're going to turn your son into a killer?" At this, Don freezes, frowning at me. Julian mewls against my neck, his breath warm. "The way you're behaving—the anger, the violence. Don't you think it will rub off on him?"

Dark bruises have begun to bloom across Don's glowering face, as if the shadows are reaching out to claim him. "Bullshit," he says, his voice pitched low. He kicks the shard of glass, which shrieks across the floor away from us. Then he pulls from the waistband of his pants the crowbar. Seeing the surprise in my eyes, he says, "I thought I'd hang on to this." Turning it over, feeling it in his hand, he gives me a leisurely, knowing grin. "It's what you used to break the mirrors, isn't it? To try to frame me?"

"Don't you care what happens to Julian?" I ask, desperate to make him see reason, my eyes never leaving the crowbar in his hand.

"That's *all* I care about," he says. "So much that I am going to take my son now, and I am going to get him out of this place and away from you lunatics."

He is wrong, I am convinced. What could possibly turn this innocent child into a killer but the violent man standing before me, willing to beat up his wife just to get at his heir? It has to be him. It isn't just that Wakefields are cursed by evil. It can't be. Yes, at this point there is no doubt in my mind that the only way to save Julian is to keep him from his father.

When he tries to take Julian from me, I kick his knee, and he grunts, grabbing me by the hair as he catches his balance. In doing so, he yanks my head down painfully and wrenches my neck to the side. Only barely do I manage to hold on to Julian, to twist out of Don's way, to dash out of the room, where I find myself at the doorway to the basement.

I hear him behind me, so I descend the creaking staircase. Entering the basement is like wading into an icy lake, wherein the farther down I go, the heavier the shadows and the more frigid the air, until I imagine that if I were able to see at all past the blanket of night over my eyes, I might see my breath in a white cloud.

Down here, enveloped in the dark, we are safe. We must be safe.

Feeling my way to the far wall, I crouch down on the floor and bend over Julian, wanting to speak soft, gentle words to comfort him but at the same time keeping as quiet as I can. He makes small noises as I rock him, and I wrap the towel more tightly around his prone form. I tell myself again that we are safe here. There is a painful crick in my neck, like the ache that sits on your shoulders from whiplash—the feeling I had when I was fifteen, driving on my permit, and someone rear-ended me, knocking my car into the one in front. After that my neck complained for a week, haunted by phantom pain.

Balancing Julian on my knees, I try to rub out the pinch in my neck, but it's no good—and what's more, I can feel a presence standing at the top of the staircase now, a shadow passing through the blind dark. The stairs creak with careful, heavy footfalls.

If I stay here, quiet, I don't think he will find me.

But Julian has other designs.

His soft cries louden into unhappy wails, and now there is no pretending we aren't down here. I try to shush him, but his cries echo around the basement, and Donovan's footsteps come faster now, pounding through the dark.

"Where are you?" he calls out.

Still crouching, I sidle along the edge of the wall, feeling the fine, tingling tendrils of spider webs on the back of my neck, trying to visualize where I am. I reach up above me, feeling along the wall until I find a shelf. There are no candles on it, my mother having taken them all to her reading room, and now the locked room, of course, not that a candle would do me any good without a match, but—there!—my hand falls on the familiar shape of a flashlight, which rolls away at my touch, clattering to the concrete floor somewhere to my left.

"I know you're down here." Donovan's voice comes hauntingly through the dark. "I can hear you."

And I can hear him, moving around, his arms likely outstretched, knocking into shelving and crates, his hands fumbling around for me, following in the direction of Julian's cries.

I cannot feel around for the flashlight while holding the child, so, bundling the towel carefully under his head, I lay him on the floor, which seems to calm him some; his cries become soft coos, quieting in the dark, and I mentally thank him for making it harder for Donovan to find us.

Now I crawl across the floor, seeking the light, and for long, terrible minutes it seems a fruitless endeavor. I am lost, abandoned. Yet as soon as I find it and the flashlight is in my hand, and I rise to my feet, grateful to be off the cold floor that still reeks faintly of water rot, two realizations come to me at once.

The first is that, with Julian now quieted, I no longer know where he is. I turn around in the dark, lose my bearings.

The second is that if I switch on this flashlight, Donovan will see exactly where I am.

For a moment I stand, paralyzed by indecision, the flashlight clutched to my chest the way I was holding Julian tightly to me only moments ago.

"This is ridiculous, Sam," Donovan's voice hisses through the dark. His footsteps move slowly around the other side of the room and then stop. A crash of forgotten objects spilling to the floor makes me flinch, the sound of metal against the old shelving unit there, and I imagine him swinging the crowbar blindly. When next his footfalls come to me, they are crunching over the glass of broken lightbulbs or shattered china.

Don gives an aggravated growl, a throat-tearing sound of frustration. "Don't make me do this, Sam."

"Is that what you said to Liz before you hit her?" I cannot help but verbalize, and I can almost feel him turning toward the sound of my voice, ready to pound across the basement and strike, and I think that now, if ever, is my chance; I switch on the flashlight and quickly scan the room, finding his form coming toward me, and I shine the light directly into his face. He stops, lifts his hand to shield his eyes, and turns away, disoriented, giving me enough time to find Julian, pick him up, and look toward my only escape.

The staircase back up to the sanctuary of the house is across the room. I would have to get around Donovan to go that way.

But there are other doorways here.

I choose one.

20

The tunnels beneath Wakefield Manor, I have heard, were once used by escaped slaves. Among the sorts of restitution the family sought to offer the world in the wake of Mad Catherine's brutal conviction, they turned to their own spiritual atonement. It became clear that the townsfolk would remain unforgiving, and perhaps this is why they turned their backs on the law and on social propriety by delivering slaves to freedom. As you have discovered, of course, their story is much less interesting than the story of those who may have once traversed these very tunnels before they became flooded and impassable. This land does not welcome underground structures. One may as well dig anthills at the beach during low tide.

I have always believed the tunnels to be, if not merely dangerous, then utterly caved in or flooded through. In all my years of living here, I have never set foot down one of them; they are the only place in all the house, or under it rather, where I have not dared to tread, and they have held less fascination for me than the locked room, for there is nothing fascinating so much as dreadful about an uncharted, collapsing catacomb wending through the earth. I've no idea where they go, how far they extend, where they come out—or if they do come out at all.

The earthen floor is wet and sludgy, shocking my feet with bitter cold, and I cannot tell, by the wild searching eye of my flashlight, how these rocky walls have held up for so long against the erosion of the ages and the deluges of the swamp. The way is narrow, closing in around me like the throat of a great beast.

Behind me, I hear the splashing footfalls of Donovan's pursuit, following the flailing white beam of my light. The farther we retreat from the basement, the colder it becomes and the more I begin to feel trapped—the more I begin to worry at where this tunnel is leading me, drawing me down its terrible length.

As I race through the dark, the air around me seems to vibrate with voices, the whispering voices of whoever once passed through here. *We should turn back*, a voice in some distant accent whispers, very close to my ear. I shake my head as if to frighten off a fly buzzing too near me. *We have to trust*, comes another whisper, amid the torrent of unintelligible ones. This is followed by humming. Did they make it? I wonder. Or did they die down here?

Now spindly roots hang down from the low ceiling, brushing me as I skirt past them, and now the icy water at my feet has risen above my ankles, slowing my pace but also slowing Donovan somewhere down the tunnel behind me. I am lithe, quick-footed; I am a panther bounding for freedom; I could have rolled out of the way and run off into the night if only my mugger hadn't been holding a gun to my head; I bring my knees high, my feet darting in and out of the water like leaping fish.

Part of the ceiling ahead is caved in, blocking the way, but there is a narrow gap. I'll have to crawl through the half-frozen water on my elbows, flashlight clenched between my teeth, Julian held up so that he doesn't get wet, mud slicking up over my knees and that shock of pestilential cold, a cold to reach out for your heart and ensnare it in the grip of death.

I make it to the other side and pause, adjusting my grip on the baby, knowing I've gained myself a few moments, or perhaps I've thwarted him altogether if he doesn't fit through that small opening.

As I push on, I hear him grunting and heaving behind me, and I turn as the tunnel curves before I can tell if he's made it through.

And I think to myself, if the exit is caved in or a dead end, I am doomed.

* * *

Upstairs and perhaps a mile away by now, Elizabeth lies bleeding on a bed that came from nowhere, in a room that is on no blueprint, a room that gave birth to itself from the void. This is a moment I will forever regret missing. Someday I will wish I had just handed Julian off to his father and let Donovan whisk him away from us while I helped my mother care for Elizabeth. If I had, everything might have turned out differently. And, of course, I would not have lost the three toes that the cold water in the tunnels took from me—along with everything else.

* * *

The passageway snakes around and fills me with the presentiment that I have gone too far into the earth to ever resurface. Julian and I will become ghosts, wandering the eternal tunnels, lost forever in the dark.

Panic begins to set in when the water is almost up to my knees. I slosh through it; I hear Donovan call out behind me, and I know he has followed. He will always follow.

And then I come to a solid wall of earth.

My breath freezes in my throat, and I turn the flashlight all around to make sure there isn't another path going in some new direction, but the walls are solid and the only branch of this tunnel is the one I took to get here, and from down its long black length, even the flashlight's glow vanishing in the dark, come the wet sounds of Donovan getting closer.

In my despair I cannot even sink to my knees or give my tired legs a rest, for the water is too high and the idea of sitting down in that icy stagnant pool is like death. Leaning back against the rocky wall at the end of the tunnel, I look up, shining my flashlight toward the ceiling—and there I see a square of thatched wood.

The ceiling is low; I can reach it if I stretch up toward it. But I have no free hand, so I bang the flashlight against the wood, and it rattles, pushing slightly upward before crashing back down. Holding the flashlight once again in my mouth, I reach up—but the flashlight is bigger than my jaw will comfortably allow, and it slips from my teeth with a splash, shining its white beam into the dirty water before it sputters out. The flashes of pure underground darkness send my heart into my throat.

With a cry, I push up against the trapdoor with all my strength, and the ancient rotting wood groans and gives way, most of it coming unstuck and swinging up, while other pieces, so decayed from water and age, simply crumble and fall around me.

I do not know what lies above, but I push Julian up and through and lay him on the ground beside the opening, then begin to slowly, agonizingly pull myself up after him. By now I can hear Donovan reaching the door below me, and I have just enough time to look up into the beaming moon on snow and ice-crusted trees before a hand grabs my foot from below.

Wildly, I kick back, kick again, and finally my foot connects with something and the hand lets go. Free, I pull myself up the rest of the way and roll onto my back in the snow, then slam the crumbling wooden door back into place.

I can see now that the reason it was so hard to push up the door is because there was several inches of snow lying on top of it, which was dislodged when I managed, through sheer brute force, to pry up the wood. The snow here is not as deep as the drifts around the house, perhaps because the trees have blocked it or the wind blew it away from here and out toward open lands. I breathe the cold, fresh air, unsure when my toes went painfully numb, having escaped, gratefully, from the dank earth.

But I know immediately, by the dark smell and the creeping whisper of stalwart trees, that we are in the swamp.

As soon as I hear Donovan pushing up on the trapdoor from underneath, I take off along the frozen bank of the creek, clutching Julian as he whines in the cold and feeling my way around the trees that loom up seemingly out of nowhere. My feet slip on the layer of icy snow, my toes numb all through and that numbness creeping across the soles of my feet like an infection. Twice I pause to wrap the towel more tightly around Julian, fearful for his delicate newborn skin and the heart-chilling temperature that blows wicked, stinging wind right through the fabric of my own clothing.

Somewhere behind me, I hear Donovan call my name, his voice repeated in the trees as the swamp gives up a faint echo. *Sam!* His voice runs ragged over the vowel, and he slurs on the *s* as if his lips are already numb from cold, or aching from the blows he has taken tonight.

"Don't worry, Julian," I murmur. "I'll get us home."

Perhaps it is cruel to lie to a child, even one who cannot understand you, but if I did not lie, then I would have to admit to myself the truth—that we are lost, and that we might likely freeze to death out here in this vast deadened wild before we ever find our way back.

The cold slows me as I go, like a clock winding down, and I have to stop and sit myself against a tree to lessen some of the weight of Julian in my arms. It is a wonder that such a small creature can, when held so long without respite, become such a heavy, leaden weight. My arms and back ache faintly, along with my wrenched neck, and I wish bitterly I were not so weak. If I were strong, I could have held on to the flashlight while carrying Julian in one arm.

The trees call out to me again in their fury. *Sam!* I know I must get up and keep going, keep moving, but my bones welcome the tree at my back that blocks the worst of the wind, and I could sit here all night, I think, blanketed in snow, and allow myself to simply drift away.

But the forest around me is alive, even at the darkest and coldest hour.

A branch snaps like a striking match. The river's current dislodges floes of ice and sends them away, cracking. An owl hoots, like the sound of the wind. Bootheels crunch on snow, coming toward me, and I crouch lower over Julian, shielding him with my slight and narrow frame, trying to make us both invisible though I know Donovan's eyes must be adjusting to the dark, as mine have. And while it remains impossible to make out any details of the forest around me, I can see the rough outlines of shapes and the glimmer of the moon touching down on the half-frozen river.

"You can't run forever, Sam." Donovan's disembodied voice snakes around the trees from where his footsteps tread. "You need to give me my son. You can't have him. You hear me?"

My breath ghosts out in front of my face. I cannot stop Julian from crying, from drawing his father to us with those plaintive, frightened mewls. When I reach inside the towel, I feel tiny fingers and toes that are far too cold.

Trying to still my chattering jaw, I whisper a near-inaudible promise to my nephew: "I won't let anything happen to you. I won't let you turn out like that. I won't let him make you into that." It becomes a chant, a plea, a prayer to the magic of the swamp to protect us from violence. It comes out loose and soft as my lips begin to go numb.

The footsteps are closer now. I can run, but he will give chase. He will hear Julian. So I sit, and I wait until the footsteps are just behind the tree, hoping he will not be able to see us, hoping the swamp's strange enchantment will envelop us. The wine cork is still in my pocket, a meaningless artifact digging into my hip, absorbing nothing, useless.

It is in the next moment that my belief in magic falters.

Donovan steps around the tree and there is a small flame in his hand, setting an orange glow upon his face—a lighter. He reaches down with a frantic, scrambling motion to snatch Julian from my hands. I hold on and try to shove him away, but he resists, the flame whipping through the air and dazzling my eyes. I start to crawl on my back, around the curve of the tree trunk, kicking out at him with my numb feet and grunting with the effort. He grabs my ankle and pulls me to him across the snow; I shout, trying to twist away as he reaches for the towel-wrapped bundle.

For a moment I feel Julian slipping away from me—and with a great effort I kick again and connect with Donovan's nose, breaking it with a crunch and a spurt of blood. He reels back, dazed, clutching at his face and snarling like a wounded animal. The lighter snaps shut and falls. I pocket it, adjust my grip on Julian, and sidle to my right, down the slope of the riverbank, down to the iced-over surface that I hope is solid. *Please*, I think, *allow me passage across the ice. Please let it be frozen at least several inches, enough to hold my weight, which isn't much, really.*

With breath held, I slide carefully onto the ice. It feels firm enough here at the edge. Unable to continue crawling without the use of my arms, I rise slowly to my feet, listening for every subtle shift of the ice. Halfway across, I am convinced it will bear me safely to the other side, and I am convinced also that there is no way Donovan will follow me on this precarious journey—but I hear him sliding down the bank, shouting at me to come back.

"You're fucking crazy!" he yells, but that doesn't stop him from stepping out onto the ice himself. "You can't have him!"

I can't help it—I turn around as he gains his footing, holding out his arms to distribute his weight.

"Go back!" I shout, throat raw with the cold. "It won't hold both our weight."

He ignores me, sliding forward, and I hear the telltale crack, the sound ice cubes make when you drop them into a glass of warm water.

Trying not to panic, I ease my way toward the other side of the river, my heart jittering as the ice complains beneath my feet—but the bank is just ahead, and in moments I am there, climbing up onto solid ground on the other side.

Donovan has made it halfway across the river when there is a great rending crack.

Even in the dark, I can see the whites of his widened eyes fixed upon me with terror as the ice splinters under his feet—and then he is gone, and all that is left is a hole in the ice, gaping open like a mouth to the dark waters below.

* * *

I wait.

My heart is a cold fist. Any minute now, I think, Donovan will burst up from the water, coughing. We will have to work together to make it back, and then perhaps we can finally put all of this behind us.

But I wait, and the long minutes unspool. I cannot stop shaking, whether from the cold or from imagining what he must have experienced as the current took him away from the only opening, the only way out.

It was terrible to be chased by someone I thought would hurt me without hesitation; yet somehow it is even more terrible, now, to look at that empty black hole in the ice and know I am alone.

I am not sure how long I walk. For a time I keep moving, directionless, unaware if I am heading toward home or only drifting deeper into the swamp, using the lighter occasionally to light my way. Then for a time I sit down to rest, and as I stop moving, the cold fills me and I begin to tremble, trying not to imagine Donovan beating against the underside of the ice, swept away in the dark. For a time I bounce Julian gently up and down to warm him, holding close the lighter's tiny flame and murmuring soft meaningless words. Then I rest him against my chest to free my hands and rub my feet, but it doesn't seem to help; they are numb as two cement blocks affixed to my ankles.

After a time, I notice that Julian has stopped crying. The stillness and silence of the swamp invade me.

"Julian?" I whisper, a terrible dread gripping me. He is sleeping, I tell myself, pulling the towel back from his pale face. I put my hand to his ice-cold cheek. He is sleeping, I tell myself.

"Julian?" Gently, I shake him a bit, to see him open his eyes, to see what color his eyes are, see what they look like after all. I never saw. Then I shake him harder.

My eyelashes have crusted over with frozen tears.

I pull the towel back over his face.

Delirious, I rise to my feet, not knowing where to go, knowing only that I need to keep moving. I need to keep moving. And as I move, I see light in the distance, and I follow it, as a moth goes to a flame. And as I move, I bounce Julian up and down and offer him soft meaningless words and try to convince myself he can hear me.

As I approach the light, thinking it is fox fire, some trick of the swamp leading me farther from home, I realize it is in fact real fire—a bonfire set atop the icy ground. I push my way eagerly through the last of the trees toward it, nearly sobbing with relief as I fall to my knees before its blazing warmth. At first I close my eyes, allowing my skin to thaw, prickling painfully as it does.

Then I hear a creak, and my eyes snap open.

I did not see it at first, but the fire sits just before a little wooden shack, with a door that has just swung open to reveal a gaping pit of darkness within that the fire's light cannot reach. I recognize the shack I saw once many years ago, when I was lost in the swamp with my sister, when we fell out of our canoe and stumbled upon a structure that should not be.

Perhaps I should turn and run away from the darkness inside the shack, which makes my skin crawl as the blood rushes back in, but I cannot bring myself to leave the fire. Out from the doorway gradually manifests a tall shape. And as that shape steps forward and the shadows peel away, the fire blazes a freakish glow on the decayed form of Clementine.

21

She moves toward me on stiff, unyielding limbs, and her tattered dress drags behind her, wet, dusted with fine particles of ice or snow that glimmer refractions of the firelight.

Her bare feet draw long, smeared prints in the snow. Beneath the ragged hem of her decomposing dress, the feet are peeling, the wet dead skin festering and ballooning off in layers. I watch those feet stalk closer to the fire, which infects the walking body before me with its livid, dancing light. Her long, yellowed toenails that curve over the edges of her toes must have kept growing even in death.

Kneeling here on the other side of the fire, I find myself carefully observing her feet because I do not want to look at her face—at the gray flesh hanging loose around her eyes and peeling back from her teeth, her lips partially rotted away.

The trembling that has started in my body becomes more and more pronounced the closer she draws to the fire, and the closer she comes, the more determinedly I stare at the ground, unable to bring myself to look up at her although I can see, from the corner of my eye, her unwieldy movement, her plodding approach.

My teeth chatter together, and I think perhaps I am going into shock.

Clementine looms over me. I can smell her, that putrid stench of the swamp, like vegetation moldering in stagnant water, like necrotic flesh. It makes me gag.

Then her hands, with their long gnarled nails, are reaching down toward me—and I think she is going to grab me by the throat like she did the Cherokee chieftain, she is going to drown me in swamp water that will burst up through my mouth in a choking torrent. I try to twist away, to fight her off, but it's no use; my energy is spoiled. The wine cork in my pocket is a dull dead thing, imparting no good fortune to me, just as all my good-luck charms have failed to provide me with anything of the sort. I cannot create context for an artifact where none exists. I have resigned myself to my fate as she reaches again toward me—no, not toward me, but toward the cold lifeless bundle in my arms. A gentle tug tries to pull it from me, but I cling harder, curling my body around it, until she lets go. Everyone is trying to take him from his mother.

"You can't have him," I sputter, my breath hitching. I am angry with myself for the tears that prickle my eyes because I know that in a few minutes they will begin to crystallize. I imagine Clementine taking Julian into her shack, into the endless darkness there that will swallow them both, and then she will have a dead baby to rock in her own dead arms, waiting for whatever comes next or for the end of time.

"You can't have him," I say again. *She is taking our children*, I think wildly. She had Julian kill Constance as retribution for the Wakefields taking Meriday from her, and now she has come to claim Julian as her own.

Then I hear her voice, a low wheezing rattle: "She can save him."

She reaches down again and gently folds the edge of the towel under his chin, revealing Julian's white face, too still and pallid for me to pretend he is still alive. I cannot look at him; I cannot bear to look away.

Clementine knows him, I realize. She remembers him, from the future.

This time, when she tries to take him from me, I do not stop her. The burden lifts from my arms, which fall with exhaustion to my sides, muscles screaming from the effort of carrying a child these many hours, and it almost hurts to unbend them. How strange that it should hurt more to finally release a burden than it does to keep holding on to it.

When I look up, Clementine is walking from the fire with Julian cradled in her arms, and for a moment I think I will not be able to push off from my knees and follow her, but I do. We don't travel far—we are yet close enough to her shack that the fire's glow radiates softly onto the banks of the partially frozen river, with its chunks of ice floating along in the lazy current of the black glassy water.

But the fire behind us is not the only one here.

Floating above the river are two small orange flames, disembodied, and I cannot stop staring at them even as Clementine bends down over the river, lowering Julian to meet it, then lowering him further still, into the cold black water. Briefly she holds him there, just beneath the surface, and I can see the towel floating around him, the water gently warbling that pale innocent face.

Then she lets go.

The sodden towel weighs him down, and Julian sinks.

"No—stop!" I cry out, rushing to Clementine, clawing at her, not caring that her flesh comes off in soft moist strips under my nails, not caring about the cold, clammy feel of her corpse, needing her to reach back into that frozen void and pull Julian's body free. But it is too late. He is gone.

"Julian!" I shout, my voice ragged, as I let go of Clementine and kneel on the edge of the river, searching the dark water for a trace of him. He cannot be gone. He cannot be gone. I cannot return home without even his body to give back to Elizabeth. My heart hurts with a thousand shards of ice piercing it through, mourning not for Julian or the life he would have lived, not really, but for Elizabeth, for my sister, for what she has lost this night.

I try to reach into the water, but the cold is so profound that it shocks my fingers at once, almost like a shock of heat, the way something can be so cold that it feels hot again, confusing our nerves. I try again, but it's no use; my hand aches dreadfully when I plunge it into the water, and Julian is nowhere besides. That is how I will lose the tip of my pinkie finger.

Then, thinking he has floated farther out to the center of the river, I trace my eyes along the surface, and I remember now the story of the Swamp Witch.

For I see her there, reflected in the water—her true, unfathomable form, beset by those blazing orange eyes that are not eyes, that stare out from an impossible face, from a face that is not a face.

Mercifully, that reflected figure begins to ripple, distorting the terrors that have been burned into my own eyes, and then the ripples grow larger and more insistent still, and at the center the water bubbles up like a fountain. Somewhere below, a shape is rising to the surface.

When it breaks the surface, Julian is there, rising from the water. He seems to float there, dripping little plinks of water back to the river, but I know, when I manage to chance a fleeting glance below, that he is not really hovering there, no, not really, but that *she* is holding him as if he is her own.

It is all so terrible, I think, my nephew's corpse floating there in the arms of the witch, Clementine standing beside me, watching eagerly, and I think this is it, I cannot bear any more of this, I will leave him to these creatures and wander deeper into the swamp to die. My brain has just reached this conclusion, filling my heart with cold despair, with sick resolution, with the unthinkable, when the unthinkable has its way with me again.

Julian begins to cry.

EPILOGUE

Many years have flown by since that day, yet it feels as if no time at all has passed.

I would like to tell you this story ends with Elizabeth's joyful reunion with her son, whom she raises into a fine young man while becoming the extraordinary mother she was always destined to be. I would like to tell you this story ends with those visions of the faceless boy dissolving, replaced now by a happy, smiling child.

I would like to tell you those things, but I am afraid to do so would be to tell another lie. If that is the way you want this story to end, then I will not stop you from pretending. Sometimes pretending is all we have.

* * *

It took me another hour to find my way back home that night. By then I was nearly catatonic, but Julian was safe and warm in my arms. When I made my triumphant return at dawn, I went all through the house searching for my mother and Elizabeth, calling out to them, expecting them to be tucked away in bed or huddling before the fire.

But I found them in the very room where I had left them. My mother sat at Elizabeth's bedside, incoherently drunk, an empty bottle at her feet and tearstains on her cheeks.

Elizabeth lay, cold, pale, and still, an enormous amount of blood drying around her.

That is how my mother and I came to raise Julian.

We tried to love him; truly, we did. I thought if only I loved him enough, then I could save him. We tried to love him, even when he started killing frogs from the swamp, even when he spoke to ghosts who weren't there, even when he insisted on sleeping in the room at the end of the hall. Who knows what he saw there—whether he ever stepped through that dark hole and saw what lay on the other side of the universe. Whether he was forced to watch his mother slowly bleeding to death in his very bed, over and over.

And how could I continue to love him when he said his mother still lived in the swamp? Even when I told him she was buried at the county cemetery, when I took him to her grave, he insisted his real mother lurked in the trees, with eyes made of fire.

Eventually my mother grew too ill, mentally and physically, for me to continue taking care of her while teaching full-time and caring for Julian besides, so I settled her into a lovely retirement home in the next town over, where she rediscovered the joy of other people and was able to cast off the worst of her social anxieties. I was very happy for her, that she had finally found a place to be at ease aside from this rambling old mansion where she had lived her whole life, but nevertheless, moving her out left me here alone. With Julian.

I have tried to leave this place, you know. But whenever I am out, I find myself stepping through doors that lead right back here, to the house. It won't let me go.

He won't let me go either.

It took me a long time to realize that whatever the witch took from him when she lifted him out of that water was something he could never get back. All the love in the world couldn't get it back.

I won't go into all the details, all the minor brutalities he unleashed on me, and all the greater ones beside. I have let it happen—have let him push me down and stomp my hands, have let him confine me to this chair, and when I talked too loudly for his liking, I let him glue my lips shut too, over and over again. I think soon he will do something to stop me looking; he does not like the way I stare at him, laughing quietly to myself as I realize the truth.

There was always something familiar about the old woman with Xs for eyes—something familiar about her face that I simply could not place. I think I would have recognized her sooner if only I hadn't smashed all the mirrors.

But I did smash the mirrors. And I did bring Elizabeth to that cursed room. And I did give Julian up to the witch when I couldn't bear to look at his cold dead face.

It is only in hindsight that I have come to realize the truth of it—come to see all my failures over the years made fresh in the memories of the house, laid out in a tapestry of disappointment, each attempt at atonement thwarted by the boy who has been to the other side of death and come back as something else—and I know, somewhere deep in my heart, that it wasn't Donovan, after all, who made him what he is.

ACKNOWLEDGMENTS

This novel wouldn't be what it is without the friends and family who hold up this madhouse. My deepest appreciation to my mom and dad for having endlessly and unquestioningly supported my dream of being a writer ever since I was a weird kid writing creepy stories. Your support means more than you know.

I also want to thank my sister Mal for always being so enthusiastic about my work, even though horror isn't her thing, and making sure I'm a part of my niece's and nephew's lives even from two thousand miles away. You and Marc are such great parents—don't worry, your kids will never turn out like the one in this book.

Publishing this book, and life in general, wouldn't be nearly as sweet without Jake, who loves me and *gets* me like no one else. Thanks for keeping me sane, for being a sounding board, for listening to me babble about writing, for making me laugh, for indulging in conversations consisting almost entirely of quotes from movies and TV shows, for always finishing each other's sandwiches, and for marrying me.

This book would not have made it this far without those who did the work to actually put it in front of your eyeballs. So many thanks to my agent, Jill Marr, who is an amazing advocate. I am deeply grateful to my editor, Chelsey Emmelhainz, who knew exactly what this story needed and helped make it so much better. And thanks also to the rest of the folks at Crooked Lane!